They Lived They Were at Brighton Beach

A Novel

By:
Iván Brave

First Edition

To be honest, the names of places in this book are real—New York City, for example, is an actual city—but the characters, what they do or say, their misfortunes and triumphs, are all fictitious; that was part of the charm of writing this novel, which I trust will translate to the charm of reading it, too.

ISBN: 978-0-9980364-3-4
$14.99

All writing is original, by the author, except where *noted*.

Literature—Contemporary, Literary, Pop Music, Language, New American Fiction

ivanbrave.com
info@ivanbrave.com

Cover Art and Design by Petya Tsankova

To my parents,
for sharing their love of music, and their love.

"There are fairy tales to be written for grownups, fairy tales almost blue."

André Breton

"Осталось написать сказки для взрослых—сказки ещё почти голубые."

André Breton

"Quedan cuentos de hadas por escribir para la gente grande, cuentos todavía casi azules."

André Breton

"Il y a des contes à écrire pour les grandes personnes, des contes encore presque bleus."

André Breton

THE FOUR MOVEMENTS
(& breaks)

I
ONCE UPON A TIME / было горе
(Overture ♀ Fermata)

II
THEY LIVED THEY WERE / с надеждой
(Interlude ☊ Half time)

III
A FAIRY TALE ALMOST BLUE / это утрата
(Intermission ☉ Double time)

IV
SERAPH / вечеринка воссоединения
(Swing time ⁙ Coda)

I

ONCE UPON A TIME / было горе*

☿

---

* You mean *grief*. Why write it in Russian, and not English? Or at least in Latin letters, not Cyrillic.

If you must include Russian, because you are Russian, fine. But give the reader something phonetic to follow along. I know you say it is pretty to *read* Cyrillic, but I would advise you strongly against using it, especially when writing a predominantly English text, which this book is, for a predominately English audience, which this book is for, as you mentioned to me last night.

True, I haven't read any of the book yet, but already, knowing you, at some point it will incorporate language few readers understand. Trust me, I have just done the research. According to Wikipedia, there are 854,955 Russian speakers in the US. Plus, Russians who speak FLUENT English (that is, fluent enough to be able to read LITERATURE in English, according to an article on Russia Beyond) is 3% of Russians world-wide. So, 4,335,000.

Adding these two numbers we get 5,189,955 of people we assume speak both Russian and English well enough to read a book that is majority in English. In addition to these, we have 31,107,076 native Russians who live outside of their mother country, not to mention NON-native Russian speakers. But we would go crazy calculating all these little factions, not to mention, we don't know how many of these ALSO speak English fluently enough as to read literature in English, or care, or be interested in a story about a DJ who falls in love.

You told me once that your fear is drowning, suffocating to death. And yet, my fear is that this book will die just the same, flooded in tangents, unintelligible letters, digressions, unless you are prepared to compensate the reader vigorously, with a message they can understand, a purpose they can deepen, and some lines to laugh along with. That's what we want, isn't it? Isn't it? Something beautiful.

Overture:

Once upon a time there lived an old couple by the beach. In the summer they would visit the shore, press bare feet to wet sand, and fill the sea salt air with their song. As the season changed, and the ocean and birds grew lazy, the couple would dance indoors by candlelight to exhaustion, or sing out loud until the last note left their breast.

But one summer, with the tide riding high and waves crashing hard, a violent storm threatened their peace. Despite making music, ignoring all fame and all fortune, even friends from distant lands toured in their youth, the old man and the old woman had never, ever borne a child.

Eager for one to call their own, the husband wrote his wife the tale of a son as a gift, which she received with joy.

One evening, as he rested softly, she read slowly. Motley feelings surged from within, as she dove into what began as one thing, then turned into two. Page after page, excited and confused, and with a pen in her hand, she added footnotes and lovenotes, like footprints and kisses, to what she loved so much, to bring it into light.

The following is that story, of a boy and his dream, by this couple that bore him, a major chord in blue.

Sound that breaks is noise, sound that moves is music. And from where he stood, Ilya Nikolayevich could almost hear the hum of a ship's haul in the distance. It cut along the line where ocean meets sky, the horizon. He longed for the silence necessary to tune in. But all around him there grew a vague white noise capable of endless distraction.

Stacy Giacometti
2:34
Sorry Ilya, I just can't . . .

He could not escape it: the diversion, the clamoring, the calls to action, the advertisements, the updates, the noise, the hit subscribe button, the notifications, the reminder to like me, the half-off deals, the pickup lines, the elevator pitch, the scheme, the sale, and that stupid text preview on his brand new phone . . .

. . . clouding the necessary silence. Luckily, he knew how to tame the noise. After all, he was a DJ. To dance between sound and silence, that is to groove, was his gift, his destiny.

Gangly and chest pale, he lowered his phone, and stood low under the light of the sun, letting himself burn for a minute, at the wooden rail of a long boardwalk that connected two beaches. Aside from needing the tan, after weeks of being sick from spring allergies and something else, he was scouting for the optimal spot to position his music gear and perform a set of original tracks. His amplifiers and keyboards were packed on a dolly, held tight by bungee cords he had borrowed.

Meanwhile, a wave crashed on shore. Gulls cawed overhead, mated. Families ambled. Ilya coughed, groaned. He needed a line.

For the past two Sundays he had performed like this, run and gun, at the beach. Usually he played somewhere in the city, some place to which he never returned: a distant tunnel between stations, a small abandoned park. But the beach he liked. Last week, this one song of his got a couple to make out. This week, he wanted to do it again, with a new song. Though, also this week, he wanted to perform together with his girlfriend, a blues guitarist, who was supposed to arrive any minute now. But had sent him that troubling text which began all wrong.

Another message came in, pushing her preview lower. It didn't make the first one go away however, not at all. Still, Ilya walked on.

To a nice spot on the wooden boardwalk, between Brighton Beach and Coney Island. There he could faintly hear rollercoasters, children wailing. He counted crushed cans on the ground, next to a pile of broken syringes and reused baby wipes in a nearby bush. Coke. He shivered until he coughed, rubbing his forehead as if someone had just thrown a red brick at his face, only the blood was sweat. He coughed again, on this cool 6th of May, suffering a fever.

Through pain and anxiety, Ilya redid a shirt button, which the breeze had undone, then unwrapped the bungee cord securing his equipment, with ceremony.

Before even finishing to set up, a crowd had formed around him. They wanted a show. Is she coming? wondered Ilya, switching on his generator. Meanwhile, fire, he searched for inner fire. Honey, he produced the honey the worker bees of this busy hive called New York City could suckle at. Look at them buzz, thought Ilya, wiping the wall of sweat like blood from his brow, turning his attention towards some cables and uncoiling them. Another coughing fit attacked him midway. Embarrassment sunk in, as the audience pulled their phones out to film the guy they had seen online. His chest burned pale, his arms burned too, so gangly. Suddenly on his lip sprouted a cold sore and another terrible cough along with it. Was she coming?

He put on a headband to stop the sweating, to focus. His phone buzzed a second time. Another notification, although not from who he wanted. Another breeze rolled in. He unrolled more cable. The phone buzzed a third time, yet again, nothing special, just fans blowing up his phone.

A young couple stopped their walk to join the crowd. They smiled like willows sway, gently and patiently, waiting. Now a fourth text came in, but again not from the one he wanted, his queen bee, who was supposed to come with her guitar and camera.

Was Stacy coming, or what? He had asked her to meet. Coke. To pick up her guitar from the apartment. Coke. She had asked him to quit blow. Coke. But then he got that prescription.

How should he have known she would find his stash just that very day, when he needed her to come to the beach to play with him? He would have sent her a message to confirm that he was at the beach, setting up without her, about to start without her. But he didn't want to read what she had sent him. Not yet.

For now, the set up complete, Ilya punched in a thick bassline, then a bright high-hat sample in rhythm.

The show had begun.

☿

Beaches and house music go together like beaches and house music.

Deeply, darkly, running five/six layers of audio, Ilya added track upon track to a compact mix of electro funk, designed to shake palm trees and bikini bottoms, adding percussion samples here and there. Feelers only he could produce, creating such an infectious beat, on the family friendly boardwalk no less. And here he was, rolling and scratching on apps and tables, his restless leg kicking its heel into hell, while a hand held his earphones to one ear. Few greater pleasures were there than to click a sample into syncopation with the established beat of a governing groove. The snaps and finger claps, the slaps and fist bumps they produced. To feel it was great, to dance even better, but to make it so grand.

This Sunday at the beach, at Ilya's hit and run set, there was magic. Even the wind swung to his music and lured people in. As the grass in the sand flowed, too. And a loose dog hopped on its hind legs. Kids made fists and shook their hips. A microphone got passed around for shout-outs. And the beat, it spiraled. Salt, sea, timeless love. Flame, good times, the sparks. Reflecting on life, embracing existence. Here the boards of the boardwalk provided springs to the feet of passersby. Some people littered too, but only elsewhere, nowhere near the music. What did Stacy say? No phones during sets, he told himself, no phones during sets.

It could be said and seen that his sweat and shaking came from a zesty self-induced trance for the music, but in reality he had slept very little the night before, was sober, withdrawing, and possessed by an inner awkwardness of spirit, which only enthusiasm could mask. By jerking a restless leg, with a dash of spit and spasm, out of pain he did self-soothe, gain strength and health, the power to move on. His music was healing him, and making those around him pour water from water bottles over their heads while shaking their long, wet strands of hair in large circles. The beat was there. The beach added to the cure. An even bigger group encircled the DJ, enjoyed his music as much as the nature surrounding them did. Everyone and everything danced.

Except for that message, buried now under a pile of social media notifications, in his pocket, clawing at him, begging for attention.

Normally, he wouldn't touch his phone during a set, but, how bad could it be? He swiped away all the messages except the very bottom one, hers, and peeked at the preview one last time: Sorry Ilya, I just can't . . .

A quivering thumb to the screen, coughing, chest tighter than a clump of sand, Ilya hesitated, waited. He would, he would open it. A goofy sample of disco trombones looped, like a skipping track, as he continued to stare at the preview of his soon to become ex-girlfriend. Part of him already knew what it said, like he could guess. But with the horn section looping senselessly, the dancing crowd, even the hopping dog, slowed down, perplexed by their distracted DJ. They were waiting for the next track, which would not load unless punched in, until the rusty horns stopped looping. Which wouldn't happen, because he was opening the message.

Sorry Ilya, I just can't believe you had me get equipment from your place. Would I not look in the drawer? And don't say they are your roommate's, they have your name on them. Clearly you have made your choice. Don't expect me to come play with you. I can't even picture us right now without hurting [read more.]

Why and why not? Ilya clicked "read more," and more there was. Stacy talked about having found Ilya's prescription pills, plus some of them crushed up like the powdery stuff he had promised to quit. Had he mixed anything in it? She knew the chance to relapse was high, their ongoing fights about it, too; but, most shocking of all, she confessed over messenger, was that after seeing his apartment that morning she realized, you know what, forget the beach, deciding instead to go sign that major record label offer she had been putting off. Her now new agent was more than willing to meet at a café on short notice, printed contract in hand.

A bomb of a text. Meanwhile, Ilya could only wonder why it hadn't occurred to him to better hide the attention deficit medication, before Stacy went to his place to pick up her guitar. Had he been able to concentrate long enough to think it through, Ilya would have realized that this was her finally breaking free, living her dream—while he was cast into a nightmare, or, rather, realized he had long ago lived in one.

His heart rate spiked. As he reread her message about the contract a third time—by now losing all the energy from the crowd—there appeared those jumping ellipses that meant she was typing again. The typing indicator appeared and reappeared, indicating thought, pauses, deletes. Overhead the sky turned dark. A nearby biker wondered if it was going to rain, chugging from a water bottle and chucking it at a recycling bin, but failing to land it. The biker rode on.

Miles away, the boat on the line of the horizon remained as distant as it did a memory. All attention fit in the palm of Ilya's hand, as he saw a new message, this one the length of a novel, weighing him down line by line, describing without any restraint the extent to which he had ruined Stacy's life, without trust, and how terribly wrong it would be to reopen wounds by getting back together again, a fourth time.

Ilya locked his phone screen and looked up at the light of the sun. The rays, which he couldn't look at directly, seemed raised like arms suggesting they also had no clue what to do. The DJ should have replied with an honest apology, could have at least pretended to be hurt, but it would have meant nothing to Stacy. Because just then, complete with a pitiful little pixel of a period mark, she wrote and sent him this:

We are over.

For a moment, an image of her came to mind, of peach fuzz and running makeup, not of how she was now, but the year before, when they first got back together after a breakup, back in college. Now, that image didn't produce the same feelings, only a bitterness of repeated mistakes. She wasn't beautiful to him anymore, no, only hot. Worse, as this image incinerated like still film in a projector's light, another image soon replaced it. Then, after that image, another then another. One of her at an ice cream shop, spilling milkshake all over herself, after a show. One of her licking her way up each note of her guitar fretboard, until her mouth reached the tuning knob for D, which she gently took into her mouth, and tightened with her lips. Another, his favorite of Stacy Giacometti, on his couch covered in crumpled music sheets and crushed soda cans, wearing nothing but jean-overalls, the left button missing, a number two pencil behind her ear, and hair knotted after sex, as she composed what would become her first hit blues single to play on air. A single that he had recorded, actually, to become the b-side of a limited edition release by an indie press, which attracted major label attention. Now she had more than enough music, talent, and, after this breakup and drama, inspiration to rerecord her songs and even write some new material for a full on, glossy, cellophane, marketed, 45-minute long album of real human pain in three chords, for mass-consumption.

Yet, there she was, typing again, watch those jumping ellipses. Meanwhile, at the beach, loopy loops kind of looped, playing plays played halfheartedly, to no one at all really, because no one was listening, or sticking around, except virtually, as his now new ex typed and typed and typed.

After wiping his face with his headband, his thumb pressed her name, then the green call button.

☿

"You have to fight." These were his father's words, when Ilya chose the path. It is great advice when you're creating art, but terrible when you're breaking up. Against all desire, all rules, against the nonexistent crowd, he turned the master volume down on the boring looping music. And he put his phone to his ear, yelling, "You want me to quit? I quit!"

There was a pause, then a crackle.

"It's too late, Ilya. Your bullshit got to me this time." Stacy hung up.

Ilya could only imagine her at some café, not more than an hour away somewhere, at a table, not alone, being asked what's wrong by the agent, and her saying, "Nothing," in an odd, cold way, as two tears fell from one eye, and she forced a smile, handwriting her signature on whatever document lay in front of her, without really reading it at all.

They were over.

Ilya thought about how at the age of 22 he was becoming a washed up loser, a Diplo to Stacy's M.I.A., a terrible breakup story among dozens of terrible break-up stories in the music industry. The worthlessness of being the dummy left behind, losing not only a lover, but his artist and his muse, not to say his self-esteem, all flimsy things, by the stroke of a distant pen.

Instead of shutting off his phone to continue the set, as any sensible DJ would have done, Ilya didn't even touch his gear. Didn't notice the crowd walk away, didn't see the couple disappointed, didn't catch a beautiful woman watching him. Instead he just texted back his ex, while other notifications piled in, bothering the top half of his screen. But he swatted those away, rereading her messages twice and replying to them directly one by one, quoting, typing, trembling.

How might he lie his way out of this one? He really had quit coke, that morning in fact, plus he had stopped taking illegal pills at work, ever since their last big fight last Friday. Why did she count prescriptions, anyway, prescriptions were legal. But then, why did he have to crush them and snort them?

Before he could tell her about taking the edge off after putting it on, she changed subjects and made it about him not releasing enough original music, being too underground. He hadn't changed, hadn't evolved. Too scared to show the real him.

The heat of the putrid day unraveled, and the beach became blistering. Boys played with water guns. Girls spun hula-hoops. Then they mixed. Drinks, too, were mixed, next served and drunk. Then, people too, and so on.

Eventually, the responses to his texts came to a halt. So he called again. But the call went to voicemail. He called again. Again nothing. She had blocked him, deleted him. He knew the signs. So in retaliation, he unfriended her, unfollowed. Her death was complete. His sorrow unreal.

The same shirt button came undone, and a breeze caressed him. One could see a thick pink scar running up Ilya's chest: from his heart to his left ear. A grisly thing that marked a certain night in Paris a year before. Over the scar hung a vial of mercury, for protection. Not unrelated.

But blocked, totally blocked. Ilya would rather be anywhere but here, nothing felt right. And it didn't help that he had a raging headache, water everywhere, but none to drink, hadn't eaten in days, save for an apple, no liquids except alcohol. He ought to have quit drinking too, because now? A pounding chest, a throbbing pain, literally throbbing in the most abject places: his eye lids, his scrotum, a muscle in the middle part of his back by his spine. His leg restless, as always. His head hurting so much that his teeth and nails ached. He should tear off a nail and bite down on the fleshy inside of his fingertip.

She wants the real me? Here it is. Take a photo of this.

Enraged, Ilya pressed his brand new phone between his thumb and achy finger. He turned at the hurt heel, and tossed that thing as far as possible. His phone soared over the beach, past rocks and shore, landing in a belly flop over the face of the ocean, which devoured the device, then forgot about it altogether. A whole, wave-like feeling washed over Ilya. It was as if a weight had been lifted. He raised his arms in victory. "Yes!" No matter what she said, he was going to quit. And win Stacy back.

"Ahem."

Behind him stood a pair of interracial, inter-gender cops, arms-folded, so close to the DJ that they could have tapped his shoulder.

Ilya grinned, rubbing the back of his buzz-cut head, and took a step back. The lady cop nodded over to the water. So Ilya went after his phone.

He was barefooted, taking his time. His sickness rising. If he moved any faster he would collapse.

Sunlight sharply burned, highlighting the crests of waves. That boat out in the distance still cut along the ocean and sky unfrozen by time, marking the minutes for everyone, for Ilya. His toes dug into the sand, seashells, and shards of broken glass underwater, which felt cool, looked good, as his knees touched the water, too cool and so unlike May, soon to be real summer.

Then, he bent and searched.

Only to pull up, like an onion from its root, a sopping wet, broken phone.

The events of the day finally caught up to him. He looked up one last time, saw clouds part. The world turned rainbow-white, as he himself fell, fell . . .

. . . backwards, flat on his back into the water, to cause, as an artist, a literal splash, waves fanning out. Wherefore from above, one could see sunk around his neck the small chain necklace and the glint of light on his vial of mercury.

A young man once full of himself, now filled with grief.*

---

* Do you know Gorée? It is a small island off the coast of Dakar, Senegal, exactly between Saharan and Sub-Saharan West Africa. "The

Brave

☿

symbol of the slave trade with its cortege of suffering, tears and death," says UNESCO, the island being a World Heritage Site.

I always thought the name meant "grief" in French, like how rope means grief in Russian *(spelled "goré" in Latin characters)*. It turns out, actually, that Gorée comes from a corruption of the original Dutch name for the port, *Goedereede*, meaning "safe harbor." Imagine that, for a slave port.

All in all, considering how you subtitle Part One of the novel, I get it now. You definitely mean the emotion in Russian. But, one last note: on *Ancestry* it claims that the American name Goree comes from the old French *goré*, meaning "deceived," or betrayed," though I have not been able to corroborate this information anywhere else on the internet. If we take this to be true, however, then that would mean its Russian equivalent, rope, would be a cognate, a *vrai ami* so to speak.

Thought you would appreciate the fun fact.

Fermata:

For a moment, the old woman folded the book over her lap, to ponder the vial of mercury at the end of the last chapter. What motivates the boy, she wondered. What has he to prove?

"Blue is the color of many things," mumbled the old man, turning in his sandy sleep. "But a dream is a dream."

Smiling at her sleepy husband, then looking out past the shore, the wife tapped the pink of her lips with the ballpoint of the pen. Ocean and sky. Gloom and calm. Deep and simple. But a boy, still a boy, like the blanket swathing him in his cradles with a mobile toy above chiming melodies.

A breath of sea salt air later, she began clicking the pen opened and closed, closed and opened, repeatedly, in tune with a tic and the tide at her feet. She would add more footnotes and lovenotes, like track marks and hickeys, on the pages she turned and turned.

She had met the boy. Now it was time to meet the dream.

"EE-LEE-YA. EE-LEE-YA."

They chanted, "EE-LEE-YA. EE-LEE-YA."

The beat sped up, they kept chanting, "IL-YA. IL-YA. IL-YA. IL-YA." In flaming letters, on a poster held by a wraith, one read:

ILYA NIKOLAYEVICH GAGARIN

The DJ's leg shook incessantly. He was repeating a nightmare. From off-stage, he counted the colors of the curtain, the heavy curtain; they were three and recognizable: red, white, and blue. His arms, the dreamer's, meanwhile, were dotted in itchy needle wounds. His nails grew yellow as he scratched the itch, cut himself open, then itched the scratch. His chest caved, realizing he had never injected himself before, thinking what a waste it was to be addicted to something he didn't remember enjoying. But now, it was too late. Heaps of glass shards, coated in slime, decorated the floorboards of where he waited, colder than alone, for his turn to perform.

His brother couldn't make it.

Neither could his father.

He had to play to strangers who continued to chant his name: "ILYA! ILYA!"

Elsewhere, go-go dancers locked eyes with one another, twisting nipples. But his set, his set, he had no idea what to play. He hadn't prepared. Dizzy spells. He opened the tri-colored curtain just a little, to peek at the audience awaiting.

Pitch empty darkness. Except for a single spotlight cast on the opener: the artist Drake, dressed as a philosopher king in a Canadian tracksuit, breakdancing onstage, in absolute quiet, save for the skidding of cleats and crown scraped against the stage floor as he kicked his legs into rotation, those clammy palms of his slapping the floor in tune to the grunts of his spinning around—not for long his only noise as he swung, because, as he swung, he spoke:

"My whole life, a waste. I've turned ashes to ashes, dust to dust!" He kicked, hopped to a handstand. "Vanity of vanities, all is vanity! My whole life, a waste!" Next he wrapped himself into a bow, before dropping. Folks clapped, some.

Nice, thought Ilya. The philosopher king mixed nursery rhyme with unbeatable Ecclesiastes. A potent combination. Drake really was a genius. And yet, the crowd barely cared, and soon began to throw rotten eggs on stage. Next, servers passed around pills in piles on rusty platers. The "I'll take one, thank you" people lost their features. Ilya saw them all, yet from behind the safety of the curtain, which shimmered as he grabbed it, attracting attention, by which the crowd spotted him, meaning they looked at him and sized him up. His judges' faces were featureless, too, with nothing but two rows of crumbled teeth, and bridgeless nose holes. The chill of being stared at by a hundred and one careless hot sauce hearted ticket holders was penetrating. By the time the pills reached him, he denied them, and accepted a stunning realization instead, one which caused him to feel fantastically afraid.

If Drake fell off, then what hope was there for anyone else? Ilya watched the crowned fool pulled off stage by his gold chain. Last name Ever, first name Never. Again.

The cold, slow urge of an icicle melting seized the boy. Where to run? Suddenly a snow white storm iced his back. He felt that if he turned around he would get slapped. Best not to turn. The ice got too strong. He froze, not freezed; frowned to feign a laugh, almost deigned to dart at last; but instead picked up a box of his dead mother's albums and stepped out, past the curtain, into that gross, sick, descending darkness of pure stage fright.

Save the spotlight cast. Now over his keyboard setup, there, just the way he liked it.

Knobs glittered, buttons twinkled.

With the laptop burning, he was ready to play those albums in the box, not his mother's, but his own original music. But what's the point, when no one you love is with you?

And that's when he raised a fist in the air, crying out with all his might: "What's my name!?"

"ILYA!"

He placed three fingers on three keys, chord prepared.

His fist still raised, he called, "But who am I?"

This time, the crowd stood detached, saying nothing. It was like throwing a rock down a well, and hearing no splash, no sound, no nothing at the bottom.

His whole spine tingling, he felt himself about to fall through a hole on stage. His index finger was on the right key, though, the E-key, his only chance for survival.

But, when he pressed it, there came not a sound.

Just silence. A drop.

☿

Breathless and jaw-locked, he awoke with a fright. It was all a nightmare. The same one lately, his name chanted by strangers, ghosts, and musicians. Ilya closed his eyes and forced air down his throat, then back out, to relax.

At least this particular Tuesday morning didn't hurt as bad as the previous morning, which had found him waking up at the hospital.

Following his faint episode at the beach, the officers handed the dizzied boy to paramedics, who rapidly administered opioid receptor antagonists, figuring he had lost consciousness and couldn't answer the question of what he had taken, so relied on how he looked, like your garden variety junkie: gangly, sun-blistered, torn white jeans, and in a raggedy black button up. Later, at the hospital, blood tests did detect trace amounts of various stimulants, possibly Ritalin or Adderall, as well as amphetamines and hydrochloride cocaine.[*] They pumped his stomach and administered a dose of activated charcoal for good measure.

---

[*] For a moment I wondered why Ilya wasn't arrested at the hospital. Apparently it is fine to have drugs in your body, just not on your person. And there is more I learned today about cocaine. Technical names: Benzoylmethylecgonine, $C_{17}H_{21}NO_4$. Monosyllabic names: Blow, Coke, Crack, Rock, Snow. Forms of consumption: snorting, smoking, by mouth, injection. Market: 1.5 million users aged 12 and over in the US, most common between 18 and 25. Price per gram: $50 in Portugal, $112 in Finland, $96 in the US, but you can find cheaper, since it is almost always cut with numbing agents or cheap amphetamine, and depends on buyer-seller relationship. Short-term effects: constricted blood vessels, dilated pupils, tremors and muscle twitches, restlessness, unreasonable distrust of others, and extreme happiness.

To their amusement, regaining consciousness, through tunnel vision as he opened his eyes, all he asked for was his equipment. "I have to produce the EP! To win her back, I have to produce the EP!" They only had a vague idea of what an EP was, not to mention they didn't care. "Must be a side-effect of the treatment," they told one another, as they nodded. No one knew it at the time, but those hundreds of dollars in amps and keys were lost to southern Brooklyn, a sacrifice for getting off easy this time.

Unaware, however, much later, when Ilya kept insisting, they replied as any decent group of overworked nurses and busy physicians would: they had no idea about any amplifiers, but he was free to go home, here's the bill, drink plenty of water. After paying the equivalent of half a month's rent for a one bedroom apartment in Midtown, Ilya did go home, that is to his couch at his best friend's apartment, where he literally flushed every single last bit of, piece of, trace of drug he had acquired down the toilet, and slept for some twenty long hours straight.

What a year. A common one, starting on a Monday in the Gregorian calendar, also known as the 18th year of the 3rd millennium. In it, the Turkish-Kurdish conflict rose, the US

Long-term effects: nosebleeds, problems with swallowing, holes in your mouth, higher risks of infections, severe bowel decay, scarring.

The trade-off must be worth it to some, at first. But after a while, it's just the low that makes you want to get high.

federal government shutdown again, a couple of monkey clones were spawned, Saratov Flight 703 leaving Moscow crashed shortly after takeoff, a couple of Russian double agents were poisoned in England, then 100 diplomats expelled from 20 countries, Trump met Kim Jong-un in North Korea who later met Moon Jae-in in South Korea, 78 people died in a fire in Venezuela, the president of Brazil was arrested, cinemas opened in Saudi Arabia for the first time since 1983 with the movie *Black Panther*, Miguel Diaz-Canel was sworn as the first non-Castro president of Cuba since the revolution; later that year, but not so much later, Russia would host the FIFA World Cup, Saudi Arabia would allow women to drive, two satellites between the European Space Agency and the Japanese Aerospace Exploration Agency would launch to explore Mercury, Facebook would report the biggest single-day loss in corporate history at $109 billion, Apple would become the first public company to reach a value of $1 trillion, the supreme court of India would decriminalize gay marriage, and some other stuff, too. Important people would pass, be born. Music live on. Love start and never stop.

But today was Tuesday, May the 8th, 7 AM, with morning light seeping into the living room of a cozy apartment in Murray Hill, Manhattan. And, relaxed now, Ilya opened his eyes.

Not technically his home, he slept in the living room, on a dyed navy non-pullout couch. "A week tops" had turned into weeks, then months. Ilya could, if he tried, find some other hole to crawl into, but his friend, the apartment owner and primary dweller, wouldn't let him. She believed in him. She didn't believe a word he said, though, but she believed he was a musician worth supporting. So she let him crash in her living room for "a week tops," knowing exactly what he meant: "I don't know."

Her name was Tiffany Voltescu. And she had even offered to have a flex wall installed in the living room, she would pay for it herself too, but Ilya insisted that drapes, held up by a clothes line, were all he needed. He didn't consider that the offer to wall him off was more for her than for him.

Like him, she stayed home. This way, Ilya learned that Tiffany spent her AM hours recording background sound, Foley, for films; and that in the PM hours she drew passionate moans from whomever was her lover at the time.

Sometimes the two activities happened in reverse, with the recording at night, and the moaning in the morning, as was the case right now. Ilya stuffed his ears with headphones and buried his burning, sweating face into his pillow, moist from so much sleeping.

Tiffany entered the kitchen feeling rosy, her hair knotted and frizzy. Twelve of her piercings gleamed, polished, at least the ones Ilya could see from over his bedsheets: there were three on her left ear, two on the right—corresponding to two freckles she had—one over her lip, four shared among her eyebrows, a septum ring, and then, a final one through her tongue: stuck out, as she poured herself a glass of OJ.

Yelling loud enough for Ilya to hear through his headphones, she said: "Sorry about Stacy!"

Ilya grunted. "How did you know?"

"She was here on Sunday, going through your stuff."

"Why did you let her?"

"I didn't let her . . . or stop her."

"Right."

"By the way, where did you spend the night on Sunday?"

He removed his headphones. Instead of *At a hospital*, he said, "I needed to be alone."

Tiffany sipped, gnawed on the pulp, and, in place of repeating herself, asked, "Where's your equipment?"

Ilya said the first thing that came to mind: "Sold it to a pawn shop."

"What for?"

"Tiff," he said, changing topics, "can I borrow your phone? I need to call my dad." Ilya and his father talked every day, almost every day. Usually about nothing. Although now the son did need something, money actually, to buy his equipment again, in order to complete a collection of songs, his EP. Now, he could have asked his brother, David, to wire him money like he had done the previous week—precisely to buy that new phone, which was now fried—but Ilya felt it was best not to ask again so soon. He could have asked Tiffany, but that would imply telling her the truth about his equipment, so he felt it best to just ask for the phone. As he asked, though, and even as he asked a second time, she became distracted by how much light was coming in from outside this time of year, this early in the day, even from the closed living room window. After drawing the blinds, she answered the question.

"In a minute," said Tiffany. "My phone is charging."

A groan came from her bedroom.

With his chin and furrowed brow, Ilya signaled in the direction of the groan, meaning, Who's that?

"You met him once," Tiffany replied. "Anyway, I want him out, so I can finish recording these footsteps." She meant for her latest Foley gig, another friend's passion project.

Tiffany reached into the bread basket, took out a half-eaten piece of sweet bread she had baked herself, and tore off a chunk. She tossed another piece to Ilya, who chewed and savored every last crumb of it. She was happy to see him enjoy her food. Really, she wanted to talk more about Stacy, about how things went with her coming to the house and leaving a little crazier than she had entered, but Tiffany felt things might change any minute between the two musicians, deciding instead to let a day or a week pass, before bringing it up, or picking sides. As Tiffany was thinking all this, she picked the scabs of her new bicep tattoo.

"I like the treble clef," Ilya said. "It matches your bass clef."

Tiffany smiled. "You know the bass clef was a mistake. It's so ugly."

Eventually the chatting fizzled, and she left. So Ilya got out of bed, sat at his tiny desk, and was about to start sculpting the final version of his debut EP's Track One. But he didn't. He would have, if it weren't for one issue distracting him, a voice that worried about work the following day, on Wednesday.

Things weren't going well at the club where he had had a residency for the past year, working Wednesdays, Fridays, and Saturdays. He had gotten the slots partly thanks to Tiffany, who used to DJ there, before dedicating herself full-time to Foley; but also partly thanks to his YouTube channel, with just over fifty-thousand subscribers, and dozens of uncanny live streams full of comments.

The front door slammed. His roommate yelled something. Ilya took off his headphones, thinking it was for him.

"What!"

"Nothing!"

"Tiffany!"

"What!"

"How do I ask for a Sunday?" Ilya was peering out from the drapes of his make-shift room.

"For a Sunday every week or for a Sunday once?" shouted Tiffany from her bedroom door.

"Just one, in July, for a party."

"Easy, just ask. Tony likes you."

"He only owns the place, he doesn't book."

"But he can set you up."

"Please, won't you ask him for me?" Ilya had hoped she would, that's why he had asked, because Tony almost always did what a woman asked of him. "He likes you better."

Tiffany shook her head, soon asking if the show was to release the EP she knew he was forever tweaking, an unfinished set of tracks, a debut that kept not debuting.

Ilya mumbled, "Yes, the EP." Then, added: "But I want to release it on my dad's birthday, Sunday July 22nd." This part was a lie, since it wasn't his dad's birthday, and because he omitted the part about wanting to win Stacy back by releasing it.

"That's nice," mused Tiffany. "But, isn't your dad, like, super tough on you?"

"You never met him."

"I can imagine."

Suddenly, Ilya's computer chimed.

"What's that?" asked Tiffany.

It was an email notification from, of all people, Ilya's father, asking why his calls were going straight to voicemail.

"Tiff," shouted Ilya. "Can I borrow your phone now?"

☿

The most philosophical, most blazingly spiritual realizations would reach Ilya as he entered one of Brooklyn's better known dingy grungy underground clubs—the place where he worked—named Zdras.

Revelations came in the form of interior monologues, usually on the nature of music and its relation to consciousness, about the dance between sound and silence, about the groove and artistic style. And other shit that tingled the boy. On this particular Wednesday, however, he felt much more practical. He needed to do three things that day, so he had come early to work.

First, he would ask about July 22nd. Second, he should collect last week's check. Last, with the tedium out of the way, he could start his Wednesday set of Dub music, set to explode into Drum & Bass.

A train passed overhead, clanking, clicking. The front door was open, as always: a red door that from afar looked like a red stick of gum, long and skinny, with a hornet graffitied on the front with a small round window serving as the eye of the vicious bug.

At the door, underneath the bug, slept three triplet, white Dogo Argentino dogs. That wasn't new. They were always there, and belonged to the same homeless man who was also always there, also always sleeping, who no one had ever bothered to remove, since he provided indirect security to the club, in that his smell repelled opportunists. Ilya got past them, though, just as always, and entered.

The secret to this club's success was that it went far, far underground. After you entered through the door, you would descend a long staircase. This meant shows could be deep, loud, and powerful, lasting till sunrise. As legend has it, back when Zdras used to host post-post punk bands in the 2000's, merch tables saw significant T-shirt and labeled deodorant sales, because folks needed clean clothes to go to work the following morning, straight from dancing. It was like they were reborn after a hard night out, ready to contribute to society. Although, these days, it felt more like folks danced a little too hard, a little joylessly at times. They still went to work directly, but they would go dirty, filming themselves with phones, and acting dumb as they stumbled outside. At least underground, the music, the atmosphere, and the clientele remained safe, pure—thanks to the foresight of the owner, Tony.

Once down at the main "landing," the owner's office lay just beyond the bar, on the other side of the dancefloor, behind the DJ booth actually, further underground through a trapdoor on the floor.

Drops of sewage fell from the corner of the office, as a light overhead flickered, and mildew flirted with pink fiberglass, in a stench and sight known only to a few. Only the fortunate enough to be invited by the boss, or unfortunate enough to have a score to settle with him.

This particular Wednesday, however, barely aware of Ilya approaching, Tony faced away from the trapdoor's staircase, wasting away on his king-sized swivel chair in agony. He would not turn right away, even though he heard the staircase creak: his face all enflamed, puffy purple, messy teary, which he didn't want to show to anyone just yet. On the wall, where Tony had fixed his gaze, there hung a row of golden records from his bygone producer days. A sigh. A creaky staircase. "Hello, Tony?" Finally, the boss turned around, and when he did the two men locked eyes for a long time, just longer than it would have been comfortable had they been strangers, and, even then, a little bit longer than that.

"Sorry," said Tony, wiping his face with his shirt collar. "The psychiatrist changed my dosage."

"I thought you were self-medicated," replied Ilya, wondering if he should take a seat or not. Tony had always told him he didn't need permission to sit, yet it was an old habit from back home. In the office, there were empty orange containers forming stacks in this and that corner, over papers and bills. Tony signaled for Ilya to sit.

"I'm glad you came early," said Tony, almost dragging the next phrase out of his mouth. "I have been trying to call you for days."

"My phone's broken."

This infuriated the boss. He stood up suddenly. "Don't lie to me, funky boy. You said the same thing a month ago!"

"No, no, for real this time."

Tony hated when Ilya lied. He stepped over his desk and grabbed the boy by his collar: "Let me guess, you dropped it in the toilet."

"Actually," replied Ilya, breaking Tony's hold on him, "I cast it out to sea."

"Great," said Tony, hovelling back to his king-sized desk chair. "There is something we need to discuss." He heaved as he sat down.

"Great," said Ilya, matching Tony's naturally low tone as best as he could, and adjusting his collar. "I wanted to ask you something too."

Tony continued with what was on his mind: "You're like a godson to me, Ilya, you know that, right?" The boss pulled from his shirt pocket a pink plastic bag, and offered a popper to Ilya. The DJ shook his hand, as nausea filled his stomach like a bubble, which burst with excruciating pain, and the sound of two single words:

Why not?

"Like a nephew," said Tony. He swallowed. "Like a goddamn godson."

A toilet flushed in the office restroom. Ilya heard vomiting. Tony ignored it.

"T," said Ilya, "I need to ask you for a favor. And I know you know I never ask for favors."

"You do all the time. Now listen."

"Would it be possible, in your infinite generosity, in your timeless wisdom, to let me have a Sunday in July?"

"Ilya, I'm dropping your Wednesday slot."

"The thing is, Tony, that it's my dad's birthday in July and I think I can draw a nice crowd that day, what do you say?"

"Elijah, did you hear what I said? You lost a slot, no more Dub, Drum & Bass Wednesdays!"

"It's Ilya, you know that. And what! Why? Folks love DDB Wednesdays!"

Tony slapped the table. Paper stacks fell. Ilya leaned in. "I play on Wednesdays, Fridays, and Saturdays. I have for twelve months! Those are my slots."

"We can't afford niche techno nights anymore." Tony motioned with an open palm at the room around them. "Look at this place!" He held out a cupped hand and caught some of the green liquid falling from the ceiling. "This place is a shitpit!" He peeled some wall paper. "We don't have money!"

Ilya figured it was a bad time to ask for last week's check. And yet, he didn't even have to.

"As for your check, that'll have to be next week. We have, what's his name, coming in tomorrow. We'll bounce back."

"You mean, Sashenka! She's a girl. On Nina Kraviz's new label."

"Sashenka, her, yeah. She's Russian just like you."

"Moldovan." Ilya fumed. "She's a gimmick, T, a fad. Ok, she's huge, opens for everyone in Berlin. Plays festivals, too, but in the small PM hours, man, c'mon she's terrible!"

"Don't be a child, Ilya, you know how this goes: she pulls. P-U-L-L-Z. Pulls. She drew two thousand heads at UNTOLD festival in Romania this year, watch the video. Anyway, as for our humble little grotto we call Zdras, the label has offered to pay for everything, her flight, her stay, her sound system, her meals, her drinks, her—"

"Backstage masseuse?"

"They will even pay us to record her set!! Dig this." He pulled out her media kit. "A masked damsel . . . the rising star of a new eastern Europe . . . mixing disco with hazy, bleached-out techno to create pop sensible tracks for the twenty-first century. . . Sashenka stands out among her contemporaries as—"

"All you care about is money." Ilya stood up out of his chair, fuming with anger, fists clenched and heart pounding. He pointed to the wall behind Tony. "Those discs up there, the gold ones, that one, and that one, and that one, that, that, that, are all a joke." He plopped back down and covered his face. "An international artist means you get to charge double at the door, plus she's already playing for free, well, shit, man, I'll play for free!" He stood up again. "I'll play every day for free, I told you from the jump I'd play for free! I just wanna play!"

"And I told you . . ." Tony walked around his desk and put his hands on Ilya's shoulders. "I told you I wouldn't do that to a friend."

"Oh, so you just drop your friend's Wednesday night, huh, is that right?"

"It's a guest night from now on." Tony looked stern.

And Ilya's eyes swelled like Tony's had been only moments before. "I'll play for free, Tony, I'll play for free, let me play."

Tony went back to his chair. "I couldn't do that to you. You're too good. Just play somewhere else . . . I don't mind, I'm not the jealous type." He rubbed his knees, then threw his hands behind his neck, turned to his wall of former glory. And then had an idea, which he postponed sharing, until he popped another pill. "Or," he said, "what if . . ."

Then, the toilet flushed, a second time. Someone was heaving heavy hard in there, heaving some last breaths.

"July, huh?" Tony asked. "What date?" He sprung open his wonky desk drawer and fussed around in search of his paper planner. "What day in July?"

"The twenty-second."

"Da whuh?"

"Da twuhny-secun!"

"Da twuhny-secun, yes . . ." Tony buttoned a middle button on his shirt, with formality, then sneezed. "Da twenty-y-y-y-f-f-f . . . da twenty-second. Your dad's birthday?"

"Yeah . . ." Well, actually, Mr Gagarin was born in the winter, acted like it too, but . . . anyway, it might help convince Stacy to take me back, since, you know, she doesn't trust me, but yeah.

"I like your old man. Swell guy."

"You never met him."

"I can imagine."

"Also," added Ilya, "I want to release my EP."

"About time!"

"Under my new name, I.N.G."

"You're the only DJ I know who has changed names so many times. What does I.N.G. stand for anyway?"

"It's my initials."

"Il-Nico-Gaga," mused Tony, with the accent he thought his ancestors might have used. "Il-Niccolo-Gagarini."

The paper planner was open. July 22nd looked free to Ilya, who almost mentioned it, when that heaving heifer from the restroom interrupted them, by creaking open the door.

Out stepped a very young, very buxom woman—Tony's second wife—wearing a kimono robe in monarch butterfly print, tied loosely over a mismatching pair of boy shorts and bra, all of which Ilya couldn't look at without awkwardness filling his pants. Her body swelled as she spoke.

"T," she called, feeling her kimono pockets, "I can't find my wedding ring."

"My little calf..."

"Where did I put it?" she asked, but without much attention, slowly fading away from her question. Tony turned back to Ilya like he didn't know what to do. Soon she became distracted by a puddle of liquid on the floor, tracing the lines of the floor tiles with her finger.

"So," said Tony, coughing lightly on purpose, then heavily on accident.

Ilya had already gotten up and made his way to the exit.

But he stopped short of stepping out. "Tony, please, you're like an uncle to me, a godfather, a friend. Give me July 22nd, please."

Tony looked so small in the back of his crummy office, even with the shiny records on the wall, even with his strange crackhead wife on her knees, playing on the floor. Ilya could tell Tony might have, just might have, said *Yes* then and there.

But actually he said: "Ask me again on Friday, and with some goddamn enthusiasm! Tell me, TONY, I HAVE THIS AMAZING IDEA FOR JULY!"

"Woah!" shouted the young wife, placing something on her head. "Check out this wizard hat!"

It was Mikey Mouse's wizard hat from *Fantasia*. When Ilya recognized it, his stomach dropped to the floor.

"Josephine," said Tony. "Get up, please, darling . . . say, when did I pay for that?"

The young Josephine, took a pencil from Tony's desk and cast a spell.

"We can't have you limp, T," said Josephine, pointing her wand at her lover's pant zipper. "This is for tonight!"

He fell on his knees before her, turning quickly to Ilya to tell him, "Come back on Friday," before turning back and up towards his wife, pecking her plump tummy with his lips, and caressing the rest of her full figure with the rest of his bony body.

☿

The skyscrapers at night shook and shambled. Each tiny window told a poem of an individual's life. That's what the mother had said to her sons, on the night that she disappeared.

Fantasia 2000 had just debuted at Carnegie Hall, December 1999, almost nineteen years in the past. The mother had gotten four tickets from an old friend of hers from her dancing days, for her two sons and husband. But her husband had made other plans. So it was only three that went. Ilya remembered that the three of them had stepped out giddy and excited from the show. Then had gone exploring midtown. At age four, this was his first time there.

The ex-dancer, mother of two boys, took them in circles, though. She used to get lost easily, just a bad habit, no matter how many years ago she had moved to the city. It was hard for her to remember left from right, unless guided by someone else. Or unless her body guided her, the momentum of art leading the way.

"Let's get lost," she suggested. She wasn't ready to go back home, anyway. Ilya had no idea about the fight with her husband earlier that day.

David, however, Ilya's older brother, knew. He was eleven at the time, a difficult age to hide things from, especially for a kid as sharp as him. David had seen it coming, and was even old enough to find out why his father made plans that night while the family saw *Fantasia 2000* together.

"This is Central Park," muttered David, his mind returning to the drama at home. "Can we go home now, пожалуйста?"[*]

"Not yet," said the mother. "And speak English to your mother." She turned up to a bright red sign in the sky. "This building is a hotel now, but it used to be where Stravinsky lived, where he lived and died. See the sign?"

ESSEX

HOUSE

The mother hoped the boys would ask her who Stravinsky was, since they had all just watched a cartoon movie with his music in it. But David wasn't about it.

"I want to go home," he insisted. "I want to see папа."[†]

"Your papa can wait."

---

[*] *"..., please?"* he asks.

[†] *"... papa"* the boy says.

I feel like sighing. Yet I won't get tired of saying this: how would anyone know папа is papa? Yes, the two words do look alike, but still. Keep it simple! A young boy in America saying "papa" already sounds foreign enough.

Ilya, that syrup-nosed boy, with a Batman shirt on under his coat, sided with his mother, whining one hundred percent about how much fun he was having and how much he wanted to stay out.

"That's right," said the mother. "Let's go get ice cream."

"But it's winter," complained David.

The mother took them anyway. Of the few facts that survived that terrible night was that she simply didn't know how to make it back to Grand Central Station, to catch the North Rail train to their small town. And that's why they continued wandering the wide avenues of New York City, in search of ice cream. Which they found.

Meanwhile, the skyscrapers were shaking, were shambling.

"This is Second Avenue, Ma," cried David, now deeply scared and worried. "We need to go back to Lexington."

"That's mama's smart young man," she said patting his head.

"I want to go," he said. "Let's turn around."

Little Ilya licked his ice cream cone, licked the drops of chocolate-vanilla swirl, smelled the air fresh, and saw the sidewalks as clear as the sky was dark.

"How come so many people are up, Ma?" asked the younger son. "Don't they have to be asleep?"

"Because, well, look, each person has his own life." She pointed to a skyscraper. "Each tiny window you see is like a poem of an individual life."

"Are they lost too, Ma, like we are?"

"Don't be silly, Ilusha. They are busy, busy bees. Some are going to sleep, others just waking up. But don't worry about those windows, those lights, just enjoy the poetry of it. Plus," she added, "they don't care about you or me, either. All those millions of windows, those millions and millions of people who will never hear about you, won't ever care about you. But that doesn't matter. You know why?"

Ilya licked his ice cream. "Why?"

"Because I care about you. And David cares about you. So don't you worry, ever, what anybody else thinks about you, ok, you got that?"

Maxine. That was her name. Ilya would never be able to say the name without conjuring the following events. That moment, she recognized a friend's apartment.

"Let's go back to Lexington," said Maxine, a sudden shrill of cold air breaking through her voice. "But first will you boys wait for me in this store?"

David cheered, then looked confused. Ilya only licked his ice cream. They hadn't captured the last part of her sentence.

"Inside, boys," she told the eleven and four year old. "David watch your little brother."

"Where are you going?"

Pointing at the house across the street, she answered, "I will be . . . right there."

"But . . ."

She hushed David, leaving the brothers alone in a used book store, where it smelled like yellowing pages. *Mom . . .* Ilya would never forget the next and last words his mom ever said, words she spoke with the crack of a smile. Those strange, strange words.

"Be right back."

☿

May 17th. Hello, journal.* It's Thursday. Day of nostalgia. Day of pain. I didn't perform yesterday, didn't work. So I went home early and slept until now. My clock says 2. It could be 2 AM or 2 PM, I would feel the same, empty. Though, I have the whole morning to mix and the afternoon to sleep, *be it as it may*. Now there's phrase you only see written in stuffy journals, never in wet dream diaries. Here is my place to fantasize, to be high, as high as the Fool in Tarot.

Make the best EP of all time. Win her back. Quit drugs. Got it.

Key change. What do you think about this: Beauty begs to be repeated? I believe this to be true.

Track one of the EP is a highly-danceable experimental opener—inspired by two of my favorite album openers, Aphex Twin's "4" and Kanye West's "On Sight"—titled, "Здравствуйте," with modulations of the title being repeated over and over, cut from a golden era Soviet cartoon, and spliced with a sample of Michelle Obama, telling Americans to "Be Healthy," and the beat going nuts at the end, a real nasty break down, into something airy and ephemeral, floating up to the ether . . .

Beautiful things. Some weeks ago Tiff read me a short something-something from a poetry collection she's been nibbling on lately. It sounded very well put, almost

---

* Hello to you too! I still can't believe you kept these entries. For you it must have been strange to read your old thoughts. But for me it's fascinating. Also, is it fair to call them "old" if they were thoughts you had when you were young? Your *dated* thoughts, maybe. Stirring my emotions.

rehearsed: "Beauty begs to be repeated." Or maybe it was something like "Beauty asks copies of itself." "Beauty calls to be reproduced." I could guess again, triangulate what was actually said, but I think the sentiment is there, between the iterations. This idea explains why I do what I do. I hear a beautiful song, and I want to share it. I hear a melody in my head and I want to craft loops of it and put beats to it, for the world to enjoy the beauty, so they can experience it too. Do I want children? I beg, call, almost ask to be a parent. Stacy was the one.

Speaking of beautiful things, on YouTube there are videographers who stitch footage together of vacations they have taken with cute models, overlaying hours upon hours of house remixes on it. I'm thinking, why would you go through the trouble of stitching together all your footage of cute women that you've invited to Fiji, to the Bahamas, to Thailand, and Cancun? The music is good, but, ok, I didn't realize this until I thought of what Tiff said about beauty. These videographers, though sleazy they may be, doing gainers off of rock faces, or chasing their top-chain influencer girlfriends, are sharing with the world the beauty they have experienced: drone shots of canyons, footage of crystal clear beaches and sandy coves, and of course the curvy bikini tops of these lovely young ladies. And make a buck! If one million views on YT gets $300 to $2000 on average then imagine this: there's one video of 3 hours of Kygo remixes, titled *Summer Mix 2018* or other, with over 10 million views. That's bank. And people like it. I'm at least ten of those 10 million views. Listening to the music, now, as I type.

When was the last time (college, for essays) that I wrote so much? I have promised myself to keep a journal each morning, from now until the habit breaks. They are called "morning pages," from Julia Cameron's *The Artist's Way*. She asks for three pages of long hand. But I'm going to do thirty minutes of typing instead, because I never learned to hold a pen right.

Yes. Stacy does these, in long hand no less, because her handwriting is clear. Girly, but clear, with loopy vertical letters and circles for tittles over her lower-case i's. My handwriting? Chicken poop. Never learned.

In fact, there are a lot of things I never learned to do as a kid. It's because I grew up alone with my father and brother. He's seven years older than me. But I've always been tougher.

Lies! Lol, how would anyone know how long it took me to write that word? Two-and-a-half minutes, before I bolded it. I simply reached the end of the word "tougher" and sat staring at the white of the rest of the page, like gazing at the white of an eye staring back at me. I could have gotten a fruit, cut it into wedges, and drizzled honey over it in the time that it took me to just sit here and stare at the page. Is that normal? No. It's sitting lazy, sitting scared. What exactly am I afraid of? "Turn on your mind, relax, and float downstream." Is that the Lennon quote? On or *off*? I'm nervous. My chest cramps. My breathing shortens. I suddenly feel the intense urge to Google-check this quote. But, as is, probably incorrect, it stays. Because, I want to be *on* one, on a good idea; not off one, a bad idea. Strange, losing Stacy hurts. I miss her.

My windows are: DAW, Mozilla, and Word—and the calculator, to see how much money I need to make this month, having now one day less of work.

What else did I not learn in school? To flow.

Yet what did I learn in school? About other people.

First grade, first week. It was one year after 9/11. And David was in high school already, a year early.

Their father was miles away and late to pick up Ilya, who sat at the curb in the part of the carpool reserved for the last boys and girls. The girls played patty cake, the boys traded cards.

But not Ilya, at carpool, alone, sitting curbside in the tardy section, none of his classmates talking to him, that is until, held by the hand of their teacher, a classmate appeared.

The classmate wore thick nerdy glasses, his skin coffee black. His name was James, but everyone called him Rashad. The teacher said a few words, then left them alone. They sat in silence for a long time. The fact that they both had tardy parents put them as equals, objectively, but they didn't consider that.

Why was Ilya alone among his classmates in carpool, and why had Rashad, from his class, not interacted with him yet? The story goes like this:

Ilya had made it a habit to brag about his Pokémon skills every day of school that first week. And not just talk, he had developed a reputation of kicking his classmates' butt at the card game. Of course he was sad on the inside, coping with the loss of a mother, but when you are six years old you don't see a classmate's pain beyond your own humiliation, or past his motor mouth bragging. Thus, day in and day out, Ilya would drop his deck on a classmate's desk and look at them square in the face. There was something chilling in the way he looked at you, even the teacher felt that. Some called it stupid, others scary, yet others beautiful. But for a class of upper middle class grade school children, no matter what, it rocked them to their very bones.

Back to cards, it was no fun playing with Ilya. He was too smart, too stacked, the cards were always in his favor. His classmates would even complain to the teacher that he was cheating. But when the teacher observed, all she would see was her top student, little Ilya, playing fair. Blue eyes and a smile, terribly deceiving. He often cheat, but talked so much and too well for anyone to notice exactly how he did, or when he didn't.

The worst part about Ilya was that he would take your favorite card at the end, since the only exciting way to play was for keeps. So, he got stronger and stronger. It was the boys who complained to the teacher, mostly because they wanted their cards back. If a girl happened to play then it would be with another boy's deck, and therefore the loss was salt and lemons to those same boys, who would cry twice as hard to the teacher, for losing cards twice as many times.

Over to the side, however, not really mixing with the crowd, instead focused on complicated board games and growing the school's small garden, was Rashad. He did like Pokémon, he just had other interests.

The teacher figured she might solve the extroverted Ilya issue by joining him with the introverted Rashad. It was during carpool that first week that she formally introduced them, when, luckily, both their parents were late.

So they sat, and stared. Until, suddenly, both of them started fighting. For keeps, that is, with cards.

Rashad was no light weight. He carried a deck as big as Ilya's, and this impressed the ruthless blue-eyed boy, at least long enough to keep his mouth shut during the game. They played: countering and attacking by finger pointing, no words, just the move on their cards, like weapons from their stack. Only children, or really old folks, could play a game with such intensity, and for so long, in total silence. The stillness magnified the imagined, animalistic sounds—of slashes, of rage attacks, of psychic spells and of quick attacks—the moves that made up their creatures' maneuvers. It was a stadium quality match, and soon more and more boys, even girls, circled the two first graders locked in a battle for the title of number one Pokémon master at school.

Narrowly—after a bitter duel of fifteen minutes, which felt like, in kid time, closer to an hour of tactical wrestling—Ilya, with a level three water type, washed his opponent Rashad's final and best Pokémon in an ocean of humility.

Some of the schoolmates covered their faces and yelled, others raised their hands and hugged one another in tears. It was brutal.

When it came down to taking the loser's card, Ilya was the first to speak.

"What's your best card?" asked Ilya.

The crowd shook and cried, told Rashad not to show it.

But Rashad flipped his deck over and showed the winner his deck of cards. Ilya had the right to take any that pleased him.

"These aren't all your cards," said Ilya, bluffing. "Is it?"

"Nope," admitted the loser. "Not really."

Rashad opened his plaid shirt chest pocket, and drew out a holographic, American-style limited edition, wide-winged, fire-breathing, orange and blue dragon-type monster card: Charazard. And as he did, the quiet, dark-skinned boy glowed, along with his card shining in the light of the hot afternoon sun.

"This," he said, placing Charazard face-up on the ground, "this is my best card. I didn't use it because I knew you would beat me even if I did. Now why would I do that to my *Flyboy*?"

Some of the classmates booed, others, the most bitter, told Ilya he still had the right to take it. Rashad didn't seem to deny this. Ilya, shocked by his narrow win, couldn't help but consider that maybe Rashad might have actually won, had he played his fire breathing dragon pocket monster early in the match. Without that dragon in play, the young player admitted, maybe Rashad had gone easy on him. Suddenly, and without words, Ilya reached down. He did not pick up the shining Charazard, but chose the card next to it: a Slowpoke.

Everyone shouted, "That's the worst card of all time!" Ilya shut them up, told them he wanted to transition from water to psychic cards, anyway, he had Slowbro and Slowking. Which meant now his three-evolution set was complete, he told them, sticking out his tongue. Everyone left the two weirdos alone.

"So," spoke Rashad, "what's your favorite Pokémon?"

Ilya said Blastoise. "I can beat Charazard with my Hydro Pump attack, you know," said Ilya.

"Yeah," said Rashad. "But I can fly away. And defeat grass-types with my Flamethrower!"

"My weakness is grass-types." Ilya turned down. "I would lose to a Venusaur."

Rashad said, "Yeah, but together you and I can defeat Venusaur, and anyone else."

They became best friends.

☿

The father arrived, finally, for pickup at carpool. He was waving at Ilya from the car window.

"Is that your dad?" Rashad asked. "What's his name?"

"Nikolai Ilyich Gagarin." Ilya took his time getting up.

"Dang, that's a long name. Do you like your dad?"

Ilya slung his backpack on. "You have to know him, you know."

"True. Hey, Ilya, see you tomorrow!"

"Bye, Rashad."

In the car the father apologized for being late, but said they still had an hour before picking up David, to squeeze in a therapy session. He was wearing a plaid blazer, the collar tousled, the ends of his sleeves curled upwards, and a button sewn on DIY with the wrong color thread. Despite this disheveled look, his chest still reamed with power, his breaths were deep, his voice even deeper. He repeated his question, but in English. This time Ilya, from somewhere deep inside himself, wishing to be just like his father, even in richness of voice, mentioned that now he had a friend, maybe even a best friend, who knew, so no need to go to therapy anymore.

The father smiled. "You don't like the therapist, do you?"

"No."

"His breath stinks like stale jelly beans, you said, doesn't it?"

"Yeah, and, really, dad, I feel better now." His leg started shaking. They drove off.

After telling him to quit shaking his leg, in Russian, Nikolai turned to his son and held it down with his hand at a red light. When it stopped shaking, the father was so caught up in thoughts that he didn't even notice the light turn green. Ilya noticed, but didn't mention anything. So they just sat there at the green light. Maybe, pondered the father, his son really was feeling better, except for that leg.

All of a sudden, the drivers behind them started honking, honking for him to go. The father stuck a finger out of the car and cursed their impatience in a dark and funny Russian. Then he turned to Ilya, and asked him a question in the same language.

"What?" asked Ilya.[*]

"I said, I have an idea. Want to help me earn some money?"

Ilya beamed. "How? Now?"

"It will be quick." Nikolai turned hard on an unprotected left.

When they reached their destination, both looked astonished, their eyes gleaming.

"What is this?"

"An antique music store. Follow me."

---

[*] What the reader wonders every time she encounters your Russian xD

The father wanted to sell his Martin Committee trumpet. Worth more than a few pennies, he told the owner, who apparently didn't know a damn, cheeks so plump they squeezed against his glasses. Nikolai made him and Ilya hear in Russian, using words that neither his son nor the music store owner, could understand.

"How much?" the father asked, again, losing patience. The owner, flustered, wanted to repeat the asking price, but Nikolai interrupted him. "What about *store credit*?" Nikolai loved this word. Especially with what he heard the owner say. The offer was low, but not so low.

"What if . . ." asked Nikolai, pointing to the electric Yamaha in the corner, with more bells and whistles than a satellite. "What if I took the 61-keys with *store credit*?" He turned to his son with the same tenderness he had felt in the car. Then back to the owner. "Indeed?"

"I-I-I b-b-believe so," said the plump man, putting a napkin to his cheeks. "Indeed, indeed!"

Half an hour later, they picked up David, and listened to him complain and praise his day as a freshman in high school, mentioning all the clubs he had joined. No one at school had guessed that he was a year younger than everyone, having skipped a grade, looking so tall. The father felt he wouldn't have to worry about his eldest, so he turned back again to his younger son, excited about the prospect of sharing his passion for music with him.

"Красный свет, папа!"* shouted David, pointing to the red light.

"Простит!"† Their father stepped on the gas.

Meanwhile Ilya couldn't take his hands off of the box sticking out from the truck, through the lowered backrest of the middle seat, unaware of anything but that box.

So obsessed was Ilya that he sat cross-legged in the living room, watching his father assemble it.

"Done." The father liked that word too. "Done! Илюша," he called, handing his younger son the power cable. "Will you do the honors?"

The 6 year old ran to the wall, plugged the cord in, and then ran back. The piano was on.

"Смотри."‡ Ilya's dad put his fingers to the piano, put his cheek to the plastic frame of the instrument, and then turned up at the ceiling with closed eyes, before playing. He

---

* *"Red light, dad!"* I know you describe David pointing to a red light, but readers will be too distracted by the strange Cyrillic to make the connection. If you're going to have non-English interspersed, maybe you write the sound of the language and set it in italics? *Krasniy svet, papa!* Doesn't it look more exotic AND understandable that way?

† *"Excuse me!"* technically, or "Oops" in this case. Try, *Prostit!* Or *Prasteet*, assuming they pronounce like Muscovites. Look . . . Language is complicated, why further complicate this tense moment of a father running a red light with his two young sons in the car! How irresponsible!

‡ *"Watch."*

played a motif, then a whole song, before speaking again: "Неплохо, правда?" *

Ilya's jaw dropped. The father had performed, with such passion, such subtly, a dance of fingers and notes like the washing of pain, the loving of sunshine and bathing in surprise, the "Ode to Joy." When he opened his eyes to his son, it looked like the light of day had been born in him. A sentiment, the father figured, he should iron out with a little irony.

"You look surprised! Let me guess, you are not into the German? Let's move east to Warsaw, shall we?" Nikolai played darkly yet lightly Chopin's "Nocturne."

Jaw dropped further, Ilya couldn't speak. So Nikolai continued, inspired.

"Let's take it home, Илюша, to where it all started."† For seven minutes Ilya watched and absorbed the "Waltz of the

---

* *"Not bad, right?"*

† I must have skimmed his name on the previous page. See why Cyrillic is dangerous? We jump over important details like how a father calls his son: *"Ilusha,"* like the mother, but in Russian.

Now, thinking about it, I know why you used the name. And yet, do you really think that anyone who doesn't know Russian, who hasn't read *Brothers Karamazov* all the way, not to mention won't remember the name of the young boy who passes away at the end—meaning 99.999% of the world's population—will ever make the connection to our Ilya's diminutive first name? The reference is light here. But fine, you rarely make references for the sake of references, instead you use references to catch an echo from the past. I remember our conversation. No one has to know Gagarin was the last name of the first cosmonaut to outer space, for this to be an engaging family, right? Sad scene, by the way. The grief.

flowers," in allegro molto, in allegro vivace, in the allegro of falling in love. Ilya stared, amazed, as the father went back in time, because music had that effect on him, especially this piece, to the night he had first seen Maxine in *The Nutcracker*'s Second Act grand ballabile, stepping her way to and fro, of his waiting out in the dead cold of November to catch her as she stepped out of the backstage loading area door of the Kirov theater in Leningrad. He started shedding tears, but did not stop playing, kept on playing and playing. Now playing louder, more allegro than before, louder than necessary. Every chord he pounded brought out another set of tears, another and another, which resulted in a more ravishing, pounding sets of notes, a reinforcing loop, which resulted in a grand finale of forearms to keys, to sobs. Again, pounding, his face over his forearms over the keys over his crying. Because she was gone, forever gone.

"Dad," said Ilya, the six year old. "Dad, that was beautiful."

Nikolai shot up, face red and puffy like the dude who had sold them the machine that day. Puffier, still, after he heard his son make the following request.

"Can I try?"

Nikolai made just enough room in the chair so that his son could fit.

The son put his fingers on the keys. The father immediately corrected his posture. Ilya didn't mind.

He almost asked, but instead just recalled the chords his father had just repeated, the last song's motif, with surprising accuracy. "Was it like this?" Ilya asked, stretching his fingers as wide as he could, to copy as many of the chords as possible, over and over, the ones he had heard his father play, the ones that had moved him to tears.

"Yes," said Nikolai, "again, again, again!"

One, two, three, four, five-five, went the chords. One, two, three, four, five-five. "Again, again, again." Ilya did. Then he got too excited, the father could tell, and the chords turned to bangs, bam, bam, bam, bam, bam-bam!

"ТИХО!"*

Ilya stopped.

"We will," said Nikolai, "start easy." He then showed Ilya how to play the Rugrats theme song on two fingers, which he picked up instantly. "First easy," said the father, "then crazy."

As Ilya played with two fingers, his father reached around on either side of his son, and improvised bass chords and high note melodies.

"Amazing," said the dad. "Simply amazing, just like his *old man*!" He loved that phrase, almost as much as he loved using it with sincerity about himself. "Don't shake your leg, keep rhythm with your foot, yes." And he did.

They played into the night, father and son, and then again every night for twelve years.

---

* *"Tiha!"* meaning "Quiet!" or "Enough!" Again, just because Ilya stops in the very next line doesn't mean readers will make the connection. BIG CYRILLIC LETTERS ARE D-I-S-T-R-A-C-T-I-N-G!!! Btw, I love how tender this chapter ends, except for . . . you know.

That first night, however, David stood at the door, seeing them play, then turning around and leaving.

☿

On Fridays, Zdras was a guaranteed make out. That's where people went right before midnight to dance the early morning hours away, ingest copious amounts of controlled substances, discover new favorite music, or explore the boundaries between love and lust.

Early to work, again, Ilya clambered down the trapdoor under the DJ booth, down to the manager's office. There he found him, his friend and boss, Tony.

The boss had trash all over the place, he always did, a veritable mess.

Ilya, blazing, repeated what Tony had told him to say: "Boss, I have this AMAZING idea for July!" He plopped down in front of the desk. The boss's king-sized swivel chair spun around. There was sweat streaming down his temples, snow under his nose, and bloodshot eyes that screamed without making a sound.

Opening then closing then opening his mouth, he slowly spoke: "You always come up with ideas." The manager shooed Ilya by fanning his hand, then spun back around, to stare as his past, the wall of golden records. "You know who I've managed in my day? Heroes, both sung and unsung. Champions, innovators. My artists have gone on to produce some of electronic music's most celebrated albums. Their music and its ripple effect can be heard on the radio even today. Some went on to lecture at universities, others to found their own labels, or start schools to teach dipshits like you how to drop a needle. And now, what?" Tony spun back around. "You want to produce a show?" He spun back, then back around. "Do you know what all my artists had in common?"—Tony stood up, he wasn't wearing pants, and must have used the restroom recently because his underwear showed wet spots—"Confidence, Ilya, confidence! When they took the stage, it was like watching lightning strike a tree. And Ilya, my boy, no one stole their lightning!" Tony began pacing around the room, still pantsless. "Not to mention, they had *business* sense. But you? How many different DJ names have you had in the short year you've been here? Four? Five?"

"The one now is the one," Ilya insisted, cotton-mouthed. "I.N.G.!"

The manager returned to his desk, snatched out an orange container among the many lying around, and popped a pill. He signaled to offer one to Ilya.

Ilya shook his hand, feverishly.

The man popped another. "Do you even know what you want? Tell me how we can work together."

"I want a show on July 22nd!"

"As of now, not possible."

"Why?"

"Ilya, let me explain to you, for the hundredth time, our little joint hangs by a pube. It's bye-bye Zdras if we don't sell, say, between 300 and 500 drinks *tonight*. Why the spread? Because we rely on the tips. And we're open almost 24-hours a day. This is a fickle business. And every morning that I wake up, I thank the gods of dance for another day. That's how we survive. It's honorable of you to envision a show two months into the future. This place needs fresh blood like you, I told you that when Tiffany brought your puppy ass in here for the first time. I can spot talent, you know that, I know that, and you know that I know that you know that. Let's say I gave you a day in . . . July—"

"On July 22nd! On."

"Whatever."

"It has to be *on* that day, it's a Sunday."

"Let's say I gave you July 22nd the two-thousand-and-eighteenth year of our Lord. What then? You'll play your songs, you'll be happy, but what about poor old me? How many heads will show? Who will buy beer? You'll dance till your shaky leg bleeds. But who *on the floor* will dance? We need asses, Ilya, asses! Asses make assets. Mouths buy beer. There's a system here. Listen, I have an idea, what if you promoted . . ." The owner lingered on his last word, as if just having performed a dance number that ended on his tip-toes. Where on his tippy-toes, he saw Ilya, saw him frozen in a pre-stuttered retaliation. "Forget it," said the owner, "I already know what you're going to say." He continued with his spiel, which led nowhere because Ilya was as determined as ever to get the date. He needed that date because it was his parent's birthday and he wanted to throw her* a birthday party to coincide with his crowning achievement: the EP, a

---

* Someone who doesn't remember that Ilya lies, even to himself, would at best be confused by this, or at worst think this is a typo, since the reader is thinking, like Tony, that the party is for the father. Why does Ilya have to lie about whose birthday it is, what a dummy. If I may, he is terribly annoying. Which I know is not your intention. Sorry.

kind of thing that makes or breaks an artist, or, more realistically, leaves him as anonymous as he started, which Ilya was determined with the gushing energy in his gut to avoid, to overcome, to surpass.

"I will promote," said Ilya, clearing his throat. "I will promote the show."

The manager slapped his bare knee. "You don't know a damn about promotion!"

"Then why did you ask me!"

"Because!"

"Give me a shot, Tony, c'mon, please, I beg you. I promise, Tony, I promise I will bring 1000 people to this show, or my name isn't Ilya Nikolayevich Gagarin!"

"Our cap is at 500. And your name might mean something online, but bots don't buy beer. What do you know about cold, hard promotion?" Tony was slapping Ilya's cheek at the end of his question.

Ilya shook him off. "Give me a shot!"

"And if you fail?"

"Then . . ."

"Then we all fail!" Tony shook his head. "No can do."

Ilya looked at his boss, his friend, his musical lord square in the face with radiant eyes, as he used to stare at his opponents in elementary school. "We share the risk."

"What?" Tony's eyes were sparkling.

"We share the risk! I am so convinced this show will rock that I will buy the first 500 people to show up a beer."

"You don't have the money."

"I'll pay it with the EP sales!"

Tony was shaking his head in approval. "Like a 'buy an EP, get a free beer' sort of deal?"

"That," said Ilya.

Tony grinned. "But not no damn domestic. It's got to be premium!"

Tony and Ilya laughed. The older one saw in the younger a glimpse of his former self. He turned to his golden records hung on the wall. If he were sober he would allow himself the joy of shedding a tear right then and there, life is a mystery like that. Instead, still pantsless, only now with the spots on his underwear all dried up, he turned to Ilya.

"July, huh?" said the owner.

"July 22nd."

Just then the toilet flushed.

And out came the same bosomy young wife, who was around Ilya's age actually: Josephine. She still had on the magic Mickey Mouse hat, a monarch butterfly print kimono tied loosely around her mismatched panties and brassier.

"Look what I found!" Josephine said, holding out a bowl of various colored grapes, and something shining golden in the middle. "My wedding ring!"

"Congratulations," mumbled Ilya, trying real hard not to stare too long at her body, so curvy and delicate it made him uncomfortably stiff.

"Do you know how Tony proposed to me?" asked Josephine, now sitting on Ilya's lap, making him even harder with discomfort.

"Everybody," said Ilya, squirming. "Everyone knows your story."

"One day, he just swept me off my feet," she said, right when Tony yanked his wife off of his resident DJ.

"Ilya. It's show time."

Josephine blew the boy a brisk kiss.

Which prompted Tony to shoot her a question, then her to give a rebuttal, and them to fall arm in arm on the floor. Laughing.

☿

The sun was preparing to set; while the DJ prepared for his, at the booth in the corner of the dancefloor, where Ilya now only played on Fridays and Saturdays, surrounded by mirror after mirror after mirror, which gave the room an infinity feeling, each dancer multiplied.

His gear lay gleaming and streamlined on the DJ table. Folks used to ask him what he played on, but he would never tell.

How he got a three-day (now two-day) residency at a not bad club he would also never tell. Not to keep it a secret, it just didn't need to be said. It helped that his YouTube channel got views in the six digits, and it helped that Tiffany had hooked him up, last year, when she stopped playing at Zdras to focus on her audio engineering career. It also helped that he was comfortable with saying *No* to offers to go on tour as an opener all over the country, while he grew roots. This way, he could build a home base, spend his time performing, in place of occupying airport lounges or sleeping on night trains. He might have produced beats there, on the run, in the sky or railing fast, but that was not his best mode of creating. Ilya would rather sculpt in peace and quiet, or better yet record live instruments. To do that, though, to get good at that, however, you had to stay put. And hire good musicians.

Most of all, before anything else, without a doubt, the single most important, defining, uncontested, undeniable, reason for his everything came down to this: talent.

And, recalling the etymological history of the word, it means desire, will, passion, weight, and is made, sometimes found, but mostly made, like diamonds. You can stumble upon diamonds, steal diamonds, or, with enough pressure and enough dirt, you can make them yourself. That's talent.

As soon as the night's guests would enter his domain, Ilya the boy would cease to exist, in body form anyway. He would become the host of the night's vibration. He would deliver what he himself did not fully understand, the first to surrender to the sound he himself would craft, unfreezing the architecture that housed the dancers' night out, would hear the cued track, and would deliver it on time. Truly, Ilya became one thing when he performed. Something nearly unnamable. Personally, he would cringe were it put to him so plainly.

There is no other way to describe it. A title so complicated and simple that Ilya would never use it to describe himself to others. That's what Tony saw in him—like all who became his artists, full of lightning shot through pipes pumping electricity—a master in the making.

Now, Ilya didn't want to become a master to control anybody; he would rather swoon, send into rapture, inspire, alleviate the pain, or help others get in touch with that most abstract yet concrete concept: the groove. The groove, that ineffable thing Ilya sought out, ever since he learned to mimic the Rugrats theme song on the Yamaha his father got him in first grade. The groove ties your shoelaces together. The groove refills your cup. The groove brushes the hair out of your eyes. The groove makes you feel good, but how, but why? Does it matter? The groove equals two opposites together, up-beat and down-beat, sound and silence, a contradiction that encompasses the whole, the little things that Ilya believed a DJ must embody with a sweltering passion, if only for a moment—for it is said that perfection is only perfect for a moment: the length of a song, a chorus, or two chords well-played, timed to fate like the glance of a pair of lovers across a crazed dance hall. Ilya could honestly say he had seen more people fall in love than dew drops on a lonely Brooklyn morning stroll back home. It would happen to him again, this falling in love. But not yet. Not yet.

Cleaning up a bit, under the club's turn tables, which he never used, he found a baggie with clear brown crystal inside, either clean MDMA or dirty ketamine, he couldn't tell without tasting it. Which he didn't do. Instead, he threw the baggie on the ground, crushed it with his foot. Then sat on a chair and crushed the baggie with the foot of the leg of the chair. He sighed.

The dancefloor was empty, but not for long . . .

Suddenly, from below his feet, he thought he heard that baggie talking, but it was Tony, yelling—"I love this song!"—from the trapdoor, meaning Stacy's hit blues single on his computer. He had been playing it nonstop lately. "I can't believe you recorded this track. Play it tonight!"

Might she magically appear if he did? "No."

"It's your song too, not just your girlfriend's."

"K."

Tony climbed up to Ilya, who was on the chair, rocking backwards. "Fine?" Tony asked. "Fine! Don't play it. Did you two break up or something?"

"Uh, nah."

"What about that other song I sent you? Did you get it?"

"Tony, I threw my phone into the ocean," Ilya said, putting his hands behind his back. "Remember? Cast it right in."

"Ah yes," Tony said, slapping his forehead. "I forgot you care as much for your phone as I did for my first wife."

"Do you think about her often?" asked Ilya, leaning back on the chair, tapping his foot and making himself rock dangerously.

That's when Tony kicked a chair leg from under Ilya, sending him crashing. "Need I remind you not to rock in your chair? You are going to bust your ass one day."

Ilya rubbed the back of his head. "You're right."

"Damn right I'm right." Tony glanced at the DJ table. "You ever use the turntables?"

"These old things?" Ilya pointed at the Tech-12s.

"They're built like AKs," said Tony. "I keep them for you. Why don't you use them tonight for a change?"

Ilya rubbed his head as he shook it.

"You know what, play Stacy's song. That's an order." Tony began sniffing the air, which smelled of smoke. "Josephine, my little calf!" he started shouting down the trapdoor.

"Vitella mia! Don't do anything stupid! Hubby's gotta work!"[*]

He had already talked to Ilya, now it was the bartenders' turn, next the bouncers who were arriving, before he could dive back down.

☿

---

[*] "Vitella mia" means my little calf? I'm just assuming based on the previous line—and I know the Italian dish, vitello tonnato, made from young, soft baby cow meat in mayo-like tuna sauce.

Zdras. It worked beautifully, with Tony at the helm. He told the bouncers to check IDs on dudes, but only if they were ill-dressed, meaning, "plain, grubby, or poor." If a fight escalated and it wasn't stopped quickly enough, one bouncer got fired. If the city came and handed the club a capacity citation, all the bouncers got fired. And yet it was always packed, especially on Fridays. Zdras. On a diagonal street in the gray zone where trendy Williamsburg ended and trending Bushwick started—better known as "somewhere," since no one wanted to say out loud exactly where this club was, because then it might stop being cool, though it had been cool for two decades. The margins were absurd, not worth mentioning either, nevertheless, no matter how much money came in, it always flowed out. So every night had to be all-in for the crew. Usually they were cool, and asked Ilya all about his gear and his music and what new music was out there. "Why you always turning them knobs?" one had asked. Ilya gave him a metaphor. "You know how you want the perfect temperature of water for your shower? You turn the hot knob first then the cold one a little, sometimes turning for a while, meticulously, until it comes out just right? It's the same with mixed music, only the water in the pipes changes pressure and temperature constantly, and there are multiple people in the shower, each with different preferences."

Moving on, Tony reminded the bartenders to sell everything, to offer customers in line a beer, even while shaking cocktails if they had to. "Standing money is money that don't move." It would pay to mention the bartenders, themselves. And how they would mess with Ilya.

As he was piecing his gear together, one older bartender lined shot glasses on the counter. Another dumped ice into a chest. Yet another opened cheap liquor and poured it into the better bottles. How they were hired sort of went like this: a frequent client would one day jump onto the bar, feeling as sexy as ever, only to fall on the other side; suddenly, when she got back up, she had an extra tattoo and a wrist band with the word "Employee" on it, hair pulled back, and an empty glass in their hand, saying, "What do you want?" This Friday, for example, they had told the newest new girl to have fallen over the bar that, as part of her training, she had to make Ilya blush. The new employee asked, "With pleasure, what's his weakness?" They told her.

She's so pretty, thought Ilya, seeing the new bartender. As soon as they crossed eyes, she put down the glass she was wiping, grabbed the bar, and jostled her breasts side to side, tongue sticking out of her smile as wide as her sway.

Ilya sunk behind the DJ booth, face blushing. The tenders sprayed spit as they laughed. Everyone part of the same organism, the hornet named Zdras.

The demographic on a typical Friday night was a mix of East Village yuppies who dressed cheap-rich, and south Brooklynites who Uber'd north to act rich-cheap: depending on the promoters, the real estate agents of the entertainment world, and who they invited. They couldn't care less about the organism, like mercenaries who suck the blood of any venue that'll take them. The real bottom line came from the bar mixing drinks, and the DJ mixing beats, and the bouncers keeping order, the trinity invested in the atmosphere. But Zdras still needed heads, meaning high numbers over the line. And there was the head promoter, who hired all the little headed promoters. But Ilya didn't pay them much mind, for now; let me, he thought, focus on the music. Music ... music ... how can one make a real living off of music? If Tony barely survived, then the industry ... then ...

Doors opened. And in no time a crowd amassed.

☿

He wasn't cool enough to use the turntables. Nevertheless, it would be great to reduce the screen time and touch something physical more often. Learn the tech, he thought, or else pretend. In the end they are just tools to reach meaning. Plus, there are enough artists keeping true to Music to worry about the abstract state of its industry, or how to penetrate it. Hadn't he? Yet how many hours wasted, watching videos online about how to do this, how to do that.

Unless you're doing it yourself, watching others to inspire yourself is as effective as trying to fix politics by watching videos of bobble dolls complain about a balding president. Presidents are status symbols, anyway, like trophy wives with nuke codes. The ones who really run the country do the best they can, and we shouldn't complain, unless we're willing to get our руки dirty, fixing the system ourselves. Or at least vote.

Ilya drew his hands from his laptop, and rubbed his eyes. It was suddenly 2 AM. Good, he thought, always in a positive mood when he got to play the entire night, because a guest DJ hadn't been booked—whereas usually at this hour he had to give up the booth to an artist on tour.

The boy jumped up and down before the crowd, mostly to wake himself up. Focusing, he saw the next three moves on his laptop, to play, like chess. Still, he was nodding off.

It was no surprise that Ilya felt extra tired these days, while deejaying. He wasn't getting trashed during his sets anymore. He was staying clearheaded, which meant a lot of time to reflect in his booth. What had him stumped now, in his fledgling sobriety, were the mash ups of languages that big and small artists alike were weaving into their music, as in "Despacito." How did the US market, in a country world-famous for its ignorance and mainstream narrow-mindedness, raise artists like Pit Bull, Jennifer Lopez, invite artists like Daddy Yankee, papi Iglesias, hijo Iglesias, or foster the holy of holies, the album of albums, *Supernatural* by Carlos Santana, one of Ilya's all-time favorites? Ne-Yo, Yo-Yo Ma, Karsh Kale, and LL Cool J, ok, that guy's straight up American, but on the whole maybe America wasn't so narrow-minded after all, thought Ilya, as he skimmed his library for the next-next-next-next track. Certainly, the US wasn't. "Despacito," a mostly Spanish song debuted at #44 on the hot charts. But when Biebz threw in his two cents, the song shot to number one, all summer long, becoming the most listened to song, arguably, of all time, with five billion plays on YouTube. And who could forget "La Macarena" in 1997. And let's not ignore how, exactly sixty years before today, in 1958, the US saw Domenico Modugno's "Nel Blu Dipinto di Blu" (aka "Vo-la-re, o-o-o-oh") skyrocket to number one.[*]

---

[*] From 1820 to 2004, 5.5 million Italians immigrated to the United States. Makes sense Modugno would sell. Today, 41 million native Spanish speakers live in the US, with 12 million Americans who speak Spanish as a second language. Spanish-English blending is possible then. But Russian-English? Russian speakers in the US are less than one million, like I wrote earlier. How many would actually read one of their own? Not to say a mixed-breed, my dear, like you.

While strangers made out, while someone vomited into the toilet, while someone else waited outside to do the same, while bar-backs danced with mops, and while blinding lights glittered, and a fervent rain of Ilya's electronic music got everybody wet, the DJ faintly heard his father's words, from one of his university seminars he had attended once, but under the chorus of today's mish-mashing tracks: "The surrealist juxtaposed reality and dreams in art, so why couldn't we juxtapose different languages?"[*]

Perhaps Ilya did have a real chance to accomplish his life-long, life-affirming dream—to produce a successful, danceable, infectious, eclectic debut EP—which maybe wasn't even to win back Stacy. But to prove something bigger.

Until now Ilya had been too afraid to act, too afraid to release his life-long dream. It remained in his head, as dreams often do, making all sorts of excuses for it. Down this road, though, he knew he would forget it, bottle it up, or worse keep it swallowed in his throat. For it was there, living and dying in him, as potential unsung. Truthfully, the fear was this: if he did share it, if he did sing it out loud, then the dream would run the risk of a diffuse, mute death, since a failure to connect with others would render its reception vaguely ignored at best, or painfully obscure at worst. Like a tree that falls where no one can hear it, a favor given but never returned, or a message sent that gets left on read. Ilya could not accept this, so instead he waited, watched. He

---

[*] You sure are going to try.

focused on mixing other people's music, on pleasing others, became more worried on securing the show he might have, than on finishing the music he needed to make that night a hit.

And yet, given that his destiny was as real as gravity, drawing him to the bottom of things, eventually he had to share his work, gamble the little warmth his perfect vision gave him for the chance that it brighten someone else's fire, that it give someone else more life. No one can do this alone.

That's why to join people who share the same dream is to break from our own contradictions, to build a sweeter reality.[*]

☿

---

[*] Us.

3 AM, still Friday night. And Ilya's friend and roommate, Tiffany Voltescu, approached the DJ booth.

She was trying out a new camera.

"Great footage tonight!" yelled Tiffany. She wore her dreaded hair in a bun over her head, which to Ilya meant she was in a good mood that night.

He had drawn something on a napkin, which he handed to Tiffany, along with a drink in a plastic cup. It was a smiley.

Tiffany took the napkin, the cup, and put it to her nose. "Nothing funny in it?"

"Just some spit."

"Just being safe."

"Who taught you to be safe?"

Tiffany sipped on her Shirley Temple, and—with the straw at her lips—mouthed the word "You," before taking a second sip.

"Any 80s in the set tonight?" Tiffany asked, after setting down her drink.

"Tomorrow," yelled Ilya, leaning towards Tiffany's ear full of piercings. "Friday has to be top-forty remixes."

"Your remixes, at least?"

"Zuh."

"Nice," said Tiffany, squinting her eyes at the madness, the crowd. "I wonder how many of these people got dumped by their S.O. this week."

"What's an S.O.?"

"Significant Other."

"What do you mean?"

Tiff snickered. "I gotta spell it out? Stacy broke up with you this week. And I wonder who else got broken up with this week. There's got to be at least one other guy in here who did."

Would talking about her materialize her thin form and heavy voice? Ilya looked around to check just in case she had, but only saw a dance floor with a "Caution" sign in the center, and bar-backs cleaning up the mess.

"When are you going to get rid of all that shit in your ear?" Ilya yelled at Tiffany.

"What?" she yelled back, turning to him.

"I said," Ilya yelled as he leaned in, "when are you going to get another piercing?"

"You know I don't have any more room," she said. "And fuck you, I know you don't like them."

"But, Tiffany, I love you!"

"Then why don't you marry me?" she asked.

"You can't marry a best friend," he said.

"I would marry a best friend."

Ilya got down on one knee.

"Shut the fuck up!" Tiffany took out a wide-angle camera lens from her bag. "Wait, wait," she said. "Don't get up. I won't want to forget this." Snap.

☿

4 AM, and the club officially stopped selling alcohol, at least on paper. That's when folks tumbled out like spilled ice cubes, and melted on the sidewalk under the twilight of early morning. Except those who, like backwash, knew to stay just a little longer, so they could buy 12-ounce cans from under the bar, and listen to their favorite touring artist perform a DJ set, or...

Ilya packed up his gear, leaving those Tech-12s as clean as new, when all of a sudden from the exit entered an old man with a swanky gait, sunglasses on, and a thick mole between his eye brows. Everybody knew his name. He looked dead straight at Ilya, ran a hand through his gunmetal hair, and smiled. He was the after-hours DJ, when a touring act hadn't been booked. In a word, the man was a legend. And a glow surrounded him. It had been one of Ilya's deepest wishes at Zdras to introduce himself to this mythical disc jockey, although he had never found the courage to say something, or the right excuse, on the off chance he stepped in to play after 4 AM, when Ilya usually beat it back to his side of New York's East River. Forget it, tonight's the night, thought Ilya, as he gathered his things, to go say hi.

But someone interrupted this fateful encounter:

A brawny man with hair like grass and sharp as needles, skin bumpier than a cucumber, and a stupid dimple poking his cheek. It was the head promoter, Jonathan Murphey.

"Place was packed tonight," Ilya mumbled, trying to make his way past Murphey.

"No thanks to you," replied Murphey, the promoter.

"You know that hair's gone out of style, Astro-Murph, you should go to my barber, so you can look less like a bro asshole."

"Your barber? Why, so I could look more like a Nazi asshole, like you?"

"My grandparents killed more Nazis than your grandparents!"

"At least we didn't lose the Cold War."

"Whatever, Femur," said Ilya, feeling the lame-nitude of the conversation busting at the seams. "You should quit hiring drug dealing promoters—"

"How would you score your drugs, then?"

"—they keep scaring the clients away."

"It's your shitty remixes that scare them away."

Without another word, Ilya slung his backpack on and stepped away from the booth, sullen.

"That's right," clucked Murphey. "Go home to your mommy. Oh wait, she's dead."

Ilya lunged at the promoter's throat. Then Tony intervened. His long arms were enough to separate the two brutes.

"You heard what this guy said to me! I'll kill him!" Ilya swung and landed a clean one on Murphey's head.

Murphey kicked Ilya in the knee, wounding him. "This piece of shit thinks he can play his own tracks? No one likes his music, they just like his face. Now pretty-boy thinks he can just have a night in July? You expect me to promote his terrible ass?" Murphey bucked at Ilya, making him flinch. "We'll lose the club!"

Ilya bled with adrenaline. The scar on his chest, from heart to ear, throbbed. But then the bouncers jumped in and firmly separated the boys. Tony ordered them to settle down, which they did. Then he sent Ilya home, whatever, he was going there anyway, to pass out, cold and pissed.

Seeing all this, the old man DJ rubbed his mole and decided to speak to the boy the following night, Saturday, for the first time.

☿

May 19th.* Saturday morning journal. Blah. Genius? I sometimes ask myself, *If I were a genius, what would I be doing right this second?* I would be doing this, this, I would be doing this. Still. Blah!

I had a run in with the tool, Jonathan, yesterday. I can't stand that leafy prick. Through my mind run thoughts of kicking his ass. Can't dwell on it too long. But how?

Tony came up to me last night thrice to tell me to play Stacy's song. All of this could have been avoided with some honesty. But I couldn't find the words. Meanwhile, he explained, "She draws. Did you see her last picture on the 'gram with over a thousand likes? One photo of her here at Zdras and that's at least a hundred heads if ten percent show up." And there I was, at the booth, and Tony scrolling through her other photos, showing them to me. If there really is a God then he or she is making sure I still get fed images of my ex. There is no escaping her. "When I make it," she used to say. Not if, but When. "You have to want it as bad as you want to breathe when underwater." It is only a matter of time before I hear her music play during the tear-jerker scene of the latest rom-com, while I get stuck playing other people's music in that tragedy of a bar underground. What

---

* I see your inspiration for adding mixed text media, like these journal entries, or previous text messages, having just read *Dracula*. The smart thing about Stoker though was that he labeled his sections clearly. Whereas you don't even introduce the chapters, let alone head them; instead you conclude them, clip them with the tiny zodiac symbol for mercury. If only your lines didn't make me feel so twisted, so fixed, then I might even be upset at you. But I'm not, you know.

injustice! Am I also supposed to play her music to the crowd, watch them enjoy her jingles and jams, not mine?

One day, once the EP is done, I'll . . . I don't know. But the single! That will be played everywhere, all over the world, played so much it will become some country's anthem, but only if they pay for the license, of course . . . (says the guy who turned off monetization on his YT videos . . .).[*]

Stacy! Not YouTube's Stay See, but my ex, my "y," ye ole Stace. Old Ecstasy, you know: the starlet with American eyes, in whose eyes I was a star, shot and crashed, while she got away, got to fly. Oh, I have ego? With how I let you upstage me every time we shared a stage? And damn these entries! No one will ever read them. There is no value in

---

[*] What's the first thing I told you when we went on tour? Monetize. I just could not believe you had this treasure trove of videos with a half-million views, and weren't willing to flip a simple switch. But even you saw how the world opened up after monetizing. You could focus on making music, you could leave your friend's apartment, you could basically grow up.

Reading these old entries really puts into perspective who you used to be. Do you see why people thought less of you? Most of them would have cheated, robbed, or sucked pecker to get views like you. And some did, like the Fyre fest folks.

But forget them, and ignore money. What about how druggy, lazy, lying, and irresponsible "Ilya" is? Who could relate with him; or worse, who would want to empathize?

Maybe that says something about people, including me, that we would shun "Ilya," when, maybe, we all have a little Ilusha inside. A whiny child who needs extra attention, or small bribes, to produce art. An unconscious youth who needs wakeup calls, or a nice kick in the butt, to get on with life. That said, you see why no one can take care of their own inner "Ilya" and yours at the same time, right?

No wonder "Stacy" left.

what I do. There is no honor in what I say. Only my beats. Only my rhythm. Stacy, you were right to stop seeing me play at Zdras, you would have only stabbed me some more. After a good set, you would tell me what needed to improve. After a bad set, you would tell me I might as well have played my own music. You never played a bad set, and you always played your own music. Sexy solo singer-songwriter, yeah yeah, you have your troubles too, but you found a way to express them that people can relate to. Your fans trust you because they expect singer-songwriters to be honest. But folks don't believe me, because they expect something else out of DJs.

On top of being a liar—can't hide that from myself—it feels like I'm left with nothing to offer except that which they already know: quick and dirty remixes of radio hits, and EDM bangers that should sound the same for smooth transitions. The deeper stuff that means something to me, which I might work on for weeks before uploading, isn't liked, isn't expected, isn't appreciated. "Obscure," they comment, on the page with my song they don't like. "We miss the mixes."

Watch—the EP tracks I'm working on now will find an audience, I can feel it, but don't tell me to share them just yet, Stace, T, World, when I know they aren't ready—so wait!

These new tracks mean so much to me, how could they not mean something to other people . . . Music in general has meaning for everyone . . . but my music in specific? What if no one likes what I have to say, could it even be called music? . . . What if they don't get it?

Maybe I change the "Здравствуйте"* title from Cyrillic to Latin letters, "Zdravstvuyte," just for accessibility. Or why stop there, I could add its meaning in parenthesis (Be Healthy), to make the track fully digestible, no experimenting, no nothing. On tenth thought, fuck it, I'll just release the click track, and people can consume that, sing over my heartbeat while I stay quiet—because I'm tired of producing only for myself. Tired of performing only for others.

There has to be a balance between performing and producing. There has to be a compromise, a dance in between. A dance for the people. A dance that means something for everyone, for us. Because to dance . . . well, to dance is everything . . . and if I can give someone the chance to dance?

Then I must. I must.

☿

---

* Forgot to footnote this word in the May 17th entry: *"Greetings."*

Now, it does make a great opening track title, if only people knew what it meant. Or could pronounce it! In a general sense, being the polite imperative of telling someone to be healthy, it makes sense. But it makes sense to me—whereas it should make sense to fans, as well. Readers and listeners alike.

At Zdras, Saturday afternoon, when and where the booth called out to Ilya like the song of a busty siren, one who wanted to see him die, but first utterly hypnotized. He set up his station, ignoring the Tech-12s, as always, looking out at a crowd that wasn't there yet, no wristbands or strobe lights either.

"Your shit better not stink tonight." It was Murphey, checking to see if the DJ was dosing up, like he used to.

"You better not stink on my shit," replied Ilya, proud to have his desk inspected, now that he had quit.

The promoter, unable to respond cleverly to what the boy had just said without looking ridiculous, said the second thing that occurred to him. "Tony might have to sell the club."

Ilya, as he often did when he couldn't say anything back, just pouted. "You do you," he blurted. "And Imma do me."

This promoter, Jonathan Murphey, had an American flag tattooed to his wrinkly freckled chest. He was forty something, maybe older, around Tony's age. He had almost been a cofounder but he didn't invest the money, so he felt stupid, and jealous of Tony, but because his main source of income was this bar then he kept his mouth shut. He would open up his own bar if it weren't so expensive and time consuming. He was the kind of person who had written on a piece of paper back home the steps he needed to open his own bar and make it fully profitable in two years. But he couldn't take that first step yet because the man was making just enough, leeching off of Zdras, to not give much of a poop; plus this place was too much fun, and Tony owed him, he told himself. So Jonathan continued hiring and firing young promoters, younger than Ilya, below drinking age, acned high school boys who snuck their classmates into the bar. More than once there had been incidents with minors. But Tony never found out, and Jonathan took the responsibility of breaking these kids' knees for letting shit like that happen. Yeah Jonathan wasn't that bad, but he was a mother fucker for sure, and he even had that tattooed to his chest, under the US flag, those actual words: "Mother-Fucker," like that, hyphenated.

He had also recently broken up with his woman. Hence his edge as of late.

Tiffany called it, someone else had gotten dumped this week.

☿

Doors opened. A crowd amassed. And the sermon began with a drop of Scandinavian proportions, cut from two sources, one from a DJ set he had found on a *Pitchfork* article in 2017, and another from a top 30 EDM anthems of 2016 from *Rave Nation*. Neither were technically throwbacks—more of a glance over the shoulder—but a good start nonetheless, for an adventure back in time. The DJ would cue the tracks himself, no auto-sync, no key-lock, for that old school slightly choppy feel, before entering the bulk of that night's deck of music, the 80s.

Somehow it made sense, since there was a graduation party going on. What better way to get nostalgic. Young folks in cap and gown cried, danced, got drunk, and hugged, and sloppy kissed with friends they had always wanted to do that with but never did, and what's more, why not, the night was as young and full of promise as them. Real happiness in there.

Amid the madness, completely improv, the wildest hour of Saturday night turned into a tribute to the first generation of musicians to mix modulators with pop, which the crowd enjoyed, singing along to the standards of the genre: Depeche Mode's song about silence, New Order's song about falling on your knees to pray, that one A-ha song with the video about cartoons and humans mixing, and even that one jam Ilya played on keys once ten times in a row some odd afternoon during high school by Human League, as the young boy nearly grasped but a shadow of the meaning of the groove, so close he came, it had something to do with repetition, something shamanic, something in its chanting "fascination, fascination"—and then Ilya closed out the 80s night at Zdras, together with the bar's official last call, with one of disco's greatest closers: "We Are Family."

Ending an 80s night on Nirvana would be too on the nose, not to say anything about the flawless mix he had uploaded recently, with 1991-Cobain singing over 1992-Jade, which he could have cued—since it did get 699,898 views, his highest to date, in just five days.

Rather, he picked a song by the lynch pin holding the disco ball of the 70's in place, the band Sister Sledge, thereby going further back in time. For months he had been doing this, playing a 70s band at the end of the 80s night, waiting for some smartass to walk up to him after and mention, "That song isn't 80s, it's from 1979"; *Duh*, Ilya imagined himself replying, but so is "Video Killed the Radio Star," and you didn't complain about that when I played it, plus nothing like the 70s getting revenge on the 80s, after all, the 80s killed disco in America like the airplane in the 1980 movie *Airplane!* knocked down the transmission tower of a disco station: something Ilya often remembered, as he ended the night with that sledge* to the dancefloor.

---

* Reading these dance sections I sometimes wonder what's more obscure, your Russian mixed with English, or your musical references spanning from hipster to bro, to retro? Very narrow market, even if humorous. Makes sense for our DJ, though, or to any DJ as woke as us. Yet haven't we discovered people can't be bothered? What a gamble!

I get the temptation, though, of being subtle, allusive, subversive—it's a way to connect beyond resentment, something that builds trust, implies commitment. Like a secret handshake.

While wrapping cables and unplugging his microphone, this particular Saturday night ended with one more blast from the past: the old man DJ—crazy enough or dedicated enough to play a set at 4 AM to the zombies who stuck around—again with sunglasses on as he approached the DJ in his booth.

One man nodded to the other. The other nodded back. "I'm almost done," said Ilya, nervous, packing up his gear, as usual, ready to make room and bolt for the exit.

But tonight would be different.

After a cough and a sneeze, the other DJ rolled up his linen sleeves and flipped through his tote bag for a record. He said something Ilya didn't understand. Actually, Ilya realized, this was the first time he had ever said anything to him at all. And now Ilya couldn't understand him.

"Sorry, almost done. You're on, right?" asked Ilya.

The older DJ did not reply. Instead he repeated himself.

"Sais-tu la phrase, 'Once upon a time?'"* the DJ asked, softening the words as he trailed off. "*Once upon a time . . .*"

This legend wasn't reticent, realized Ilya, he just barely spoke English, this old man as tanned as chai, wearing linen as white as ceramic, responsible for more than one of Tony's golden records.

"*Once upon a time,*" repeated Ilya's hero, air under the words. "Know you this?"

---

* *"Do you know the expression . . ."* Or, if you want it to sound foreign but have readers understand, try translating it here literally, *"Know you the phrase . . ."* like you do later, on the page.

"Yes," said Ilya, light-headed all of a sudden. "I know. *Yada-yada, in a land far away, there lived a king and a queen.*"

The other DJ smiled, as he laid an LP over the Tech-12.

"John Rocca, 1984?" asked Ilya.

The DJ nodded. "First disc I ever spun." He continued: "En français, we say 'Once upon a time' like this, 'Il était une fois.' It is a simple phrase in French. *Il était une fois.*"

Sir Il-était-une-fois blasted off, it seemed, straight up flew away, as he kept the 80s alive with that disc he had laid down, a legendary house music a-side, titled, "Once Upon a Time," showing Ilya how to drop the needle gently yet with precision.

Back home, that night, Ilya fell head first into bed, his heart on fire, his mind flooded by a thousand facts, and a mad night's dream beginning to swirl in his mind.

In this vision, a brunette, with cream cheeks and sandalwood eyes, beckons the boy, in a soft and soothing русский язык,[*] like casting a spell, with two simple words:

"Жили были,"[†] she says, holding milk in one hand, honey in the other, pouring both over herself and him. "Жили были."[‡]

---

[*] In Russian (literally, in the Russian "tongue.")
[†] *"Jili Bili."*
[‡] To begin a fairy tale Russians say Жили были, similar to *Once Upon a Time*, although it actually translates to, *They Lived They Were.*

II

THEY LIVED THEY WERE / с надеждой*

ॐ

Interlude:

They lived, they were, this old couple by the sea full of love and timeless, beginning each day at the shore with a dip in the water.

Standing together in the vastness of ocean over sand, the old man would focus on his lover's lips as if for the first and last time—noticed crinkled curves, counted wrinkles, saw where the pinkish hue of lower lip turned to white skin, a mini-mole twinkling by a drop of salt water dew.

She too would spot drops of life between the mounting folds of his shoulders and arms. Or would splash him and make him laugh like old and new times.

Eventually, and for a while, they might go their separate ways, along opposite sides of the shore. But waves brought them back together again, their hearts in song, singing, I will love you, I love you always, in any language anew, and in any part of the world. I will always love you. That's true.

This thing they were creating, not a symbol of their union, but the union itself, did not come from nowhere. It sprung from without, from all those fans and friends, who dared dark forces to realize a birth. The imperative to continue.

Before the young DJ sat a clean-shaved, buttoned-up, bald-headed sales manager with a lazy eye. Lazy as it was, Ilya couldn't avoid feeling out of his comfort zone, with all the staring this interviewer was doing. Plus, he really wanted a job.

"Your resume states you want to work in the production department," the man said with a sigh. "But you applied to be a sales associate?"

Ilya—wearing torn white jeans and a wrinkled black shirt, from where his rose-colored glasses hung over his vial of mercury, and under a dopy smile—replied: "You know how it is! Gotta get my foot in the door somehow. This is a big radio station."

"We're a conglomerate."

"So, you prolly got room with the production team, huh?"

The sales manager kept staring, both at Ilya and at Ilya's glasses simultaneously. Why, he wondered, why had he blocked out thirty minutes to speak with this ill-dressed loser? "Prolly?"

A moment of silence passed, with the DJ feeling the need to elaborate. He coughed. "You see," he began, "I work at a Brooklyn night club, two nights a week. It used to be three. Now I'm looking for some extra work. I figured this would be the best place to put my industry experience to the test, creating real-time solutions for real world problems." He felt especially proud for that last turn of phrase. He had picked it up in an ad.

The manager couldn't help but feel his interviewee turning soft as he spoke, like soggy cereal. No way he could ever close a cold call. It wasn't that the manager took issue with hiring college dropouts, like this kid, youngsters with no miles but big engines—he had turned the worst of them into sales machines—yet they at least showed some potential under the hood. But him, this kid?

In any case, he looked at both hands of his watch, sighing a second time, before holding back an acrid burp. The manager needed someone on this floor, in this office. "If you are interested in production, you should visit our jobs page and apply for other positions." With licked fingers, he smoothed out his eyebrows. "You know, a job in sales—"

"I did visit," Ilya explained. "That's where I uploaded my resume and booked this interview!"

The manager rested his head on his hand, as he ignored the rumbling call at his thigh, of a device begging for his attention. It was his cellular work phone. And he resisted the urge to scroll through it, a thing of constant vibration this time of day, during which he felt his worst, his most tired, the afternoon, vibrating with every client who had to drop him a dumbass question, or insist on some dead end event they wanted promoted on the air, dozens of nonsense deals, while actual partners asked for more and more favors, free promo, help with their client platform experience, the endless corporate banalities for which he desperately needed assistance. But would have been more fun than sitting through this water torture of an interview.

One after the other, Ilya answered the standard questions always asked of prospectives, while the man behind the desk leaned back to stare at the ceiling. He recalled how that past spring a most exciting thing in his life, aside from running marathons, occurred, yet not for the better. His wife had read through his DMs—his, a grown man's—in which he chatted a little too friendly with a handful of IG models. If either the manager or his wife had been any younger, or a little more aware of how social media worked, then one of them would have noticed that most high-profile models assigned AIs to reply to DMs. Still, the wife threw a fit, one of her finest, and ordered her husband to delete his account— him, a grown man!—and to fire his secretary, Ananda, for no reason.

This dumb boy, what's his name, doesn't know when to stop talking, does he? realized the manager, concluding that he would be a terrible member of his sales force. Still. He at least needed an assistant.

Ah, Ananda, the manager mused, now that was an assistant. He recalled with tenderness how her French-manicured nails would rap at the keyboard, how it used to annoy him, yet how he missed that sound; by comparison, who was this strange, idiot running his mouth about how much "value" he would bring to the "table"? Ananda was the best secretary ever: quick to learn, thorough on edits, soft-spoken at the office, yet the type to jump on a table and spin her sweater in circles at the annual Christmas party, an act that would showcase her half-Indian, half-Polish raw sugar arms, to which our withered, seasoned, hard as oak sales leader only ever dreamed of becoming entangled in, yet never really did. Why? Because he would never ever cheat on his rotten, equally calloused, equally tough woman who some still considered his wife, unaware of the resentment she inspired, like the granular drops at the bottom of an old espresso that could be avoid, but he had to drink, having married her.

In the end, the manager realized, if he had known that he would be letting go of his best secretary, then he might have pinned her shoulders down against the fresh coat of egg-shell paint along the hall, that one time they brushed shoulders four months ago on the way to the restroom, and nailed her good, released all of himself inside of her, and watched her enjoy it too.

Ilya was rounding third base in his sprint of a monologue: ". . . that's why I think I could start off in sales, and then transition to a more creative position. What do you think?" Ilya remembered to look when at the manager as he spoke, but noticed that the manager wasn't paying attention. "Do you think that—"

"Stop." Just then, the man with the lazy eye, snapping back to reality, raised his hand to interrupt his own spiraling depression, together with the verbal diarrhea spewing from this obnoxious youth before him: "What kind of lifestyle do you want?"

"Me?" asked the DJ, pausing to ponder the question.

"Yes, you. What kind of lifestyle do you want?" The head of sales leaned forward, making the leather under his seat crinkle. "The answer to that question should determine what kind of job you get."

"I want a job that allows me to create beautiful things, for myself, for other people, whatever your team needs."

"My team is with sales."

"For the station, then."

"Why do you care about us?"

"Because . . ."

"Why create at all?"

". . . for connection . . ."

The manager pushed himself out of his chair, then showed Ilya the door. "I don't think this is the right fit. Please."

Once outside of the office, Ilya tried one last time: "What about the production team?" he asked. "*Whom* may I reach out to?"

The man gave Ilya a phone number. But Ilya couldn't call, he explained, since, you know, he didn't want to bother anyone, although, really, it was that his phone was broken.

"In that case, email the production department." The man gave Ilya the address of the station's head producer, but it was such a weird name that Ilya had to ask for it a second time. The head of sales repeated it, but faster. So Ilya missed it again. "Wait—"

"It was good meeting you," said the guy, "break a leg," quickly locking the door behind the youth. After a second, he caught his breath. "And break your face."

As he relaxed, a recurring thought dawned on him: down the dark avenue which was his life, beyond the slings and arrows of misfortune, the twists and turns which had defaced him, he had to wonder, what circle of hell was Ananda in today? When, finally unlocking his phone, he discovered who had called then sent a text message.

Both of his eyes met with Ananda's full name, and a message to grab drinks that night.

He smiled to see that life still brought with it surprises and coincidences worth a damn, even after all these years. Let middle age be a new age! he thought, pressing the green call button. Each dial tone ring was sweeter, more cloying than the last, until . . . she answered.

"Hi."

ౚ

June 3rd. It's Sunday morning, my journal. And fuck radio. Coke blows. Say "no" to drugs, lay snow to Dougs, day dose to does. Or, rather, "Come As You Are," *as I want you to be; waiting just for you*, singing, *I'll* "Be Right There" *for you, don't walk away*. Please, stay . . . That is from my Nirvana + Jade remix, not unlike Diplo's cover, though mine samples *Nevermind*, eh?

Nonsense. And no sleep again. I'll sleep at the beach today. Another booty pimple. Another earache. I'm restlessness, my leg won't stop. I need more power. Where is it? How can I inspire others? How does music move us? A genre a year keeps the ears a-grooving. Click the click track, then track vocals for Track Two of the EP: "Body Language," a pop pastiche that micro-samples a dozen songs with the same title, including Kid Ink's and Queen's, and "Тело" by Belarussian ЛСП,* even a sample of "You Can" from an alt/electro band called Body Language. Me? Make my shit stick, free of wack. How? Ain't got a damn dim idea. Call Pa. Feel. What do I feel?

Life granted me the moment to write, and my soul the words which flow outwardly, so let it be done. My weed words, pointless. Whereas real weeds in the ground serve a purpose, their own. But my garden knows no weeds, no orchids. I have not one rose. Only an onion, which grows one flower. Onion, like in the story about hell and the angel in the *Karamazov* tale.

---

* *LSP*, a Belarusian electronic outfit, makers of "Telo," pronounced "tiela," meaning "body."

But where is mine going? Impossible to exist without a fix. My every non-dedicated hour, no, minute, is spent in pursuit of a goal unattainable. Words deleted. I type. Forgo long-hand. My рука[*] is fuka. Stacy wrote by hand. And I? On a Julia Cameron roll, one lesson a week, one entry a day.[†]

Synchronicity, not so interested in that idea, as much as its two components, spontaneity and simultaneity. Big words. Big boys. What we gotta do? Keep applying to jobs, shower, laundry, lunch, train to the beach for the afternoon—have a beer and walk the boardwalk where my equipment disappeared.

For the longest time I told myself life was fine. But then I came back to New York after the bitch in Paris. Freddie Mercury asked once, "Why can't we give love, give love, give love, give love, give love?" And that's all I'm asking of myself after Paris—not with words, but with action.

After I came back, I announced to the world, that is, to *Papa*, that I would dedicate my life to music. He insisted he could help me get a job at the university, but that implied

---

[*] *Ruka*. You used it before, at the bar, when he pulled his hands away from the keyboard at 2 AM. I forgot to note it. Also, should we fix that *fuka*, or is it not a typo, but a silly rhythm? There was a book about fukú . . . remember?

[†] Teaching artists "how to guard themselves against the tides of negativity," according to *The New Yorker*, in an article celebrating its 25th anniversary edition. I remember when I bought you the first edition for your birthday, and I practically had to hit you over your head with it a year later, because you were complaining about all the problems which Cameron provides solutions for inside, without having even read a single page. It helped you, in the end, didn't it?

finishing school. I told him *No*. Then he calmed down, having seen it coming for a long time. He understood, more than anyone else. What I want is to connect with people in a universal language. Do I even realize this, consciously? If I am writing it, yes. And yet here I am, ambling through my mind as if through Brooklyn on a jobless weekday, thinking thoughts in-loud; then Sunday, more going in circles, pretending as if music is all that matters, or it actually does, after all the four-four beat can be found in almost any culture, in any language, it's so necessary. Ilya, O Ilya. Forget not the lessons. Love, love, love. Love everyone. Love.

Empathy. I aim to connect on a broad level; and if that sounds too vague or too grand, then you don't understand how vague and grand language is. Let the world share a common language, one music, filled with variety.

If more Americans spoke Russian, and if Russians spoke better English, and if the French were kinder to people trying to learn French, and if the Chinese were less strict about intonations, and if Arabic words were always written with vowels, and if South Africans made more music in Xhosa, then maybe the world would be a whole lot better. It's a matter of sharing and caring. If that doesn't make sense, then we have to start over from the beginning.

"In the beginning . . ." Remember Pa reading his parallel English-Russian Synodal bible, to David and I, one or two passages at a time, then discussing, reading another passage or two then discussing—except the very original first line in Genesis, which we read word by word, like a middle school science teacher dissecting a frog, bone by sinew, showing us how gross it is to tear open something beautiful and point out its parts with a scalpel. David thought it was BS. Pa liked that reaction, but he liked my reaction even more, when I asked *Why?* The father was eager to respond.

"When we study His creation, we get closer to Him," Nikolai explained. "Heaven and Earth did not exist until the Lord gave them a name.

"Consider a shop. By analogy, it does not begin to exist when the material building is completed, but when the owner opens the doors for the first time; only then does it begin to exist, only then can customers fill it.

"Do you know, Илья,* the first man? He did not come alive until breath was whispered into his dead clay body. From this stuff, two names were given, Адам и Ева,† a creation by separation, a labeling of what was already there."

"You're saying," David replied, "that something exists only after you say so? Sounds wrong."

"Did you notice I bought groceries this morning?"

David peeked around the corner, at some fruit in a bowl gleaming. "No."

"Not until I mentioned it, you didn't. Now go eat your fruit."

ॐ

---

* *Ilya.*
† *Adam and Eve.*

The sun was shining on Brighton Beach, the last stop of Russian immigration in America, where young couples made out in nooks between apartment buildings. The boardwalk was too busy with trippers tweaking, bikers peddling, and strippers washing down a simple pain reliever with a glass of sparkling water. All around a cool breeze rolled along, having entered from shore. With weather like this, everything fell into its right place, like a house on the beach, a guitar in your lap, or a bird in the sky. Only chapped lips and an empty stomach could do one wrong, but nothing a cold beer couldn't fix.

Ilya found a seat outside a restaurant he hadn't had the courage to try yet, because the waitresses were speaking in a hood Russian with their beach bum Russian patrons every time he walked by. This intimidated Ilya, most of all, along with a certain woman, who always happened to be there, like today, two tables over.

He recalled the trash his father used to talk about Brighton Beach, how rough the sand was there, how full of Russians too. Ilya didn't pay attention to his dad's comments about the братоки[*] in FC Barcelona shirts, or the девочки[†] with French-manicured nails. Ilya made it a point to go to this beach at least once a week, if not to perform run-and-gun sets, then as part of his Sunday walkabouts through Brooklyn, to visit this nest of distant comrades his father wouldn't even hold his nose over, unless it was on the way to

---

[*] The *bros* . . .
[†] And the *hoes*.

the more American side of the beach, Coney Island, meaning more full of different kinds of Brooklynites from the rest of the world.

Ilya was wearing his rose sunglasses, when he saw in the distance that same ship cut along the horizon. He brushed the bottom of his nose, nervous the way one feels when plugging a phone to a charger, when for some reason the battery won't load, that awkward try and retry to plug and replug the cord in and out of the phone, until suddenly, the green battery signal pops up on the screen and you sigh with relief. But Ilya didn't have a phone anymore. Nor did he remember the Russian his father half-tried to teach him once, the way he and his grandparents managed to teach his older brother David, who spoke fluently, through repetition and clarification. Today, above all, it would have been handsomely useful to know.

"Dievushka," Ilya said, calling, with an accent, to one of the waitresses.

The one assigned to his table licked the ball point of a pen, an old habit, before putting it to the notepad in her hand. She had on a white apron, undone at the top, and a purple shirt that in graphic lettering read: *UNTOLD*, which, any woke DJ knew, was a mega music festival in Eastern Europe.

"What can I get you?" she asked, in a calm, neutral American accent.

Ilya subtly insisted they speak the language of old Tsars, when he ordered the national beer in a tragic, painful American accent: "Pazhalusta, ya budu baltiku."

Here, the waitress stared at Ilya like he had spoken in Cantonese.

Ilya repeated himself, this time with added stress. The waitress understood.

In a fast, natural, open-mouthed accent that stressed the O's, she asked what size he wanted the beer, "Большое или маленькое?"

Ilya stared at the menu, pointed at the item he had ordered, and just repeated the order, still in his star-spangled accent: "Ya budu eta baltiku, pazhalusta." Patience was wearing thin, as nerves turned from steel to butter.

On her end, the waitress saw what Ilya was pointing to, had actually understood him, and knew what beer he wanted, yet turned as soft as overcooked pasta. Why? She recognized him as the DJ who had fainted the previous month on this same beach, Ilya N. Gagarin, her new favorite YouTuber, who she had discovered recently, for his videos of him playing sets in random places around the city. And yet, and yet, what she didn't know, didn't understand at all, was whether the DJ wanted his beer large or small. That's what she had asked him earlier, and was prepared to ask him again: *Yes, but large or small?*

"Да," she said, repeating herself, blood rushing to her face, "но большое или маленькое?"*

---

* No need to subtitle the words of our waitress, since the context is clear. Not to mention she repeats herself! The woman :)

Ilya got nervous too, but for his own reasons. Nevertheless, he insisted on speaking Russian; and insisted the drink be draft, randomly.

"В бочке, mkay," the waitress said, not even jotting down the order in her notepad. "Draft Baltika, right up!"

The waitress rushed back inside the restaurant, peering over her shoulder at that handsome boy her age, as she filled his glass past full, making a mess. Meanwhile Ilya eased the muscles of his jaw. His teeth hurt from so much pressing them together. It was terribly hot outside, the beer would be nice.

Two tables over was that woman, the one that had intimidated Ilya the most. She sat alone at a table today, June 3rd, with a half-eaten birthday cake, on which Ilya counted six candles. The woman, whose gaze Ilya had felt this whole time in fact, or imagined having felt, wore oversized sunglasses. By pointing her nose just off to the side, she seemed to want to fool Ilya into thinking she wasn't looking at him, but Ilya could tell when someone was, especially when the lenses were a clear yellow, like hers. She wasn't happy, he could also tell, when she wiped a bit of icing off her lips with a handkerchief, and then wiped a tear, though Ilya could have been wrong about this last bit, though, it seemed to him, in this dizzying moment, that she had been crying even earlier than now, because she brought the handkerchief up again, and this time blew her nose in a very wet, snotty way.

Suddenly, her phone buzzed. But she locked it instead of answering. And ate more cake.

The waitress came back. "Baltika в бочке," she said, still blushing.* "Six dollars, please."

Ilya confused the blush for a sunburn, a little annoyed by how the waitress had asked for the payment so soon, despite his planning to stay longer. Also, Ilya noticed that the first beer he had ordered after one week of sobriety was now being handed to him in a small, plastic cup. Ilya looked up at the waitress.

He said he would like to stay, pazhalusta,† and maybe order another.

The waitress left to help someone else, peering back at Ilya from time to time.

All the while, the woman two tables down continued to stare at Ilya, too. He became self-conscious of this, and of his breathing, as she stared. He looked at the fizz inside his glass he sipped, and as he sipped some carbonated bubble shot up to his eye, behind his sunglasses.

She smiled, going for another bite of the birthday cake, on which one saw, between the six candles, all unlit, a rather large, red, wax letter A.

---

* She mixes language, she blushes. Mhm.
† Maybe I was wrong. It looks ugly transliterated, пожалуйста, *"please."*

"Dievushka," Ilya called. The waitress came over. "Ya budu droogiu baltiku, pazhalusta." This time Ilya indicated with his hands just how large he wanted it.

"Большое?"[*] asked the waitress, eyes wide, glazed.

Meaning Yes, saying Da, Ilya replied, "Да."[†]

The waitress let Ilya see her first smile of the day, brought out a healthy draft of large Baltika beer, telling him that that was actually the last of the barrel, and that he should consider himself lucky. Ilya didn't pick up all the words she had said to him in Russian. Instead he knocked back the beer. And smiled, before turning away.

Up above were stars hidden behind a dense blue oxygen, lit by daylight. Down on the boardwalk, a dude with a reversed cone-shaped afro rolled by smooth on fresh rollerblades, humping the air to the beat of the music blaring from the boom-box on his shoulder, playing a trap remix of the Jackson song which begins with a panther roar, a HEE-HEE, and the lines:

Pretty baby with the high heels on / you give me fever like I've never, ever known / You're just a product of loveliness / I like the groove of your walk, your talk, your dress

---

[*] But still, I'll keep translating, *"Bolshoe?"* she offered; *"You want it big?"*
[†] *"Da,"* he replies.

"Excuse me, Miss!" shouted Ilya, as he ran after her.

The woman with the yellow sunglasses was not the only one wearing heels, tapping and clacking her way over the boardwalk at a pretty fast clip; faster, even, after having heard this stranger call out to her, and wanting nothing to do with him.

"Hey, hey!" Ilya caught up. "You left your phone, miss."

The woman whipped around, scowling to sting Ilya with her venom: "It's Mis'ess—"

This made him step back; she was used to strangers bugging her. And true, Ilya was stung by her words, right in the chest, and from this up close he could barely keep from stammering.

"You f-f-forgot your-r . . . here."

Ilya held up a rather large phone in a soft bumble bee case. She scanned it up and down, then scanned Ilya, his rather square face, his curved smile and sharp jaw, a head taller than her.

"Actually, I'm not sure if it's an iPad, an iPhone, or what," he said, "but I assume you want it back?"

"It's pretty big, isn't it?" She had a rich voice, Ilya noticed. She pinched the device, and put it in her large purse.

They stood before one another.

"Haven't I seen you somewhere?" Ilya asked.

She snickered. "You and five-million New Yorkers with a television."

"I don't have a TV," Ilya said, with sincerity. "I mean, my roommate does, but no, I've seen you at that restaurant before."

She raised an eyebrow out from behind her oversized sunglasses. "I go there every week."

"On Sundays?" Ilya said.

A dimple appeared on her face, the shadow of which made his heart thump.

"Vv vaskresenye?" Ilya repeated, swallowing spit, and heart still thumping. "Like me. I come to the beach every Sunday."

She snapped off her glasses, and put her face right under Ilya's. It took all of his courage not to drop his lips onto hers, or completely collapse onto the ground, like one of those souvenir push-puppets. Then she tilted her head.

"Да или нет,"[*] she asked, "are you American?"

"Да и нет!"[†] he said, swallowing mucus. "What's your name?"

She snapped on her sunglasses. "I'll tell you next week, if you really do come here every Sunday . . . and really don't own a television. Hah!" She walked away swaying, as if wearing a sable pelt on her shoulders, full of grace. Had Ilya seen her face, however, he would have seen a not so subtle face, her biting her tongue, her brimming with an all too familiar, yet all too rare, feeling.

---

[*] *"Yes or no . . . ?"*
[†] *"Yes and no!"*

"Wait!" he called out, snapping his fingers, zero idea of what to say next. "For real, what's your name?!"

The lady kept walking.

"HEY!"

The lady halted.

"Give me something to remember you by!"

She didn't turn around, but replied: "No handkerchief for you, young knight." Then, waving her cloth with icing and snot in the air, she added: "But a word: Любовь!"

"Liubof? That means love!"

"Любовь!"

Where in real life she had turned off the boardwalk, in Ilya's mind, in that instant, she walked straight into a folder in his mind titled "Forever."

ॐ

"EE-LEE-YA. EE-LEE-YA."

They chanted, "EE-LEE-YA. EE-LEE-YA."

The beat sped up, they kept chanting, "IL-YA. IL-YA. IL-YA. IL-YA. IL-YA." While with six flaming wings a seraph, the highest celestial being, came down from the ceiling. She illuminated everything. Then, burst into a nothing . . .

. . . Ilya's leg shook, tapping his heel against the wooden floorboards of the stage. (Do you hear it?) He was repeating this nightmare for who knows what time. (Do you feel it?) He stood behind a curtain, peeking out now and again at the mass of blank stares and anonymous faces, featureless save for two rows of crooked crumbled teeth that chewed sunflower seeds then spit them. (Do you taste it?) The curtain glowed in three colors, this time: white, blue, and red. (Do you see it?) It attracted no attention, which is to say it distracted not one jot or one tittle from the performer on stage overcome by flatulence. (Yes.)

It was a different artist on stage in every dream, tonight's from New York, someone easy to love at first, fun to keep up with later on, but who like the others fell off with a shebang, only to return here and there with cameos and acoustic albums, the occasional a cappella or duet. Never-da-less, dreamers wondered what world this would be were one to mention her name, or to have never known her at all.

Lady Gaga performed petty magic tricks. First, she sawed chocolate bunnies in half, then pulled ribbons out from her top hat, amid the putrid odor of fuzzy bluish eggs that surrounded her. All the while, she kept repeating a line from an Italian movie, which, if you consider Gagic *herstory*, isn't too far-fetched: "È solo un trucco!"[*]

"F'course, muh'lady!" shouted a jester in the audience who'd seen the Sorrentino film.

Unfazed, the act merely repeated herself, "È solo un trucco," words echoing bassy in the room so spacy.

One half of the crowd cheered, the other booed, in between caws and moos. She insisted it was only a trick, and this gave the impression that she meant to say something along the lines of, *Don't take me too seriously*. Yet, one did.

Around the time she started applying lick-on tattoos to her shoulder blades, she was dropped through a hole onstage.

"You're up," said nightmare Tony, over Ilya's snow white icy shoulder full of frozen gumdrops, lollipops, and bedbug poison.

Whipping around, Ilya saw, instead of his boss, a fire the height of houses. And in the flames he saw a man, not Tony, but someone like him, with horns on his head. Ants falling out of his mouth, fire ants, with pincers as sharp as shrapnel, the fragments of a bomb. His horns bumpy. And his eyes roaring as he spoke again:

"Did you pack your jelly beans?!"

Ilya trembled. The crowd chanted his name. Meanwhile the seraph reappeared to hush them. They did.

---

[*] *"It's only a trick!"*

He stepped out, taking center stage: "What's my name!"

"Ilya!" they cried out. "Ilya!"

Ilya raised his fist with one hand. And with the other placed three fingers on three keys. Tension was rising. All depended on this first moment, his first stroke, but there was doubt.

The laptop burned. The keys glowed. And Ilya shouted: "But who am I?"

He stuck an E key. But not a sound came out.

He dropped.

ఉ

The DJ burst awake from his feverish nightmare, screaming. Afterward, everything in the apartment seemed calm, bright. It was a non-work day, Tuesday. He needed another job. He needed coke. He needed something. But swallowed his spit instead, all of it, swallowed it twice, thrice, whatever comes after that. Then got out of bed.

In the kitchen lingered the smell of Tiffany's traditional sweet bread. She had just baked a loaf.

"You good?" she asked, referring to the scream. Behind her, in the cinnamon powdered air, was hung a large tri-colored flag—the flag of her home country: Romanian, with its blue, yellow, and red primary colors making themselves proudly seen. She called out again: "Eh?"

"Yeh!" replied Ilya, rubbing the boogers out of his eyes. "Just a crack dream."

Her national anthem started playing from a laptop in the kitchen.[*]

"Good." Tiffany happened to be cleaning the cabinets, when she found an empty pack of cigarettes, save for a nail and a lighter in there. She shook, her body craving a smoke. But threw it away, seeing Ilya, and remembering his promise to quit, and her promise to quit with him. They sat in the kitchen together for a long time. Until one of them spoke.

"What do you call this again?" he asked, wanting to break off a piece of sweet bread, but having his hand slapped by Tiffany.

---

[*] How are we supposed to *hear* the anthem, if you merely *tell* us about it? I had to search it on YouTube. It's good.

"Cozonac." She put the tray she had used back into the oven. As she closed the oven door, there floated a rich aroma of battered eggs, flour, butter, nuts and raisins, toothy rum and warm crust. Put bluntly, the smell of yellow bread that tastes good. Ilya reached for it. But Tiffany slapped his hand again, told him to wait for it to cool.

"You know the joke about the hipster burning his tongue?" she asked.

"What?"

"Why did the hipster burn his tongue eating pizza?"

"Why?"

"Because he tried to eat it before it was cool."

On one side of the Romanian flag hung Ilya's Russian flag, while on the other side hung their joint Stars and Stripes. Ilya had no doubt why drapes and flags kept figuring in his imagination.

"Could you repeat the name of this stuff?"

"It's co-zo-NAC. My mother taught me to make it this past Easter. Now I want mine to be as good, if not better than hers. So I practice."

Soon Tiffany softly cut herself a slice, then Ilya one too. Making bread was like mixing music, he thought, all those ingredients coming together to make a sum greater than its parts. While, moreover, baking the bread is what really brings it all together . . . in production this is called mastering. Who should master his tracks, bring them together, slowly bake the ingredients? Should Ilya himself? Or someone else?

Wondering when was the right time to ask his idol to master his EP, if after getting to know him better, or after offering some monetary compensation, Ilya chewed and chewed, savoring each bite, the flavors of her childhood.

ఉ

First grade, second week. And his father was miles away and late for pick up, again. Ilya sat curbside in the tardy section, but not alone. He was playing Pokémon cards with Rashad.

"I don't like Yu-Gi-Oh."

"Me neither," said Rashad. "You know, I think you are the smartest boy in class, maybe even in the whole school."

Ilya felt water in his eyes. "Thank you. I think you are the fastest boy in class, and the school, maybe even the whole world."

"Thanks." Rashad took off his nerdy glasses and winked at his friend. "Wanna race?"

Ilya shook his head.

"See, you are smart." Rashad slapped his frames back on.

"I'm not as smart as my brother," Ilya said, picking his nose. "He skipped a grade, so he is in high school already."

"You pick your nose?" asked Rashad. "Me too." He put his cards down. Next, he mentioned also having an older sibling, a sister, as he drew from his backpack a piece of paper.

"Do you know what my sister is doing this weekend?"

Ilya asked, "What?"

Rashad wrote a three letter word on the paper, wrote it in big letters, with a pencil.

"She is going to have S-E-X with her boyfriend."

"What's that?"

Rashad crumpled the paper and asked Ilya to put it in his backpack. Ilya took it, but didn't pack it just yet, instead he repeated the question. Rashad told him he didn't know what a boyfriend was exactly.

"No, what's S-E-X?"

"It's when you . . ." Rashad stood up and humped the air.

Like a dance, thought Ilya.

Rashad sat back down and in a hush explained how he had seen his sister on the couch with this boy she called her boyfriend, and he just repeated the humping motion. "Back and forth, back and forth."

Back and forth, thought Ilya, definitely like a dance. He unrumpled the paper with the word on it, and tried to read it. "Seex."

"S-s-eh-x-x," repeated Rashad, stressing the "s" at the back and front of the word, and the "eh" in the middle.

Ilya pulled out his own pencil and, underneath each letter, wrote down the following words: "silly," "energetic," and "xtrordinary."

"What's this?" asked the best friend, receiving the paper back.

"It's a poem, my gift to you."

Rashad didn't know what a poem was, but didn't ask. He started smacking his lips. It meant he was happy.

"You really are the smartest boy I know."

"Thank you."

"But I think 'extraordinary' has an E."

Ilya said, "No, it doesn't," but wasn't sure. So he erased the word and wrote instead: "хорошо."

"What's that?" asked Rashad. "Ksopa-what?"

"Hah-rah-SHOW. This letter, "ш," is like the "sh" in your name, Rah-SHAD, xo-po-ШО."

"What does huh-ruh-show mean?"

"It's more like hah-rah. Pretend you're laughing: hah-rah-hah-rah-hah-rah. It means 'good' in Russian."

"Like good, good?"

"Yes, yes," said Ilya, seeing his father's car rolling up, but not wanting to leave just yet.

Rashad got even antsier. He didn't exactly know Russian, but he liked the "ш," because it was like the "sh" in his name.

"You're хорошо," said Rashad, winking.

"You're хорошо," said Ilya, smiling.

"Let's race."

"Can't, gotta go," said Ilya. His father had pulled up.

"Next time," said Rashad, waving his friend goodbye.

ॐ

"There's no fool like a young fool," noted Ilya, hearing the words of his father who didn't like him going to the beach. But there he was, the air as hot as last Sunday, with the smell of sand and seafoam.

And there she was.

The same waitress working, wearing an apron over the same festival shirt, but who cares. Ilya was distracted. There she, who really mattered, was. He could not but notice her; not but see that she sat by herself again. So, in spite of common courtesy or even his own habits, he took the seat in front of her. She, surprised by his boldness, left it to him to say the first word. But he didn't know this, his boldness ending as soon as he took the seat.

As a result, both sat there glancing at one another in an unspoken, No you go, no you go—looking away and looking back—letting the smell of the beach dance around them.

Reflected in his rose-colored glasses was her striped sundress. Sleeveless. Long. With blue tulips. She had on the same oversized sunglasses with the yellow tinted lenses from the week before, and reflected in the lenses was Ilya, thinking she looked so cool. She made Brighton Beach look like LA. He had pictured her all week in just this way, too, which was odd, because on average he had terrible memory, and would make up for it with wild imagination. But in this case, today, Sunday, from his first impression of her last week to his impression of her now, there was a match. Best case scenario his life changes forever, worst case this stranger hates and forgets him. What's there to lose?

"Do you mind if I sit here?" asked Ilya.

"A little late to ask for permission, isn't it?" She left her mouth agape, to smile. "I hope you like mimosas. I ordered a carafe."

"What's your name?" he said. "Not Love, but your real name?"

She looked remarkably serene, unflinching in her seat, as she replied, "Some do call me Love."

He looked down, but only after asking: "What do people who really know you call you?"

"You tell me first, young knight," she said, folding her arms in a flattering way, under her bosom. "What's your real name?"

"They call me Ilya," he said, looking away, slightly.

"Илья . . ." she said, as if musing it over. "Так ты русский тогда?"[*]

"Нет и да," replied Ilya, flustered, "я тебе сказал," dousing his own enthusiasm with words that sounded foreign to him. He switched to a more comfortable accent. "Ya americanietz."[†]

---

[*] *"Ilya . . . So you're Russian then?"* I image this woman with smoldering eyes, so hot she melts poor Ilya with just her gaze. Our boy! I know you live real life as a fairy tale, and treat stories as reality. But this straddles the in between! Where are the castles, where are the curses? Unless he's building the castle, unless the curse is the mystery we're unraveling together. Her eyes, though, her eyes. Who could blame anyone for falling for her eyes?

[†] In clear Russian, he replies *"No and yes, I told you."* Then, in Russian with an accent, blushing, he adds: *"I'm American."* Finally. It took me

She hummed. "Но ты говоришь по-русски."[*]

"I don't speak Russian," replied Ilya, as if there were an ice cube in his throat that wouldn't go down. "I'm not Russian." Most times it was the automatic response to the direct question of his nationality, where are you from. But he knew it was flat out wrong to say he wasn't Russian, just because he couldn't speak the language. And yet, if you can't speak the words, how do you answer the question? Worse, other people's opinion always sound more convincing than your own on this one, a case you had no decision on to begin with. Even now, it remains a complicated matter—all the more reason to give easy, incomplete answers to difficult, simple questions.

Soon, full of sun-flush and blush, the waitress placed the carafe of mimosa on the table, along with two flute glasses between the two strangers. She stepped away in a hurry, nervous, wondering if Ilya recognized her from the week before. But he didn't notice.

Rather, he paid attention to the froth. The froth, he thought, of the juice as it is poured is like the foam at the mouth of a beached jellyfish. Unsure why his mind had taken this wild leap, he began to tap the table with his fingers, nerves blistering, and leg tapping, eventually

---

100 pages to understand why you insist on Cyrillic for this novel: it is all in the accent. Book about a DJ, something about sound being sonic, et cetera. And the prettiness of the letters, sure. But still. Not a strong enough reason, especially if the majority won't get it.

[*] She is almost insisting, isn't she, when she says, *"But you speak Russian."*

pulling out a pocket notebook, and tapping his leg even louder.

"What are you writing?" she asked, resisting the urge to peek inside his notebook, or to comment on how the table was shaking because of his leg. "C'mon, tell me."

"Nothing," he answered. And kept writing, kept shaking.

Pressing down on the table to help keep the flutes from falling, while also succumbing to the temptation to read, she peered over and caught sight of two crossed out words in the young man's notebook: "Orange, itchy . . ."

Ilya closed his work. Glared back at her. But softened when he noticed how she was peering over him, so sexy. So he opened up and looked at his words, more to avoid staring at her, as his eyes traced the line of words as he just written:

Poisoned Man O' War / bubbles of a wish ignored /
on its mouth no more.

She gave an honest, two-finger clap. Ilya, blushing, held his legs down with his hands, and asked: "You like it?"

"You have more?"

"Yes." Ilya turned back one page, his leg restless, shaking the glasses on the table, saying, "I wrote this two Sundays ago, for my ex, who broke up with me, just before the police threw me in an ambulance headed for the hospital."

"Who did what and why?"

"Listen . . ."

All alone / all on my own / тоже ты / тоже мы /
connection breaks in two / our different langs / while
through my heart / you drive a stake.[*]

"Your leg ... does it always shake?"

Usually, *yes*, but he wasn't going to admit it. Nor admit
that now it was positively at its worst, so stressed, nervous,
exposed.[†] When, quickly, sharply, uninvited, this nameless
Love woman got up, walked around, and kneeled next to the
boy, looked the boy in the eyes, and put her hand on him,
that is her warm hand on his thigh, to ever so softly caress it,
caress it, whispering things in Russian he hadn't heard since
he was a baby, the baby, with lullabies with melodies like
angels of angels, cuddling and soothing, loving slowly.
"Now, now," she said, standing up, "isn't that better?" She
walked around, back to her chair, pleased at having calmed
his restless leg. Which astonishingly seemed cured.

Birds. Waves. Beautiful silence and sweet sound danced
around the couple of strangers staring at one another,

---

[*] I can't help myself: *В одиночестве / все в одиночестве / you too /
we too / нарушает связь в два / наши разные языи / через мое
сердце / ты забиваешь кол.* It is choppier in Russian, which, for this
verse and this scene, sounds better.

[†] Hypnotic self-soothing, the symptoms of an abandoned child. You see
it when a baby has been left in a crib alone for too long, they rock back
and forth uncontrollably, or grabbing on to the edge with dead eyes
staring into space, waiting for their mothers, or someone to love them.
Until ...

saturating the world around them, colors intense, warm on the outside and cool on the inside.

After the astonishment disappeared, Ilya spoke up. "You're really, really pretty."

The lady rolled her eyes. "Don't you want to know my name anymore?"

"I'm tired of asking," said Ilya, folding his arms, flexing his chest, calmly.

"Then you'll never find out," she said, pouring him more mimosa.

He went back to writing, no longer tapping his heel, just writing, but not for long. Because the ink in his pen would run out.

A fresh one from a large bag was tossed to him. Printed on the side of the new pen, Ilya saw, was the insignia of a local news station.

"Is this where you work?" he asked.

"You really have no idea?" she joked. He didn't. So . . .

She explained, as they drank, in detail.

ర

But Ilya didn't pay attention. He was too busy resisting the urge to talk more than her. Just listen, he thought, just go with the flow. And yet, in fighting his desire to comment, or to interrupt her, Ilya zoned out, contributing little to the conversation. And forgetting details along the way.

His eyes maneuvered from her mouth, to the vertical line at her chest, to the folds of her sundress, to her tanned, freckled arms almost at rest; as his ears followed the sound of her words, rather than their meaning. Sometimes, it wasn't that he zoned out, so much that he was zoning in, just in the wrong direction. Amid the caw of birds, the blaring of radio music, and a monolog by a stranger presenting herself, Ilya could hear the sipping of her mimosa between phrases, and the licking of her glass rim clean.

All in all, however, if blame had to be assigned, it was that native language of hers, which made a long dialog difficult to maintain.

"Могу спросить, сколько тебя лет?"*

"Hm."

"Почему мы не говорим по-русски?"†

"Почему? Потому что."‡

Ilya felt sweat stain his armpits. He wished to say more, but couldn't. She probably wished he would answer her

---

* She is curious. And right. I know how old Ilya is, but everyone else has to guess? He won't answer.
† *"Why don't we speak in Russian?"* Because no one would understand you. I like Ilya's response . . .
‡ *"Why? Because."*

questions, or speak in Russian. She didn't look like anyone he had ever met, and yet, not knowing her well, she seemed like all the women he had ever met put together. She unfolded her arms and placed her hands neatly on the bottom of her glass. A ray of light broke through a pretty cloud as she spoke.

"Julia," she said, "my name is Julia. Though my parents called me by the Russian Юля. The rest of my family did by the Spanish Julia."

"So you're either Hulia, Yulia, or Djulia?"

"Or all three. Very sing-song, isn't it?"

"I like sing-song." (Ilya was smiling now, thinking, oh sneaky synchronicity!)

His leg stared shaking again. And that's when Julia's foot brushed his knee, before swinging it under the table. Ilya relaxed his leg, yet calmly trembled elsewhere. He had come here, hadn't he? And he was the one falling apart. Her big narrow eyes crushed him. Her freckled arms and tanned shoulders enthralled him. Ilya, O Ilya. A very real force overcame Ilya. He suddenly wanted to embrace this sing-song Julia across the table, to hold her in his arms, to press her, but instead he just sat there walled in by the chatter of his mind. All he could do was think too much about her gaze, then think, *Match her*, and gaze:

Strawberry hair, eyebrows cacao. Lower. White chocolate neck, and white chocolate bust. Lower. He tried not to look, but the way the dress opened like that parallel to her cleavage, where the freckles did crowd. Her arms folding again. Oh God. Lower. He imagined they were filled with chocolate milk, those white chocolate breasts, how generous.

This time Julia caught Ilya staring, as her chest popped. "Илья!" Her hand went to her mouth. "Пожалуйста!"*

He turned red, shaking, wondering if he should sprint now, or when she's done laughing.

She started to tell him something, but he didn't hear.

"I was saying thank you."

"For what? This is a mess . . ."

Julia tilted her head, and with that had Ilya listening.

"For bringing back my phone last week."

Ilya felt her hand on his, above the table.

The thought, "I've known her my whole life," stung Ilya like a sunburn, untrue as it was. He inhaled to relax, like one does to float in the ocean. Meanwhile Julia apologized for staring herself, complimenting Ilya on his chest hair, wishing yet restraining herself from asking about the long pink scar or the shiny metal accessory hanging, instead giggling at how oblivious he was to her staring, which he wasn't. She drew her hand back.

"I have to leave soon," she said, drawing her hand away, and taking her pen. "My baby sitter is like a magic pumpkins: she can show up last minute, but disappears all too soon."

---

* It was only a matter of time. *"Ilya! Please!"* she shouts, jumping up in her seat. But how surprised could she be? She's toying with this young boy, this cougar. She doesn't even cover up. She is smiling, watching him squirm. She is talking, proud of herself.

She took Ilya's notebook from his hand, so as to write her name and number in it. Any calmness Ilya had had until now left him, as he dropped back into a foamy form of anxiety, worried she might read one of Stacy's notes to him. But Julia didn't. Instead, she found two blank pages. On one side she wrote her information, in big letters and big numbers, big enough to take up the entire page; while on the other, in much smaller letters, in the middle, she wrote something else: a two-word poem.

"You don't have to call, but I do expect you to text me," said Julia. "And I expect it soon. I don't like my new friends ignoring me." She closed the notebook.

Ilya snatched his notebook, eager to read what she wrote.

"This," he said, "your poem is ... really good."

Мы
We

She smiled a stewed-cherry smile. "Do text me soon, Илья."

"I can't," said Ilya. "Julia, I'm sorry, but I threw my phone into the ocean ..."

ಠ

Julia was in a hurry, but like the saying goes, there is more time than there is life. She grabbed hold of Ilya's arm and led him to one of the phone repair stores a few blocks up from the beach, just before it closed.

She pecked the grubby store owner on both cheeks and in a casual Russian asked for a favor. The owner grumbled, flirted with Julia, then eventually handed her a new phone— not the latest model, but not a first gen either.

Ilya had been standing there next to her like a turtle.

"Do you like it?" she asked.

"This is too much," he said, handing it back to her. "I can't accept this."

But Julia pushed the phone back. "You have no excuse. Text me this week."

As they stepped out, Ilya pulled up the call keys and played with the various tones of various numbers, like he used to do as a little kid with the house phone.

"You like it, don't you?" she asked, watching him play.

"I do," he replied, "I do. Same one I had before."

Vermillion on one side and magenta on the other, the sky turned. The two parted ways, but not before they walked for a minute under the train tracks, over the main boulevard of Brighton Beach, heavy car traffic this time of day, people eating hot dogs, and dogs being walked, one lapping a puddle of vanilla ice cream that was inching along a crack in the sidewalk.

Julia watched Ilya as he squatted next to the pup and pet its head, as he scratched the pup's belly in such a way that it could continue lapping the melted vanilla ice cream puddle. She watched the dog's owner, noticed how jolly this lady looked to have her pet admired, while also noticing that Ilya hadn't even looked up at its owner. He was too entranced, humming doo-doo-da-das to the dachshund, too busy even to notice her, the holy, beautiful, never-ignored Julia. She tried for a moment to get this young man's attention, by clearing her throat a couple times, when suddenly a button on Ilya's shirt came undone, and his metal chain with the vial fell out.

As Ilya got up, Julia's eyes moved from his heart to his ears, tracing that scar that trailed on his chest. Might as well ask, she figured: "Why the vial of mercury around your neck?"

"It used to be my dad's," he said, putting the vial back inside his shirt, fidgeting to fix the button that had come undone.

"Your dad's?" she asked, caught off guard by that familiar yet foreign, tender-sounding American word, "dad." She recalled why she had to leave soon, because of her kid. "Kid," another super American word.

Ilya didn't notice how the word triggered Julia. Rather, he spoke honestly, briefly, regarding her question.

"Technically, it used to be my mom's, but then she gave it to my dad one day, before she . . . passed away." I'm sorry to hear, she seemed to say, Ilya could tell, by the look on her face, although he failed to grasp the full extent of her thoughts at this very moment. She was starting to worry about getting home. But he continued. "He gave it to me soon after," Ilya said, referring again to the vial, "Now I keep this little piece of the past with me, for protection I guess, or luck."

"You believe in luck?"

"No, but wouldn't it be nice." He leaned in to kiss her.

She turned away, her lips evading the young man, as they smiled. "It would be nice," she said, "it would. But will we meet again?"

ఐ

The following day, Monday—cooped up in the apartment in Murray Hill, feeling cramped, but accomplished, all errands done for the day—Ilya texted Julia, I can't stop thinking about your two-word poem. Immediately, an inner voice told him he should have waited at least two days before messaging her. And then, yet another, deeper voice entered, saying, *Ah, but she replies in seconds, read*:

The poem is inspired by Muhammad Ali's speech at Harvard in 1975. Try to find it online.

Ilya spent the following ten minutes watching it. So good, he replied.

She typed, Want to know how I put your name in my contacts? adding the emoji with the side-eyes.

Tell me.

Илья Муромец. Like the monk-knight.

Ilya looked the "monk-knight" up, embarrassed he didn't know.[*] Fifteen minutes later he responded: I settled for

---

[*] At long last, a real fairy tale in this book supposedly a fairy tale. Do not bother with Google, little guy, I will help you . . .

'Julia' in my contacts, since the 'J' kind of encompasses all three pronunciations.

Nice.

Plus, I added your other name, too. The one you gave me to remember you by.

They lived, they were, a pair of strong and beautiful farmers, with a house and a magical well, deep in the woods. The husband worked from when the birds started singing to when the sky went to bed, while the wife fetched water from their endless, delicious watering hole, pickling vegetables, and weaving clothes for a neighboring village. They were the happiest couple anyone had ever seen. But as they grew old, the couple grew sad—despite all their richness of heart, and all their purity, they could not conceive children. It wasn't that a witch had cursed them, nor an evil king forbidden them—they simply could not make a child. Every night, after working all day, the husband and wife would kneel together on opposite sides of the bed, hold hands over the sheets, and whisper the same prayer. And every night they fell asleep hopeful. But woke up, just the same, just them.

One day, however, their wish was granted. The husband was out hunting deer, when he saw drifting down a river a basket-sized, fresh, round, soft-red and fuzzy-orange peach. Little did he know what he would find inside, when he took the strange fruit back to his wife . . .

. . . "Where did you find this?" she asked, her eyes wide and shaking.

The husband explained.

"And where did it come from?"

The husband couldn't explain.

Suddenly, the big, fuzzy peach began vibrating over the table. The man and woman stepped back, and saw with utter amazement the bright light that broke through the flesh of the magical fruit before them.

Inside was a baby boy.

And they named him Ilya Muromets.

A typing-sign appeared, disappeared, reappeared. She hit send: Not in Latin letters, right? Liubof . . .—adding the face emoji that vomits.

Ilya had already added the extra keyboard on his new phone, when he replied: Nah, Любовь, in Cyrillic.

She sent him the mind-blown emoji, adding, I could pinch you right now.

Here, Ilya put the phone down. Любовь. Pinch. This rang deep, like déjà vu, a thing that feels like it has happened once before, but not twice. Meanwhile, Ilya told himself to play it cool, as he reread their conversation. He put his phone down again. In his head, Julia might have been on silk bedsheets, silk-naked, about to utter the world, inhaling baby-softener air, her lips unlocking, then, finally, fully, with all her chest and all her abdomen and body, exhaling that tiny, meaningful word. The vision was all in his head, of course, but it didn't feel like a fantasy, so much as a promise, because Ilya trusted, and not without reason, she would say it to him again, sometime between now and forever from now.

Once, Stacy had asked Ilya how to say that word, *Love*, in Russian, but it had seemed to Ilya that she was asking in passing, plus she never brought it up again, though she said the word often enough in English. How casually Stacy said it, and this only after many months of being together.

Julia, on the other hand, said the word with such freedom, and right from the start. With Julia, where one romance ended, another began. Julia . . . mind-blown and open . . .

Waiting before replying, knowing he was maybe playing games, Ilya went to sculpt the second track of his EP, distracting himself with work, then with the following thoughts, in a murmur: *"Мы" and "Me" are nearly the same sounds, but mean the complete opposite. While, "I" and "Я" are exactly reversed sounds, but mean the same thing. Which one is backwards? The one you're not willing to understand. All are correct, and simultaneously so, without stepping on the other's foot-serif. Fonts are either serif, weird, or sans-serif. Serif, seraph. Sad, sans mère. Мы. Me. Mama. Maxine. How long will her song remain unnamed?* pondered the boy. *Must complete the EP.*

Soon after his mother's disappearance, Ilya wrote an "R" on his forehead and stared at himself in the mirror for a long time. Hence the psychologist who smelled like jelly beans. As it went, he had opened the old Synodal on this father's night stand to a random page, to Exodus 3:14, and stumbled upon its passage. *Boyod,* the same inner voice had told him, *God's name in English and Russian are mirror images. God – bog / Khod – bokh. God = Бог. Bach? That, or Бог's name is Sushi. It's a coincidence.* And here's another: *In Russian, "Я" is the last letter of the alphabet. Arbitrary, sure, but as arbitrary as 3.14 being the number pi, or the Russian letter "П," or attending child therapy at age 4 . . . 4 − 1 = 3. "П" is symmetrical, another mhm.* More mhms: *in the word "Russian," isn't "Я" its first letter backwards?* All thoughts Ilya had not once, twice, but many, many times, most times in times like these: all to distract from his work, from replying to Julia's text, from anything. Then an image of Muhammad Ali kicking ass out of nowhere came to mind. The kid remembered Julia's poem. Her candor. Her attentiveness. He must reply!

So at last, Ilya replied with the upside-down smiley emoji, adding: Only if you let me pinch you.

She replied instantly: If we ever see each other again.

At Brighton Beach? he asked. What time, what place?

No planning, she wrote. It's more fun that way.

ಠ

June 12th. It's Tuesday morning, my beautiful diary. Fort Greene Park today, to count the cigarette butts on the ground, mind my own business, and relax. But until then, morning pages, mix, eat and go. Go. My favorite word in English: Go.

How did the first people talk to each other, if there wasn't language yet? Did they make it up as they went? As they goed?

On another note, days go by and I don't count them but by the number of entries in this Word document, by the number of tracks uploaded to YT. One track a day, minimum. Don't care about much else, except looking forward to Sunday, when I can see her again. Until then, I make music, apply to jobs, bomb interviews. Text her. Tell Tiff? And I know most tracks will be horrible, at least I feel that way, but I am ok with that if every now and then a good one is birthed, a sharable track that listeners enjoy. How to measure enjoyment? Views, likes and reposts. Make statistics out of people's emotions, and you have a virtual world of low self-esteem. The most sugary part of "making it" is that you can't, unless the crowd says you did, please see reviews and show blurbs and critical essays and comments and count the replies, or skim the belle-lettres of your local library. "Making it" should mean making stuff for others, stuff that lifts up the people around you—you know, being more serious about the verb "make," and being less serious about what others say, or comment, though it's generally for others that you are "making it" for.

I am watching the TED talk David sent me. In it a speaker tells the story of his attempted suicide, but by reading the Stoics, he came to the conclusion that one should be wary of the opinion of others—or its evil cousin, what we *think* is the opinion of others—and instead find hope beyond despair. Seneca: "It is the power of the mind to be unconquerable."

Later I'll cut the audio of the speech, modulate it, and insert it to the tail of the "Body Language" track to create an ambient transition to Track Three, something else I hope people enjoy, positive self-image, that sort of thing, lest they be bored.

---By Jove! I want passion, I want dance, I am here to make people fucking dance! What is this sonic shite? New track! Add a funky breakbeat, a washboard, some popping noises to a pentatonic scale. How is it I can throw down drums, and make heads bob? The two actions are connected—throw a beat, shake a leg—though they look and sound different, they are as connected as lightning is to thunder. Add a thick low-end bass line, which listeners might not even realize is a layer of wobbles at 800 Hz, but their hips move, move, no longer stunted by self-doubt, the raver revved into 1990s ecstasy—can't spell ecstasy without Stacy; sad boys club, hope to tender my resignation soon; soon, but before, a melody from old chords like jewels in a treasure chest, or Jules, I'll call this new track Jules. I'll message Jules when I finish it . . . add some dropping coins . . . Music is organized sound, even when experimentally arranged. But no one thinks like that, because music is mirage. The illusion of music is so great that no one enjoying it needs to count the beats governing their bodies. No admirer needs to note the tempo change in Pink Floyd's "Money" at minute 3:06; but you would have to be sex-deaf not to feel the change to rock and roll. The sax just spanks you. You feel a chill up your chest. Jazz to rock. What a mix. Or, consider this, how music marks time. Think about it for two seconds, for what is a clock but a click track set to sixty beats per minute. Music is the soul's highest art! I exaggerate, but to make a point. For visual arts, you need paints and canvases, yet no matter what it rots—even The *Birth of Venus* will fall apart, the *David* collapse at the next minor earthquake. In sports, if those are considered art, you need the body, which will perish. Even ballet, which uses music, by the way. While Music itself? Music raw? Any composition can be played by anyone, anywhere, so long as it is remembered, repeated. This isn't theory. It's fact. Is not a soul, like music, just as anywhere, just as timeless? Hear the music of birds, the music of a river. Ah! Rivers and birds, the mourners of Orpheus, the timeless liar with a lyre. And here enter the *Gearslutz* comments to my failed threads: "How can music be timeless, if music marks time?" "Smh." "This sucks." "Lame." "Half-baked, boring." <Cough, cough.> To you, friends, I stand to face your spit! Fire away. My heart has found peace. I will not hide. Hurl your stones at me, insult me deeper. Too late, I hand you your ammunition in advance: privileged, selfish, vain you can call me. Well, is it vain to challenge you? No, it makes me humble. One cannot condescend to meet you, one must climb to your judging heights. You, who would read inside my mind and criticize my thoughts, while you shut out others from looking inside you. You, you high post-count lords up there, who berate me, yourself sometimes and others, so desperate are you to fit in or push away; and yet not I. Self-deprecation is self-regard. Ask Woody Allen.

Dear World, I still love Stacy G! Fuck you! There, I said it! Yet there's Julia L! Do what you please with my fruits, my music! But before that, what I want to say is this, music is timed and timeless: when I hear a song I am teleported to the moment when I first heard that song, because music does not just mark time, in that it keeps the beat, but it marks time in that it stains it with nostalgia. Where were you when you first heard Rihanna, Madonna, Bush, Franklin, Fitzgerald, or the freaky French sparrow? I was in my bedroom, learning to strike keys, and wishing for things outside of myself.

Today, when I hear those artists I am different, yet I renew. Call me, my strawberry Blondie, and ask: am I here? Here I am!

Go.

ॐ

The green leaves of summer rustled brightly in the wind. Ilya sat on a park bench at Fort Greene, counting the cigarette butts on the floor like he had promised himself earlier that day. Nearby, some elderly woman threw candy pop rocks on the sidewalk, a spark of afternoon light dashing across her grin, as Brooklyn pigeons ate the candy, shook their heads, then ate some more pop rocks. Ilya jotted this down. Jotted some other notes down too. Mostly, the realization that birds, these here and there everywhere, are never just standing around pointlessly. They're always doing something: chilling, mating, feeding, or mourning loved ones. Ilya needed a job, he wrote, then closed his notebook.

That's when his father called Ilya, on his new, new phone.

Being the kind of parent to keep his child on the phone for an hour, they chatted for a long time—Ilya making up a story about how he got this new phone—when out of the blue the son asked a totally unrelated question:

"Dad, could you tell me the story of Orpheus, again?"

"That old story?" The father huffed. "You aren't on drugs, are you?"

"No." Ilya could never get used to that particularly funny feeling of relief, when what he was supposed to say matched with the truth.

"You really want to hear it?"

"Yes."

The father, soon to ask why, told the story.

"Orpheus was greatest poet the ancient world had ever known," said the father.

"*The* greatest poet," said Ilya, correcting his father's slip.

He continued, unfazed: "And not half-bad at the lyre either. His music could elicit any emotion, from fist-shaking wrath to toe-curling ecstasy. Notwithstanding, he was charmer, with—"

"*A* charmer."

"A charmer, with throngs of women falling at his feet."

"But," said Ilya, "he only ever loved one, right? Eurydice."

"Да."

"How beautiful was she?"

"Prettier than birthday cake. And she was as crazy as him, crazy in love that is. They decided to marry.

"On the day of their wedding, however, a terrible snake squirmed near Eurydice and injected her with a poison so horrible it ended in her agonizing death."

"And then?" asked the young son.

"And then, what do you think, madness, followed by sadness. He stopped making music, and, soon, so did the birds and the bees. In fact, eventually the whole earth wept for the poor boy. Luckily, Orpheus was son of Apollo the god of Music, and Muse the goddess of Lyric, a powerful combination. While his aunt was Aphrodite, the goddess of Love. Taking pity on her nephew she sought out Hades and Persephone. She almost arranged an audience for Orpheus, for him to bring his dead wife back to life. But Hades, being the nasty guy that he was, told her no. Despite that, however, Aphrodite told Orpheus to go down anyway.

"So Orpheus ventured to the Underworld, to beg the king and queen of souls to grant his wish of reviving Eurydice." Here, a breath, then the father continued.

"It is nearly impossible to reach the Underworld, a passage fraught with perils, ghastly beasts and ghouls. You remember the three headed dog that guards the gates of hell? Cerberus, ready to rip a wonderer to shreds?

"Well, a dog is still a dog. As the poet approaches, he pulls out his lyre. And puts Cerberus to sleep with a beautiful combination of lullaby and ear-scratching.

"Next, he must cross the river Styx, the river of death, which divides this world from the next. The only way across is to pay for a ferry ride. Again, Orpheus's cunning and talent helps him across. After greeting the ferryman Charon, the poet Orpheus charms him with a song in honor of the working man's efforts, some Bruce Springsteen tune, surely.

"Filled with gratitude by Orpheus, for recognizing his labor, Charon grants the poet a ride, telling him that not far from shore lies the castle of the king and queen."

"Hades and Persephone."

"Yes, the rulers of the Underworld. The two aren't exactly famous for their hospitality, but they greet the poet with enthusiasm. They host a party. And no one asks anyone for any favors just yet.

"At the height of the festivities, the young poet seeks audience with royal overlords. Orpheus pleas for his wife back, saying she was taken from him too soon, on the day of their wedding. 'What are a few more years of life with me,'

Orpheus asks Hades, 'compared to the eternity she will spend here when she must return for good?'

"Hades, sobering up, cuts Orpheus off, saying there is no way in hell he's going to return a human soul to earth. Persephone doesn't appreciate her husband's aggression, however, and implores Hades to listen to the boy."

Ilya tensed up. He had forgotten this part. But the father continued.

"Orpheus, of course, having anticipated this reaction, recites a ballad especially prepared for the king and queen: essentially, the most beautiful song ever composed.

"On the one hand, his melody reminds Persephone of her earthly days, as sweet as the walks with her mother Demeter. On the other hand, his lyrics sing of Hades's heroism in the war against the Titans, singing of the clashing of swords and breaking of horses. This combination fades into an outro, eloquently, about the power of love, even at the edge of existence, between the royal couple.

"After a performance like that, taking the breath away of everyone in the Underworld, Persephone speaks: 'Bravo, Orpheus, if it were up to me you would have your wife back, for a second chance at life. But let us see what his highness, my husband, believes to be correct.'

"Hades, a little annoyed by his wife who is always right, yet genuinely moved by the poet, agrees to let Eurydice accompany Orpheus out of the Underworld, but on one condition. 'As she follows you out of the underworld, you must not look back at her, not even speak to her . . .'"

As Ilya started heading home, the sky darkened. The father, completely enraptured by the story, continued.

"So the lovers leave, together, following the path back: over the river, past the gate, and through the perils and obstacles, back to solid ground above.

"All the while, Orpheus remembers not to look over his shoulder, as he was told. But Eurydice doesn't know the rules.

" 'Orpheus,' she calls out, 'my love, Orpheus, why do you ignore me? Why don't you look back at me? Don't you love me anymore? Won't you say something to me? Talk to me, my love, speak your mind, look me in the eyes again like you used to. What nightmare!'

"The world's greatest poet does his best. He holds strong. He remembers the words stating he must refrain from even looking over his shoulder. As the light at the end of the tunnel shines, however, what happens? Eurydice calls out one last time.

" 'Orpheus, why, why do you ignore me? Cruel, cruel Orpheus. Don't you love me?'

"Passionate Orpheus turns around, screaming that he does love her, that he does. But no sooner came the reply does she tumble back down, down, forever down."

"No!"

"Да. Orpheus went from being the world's greatest love poet, to the world's greatest poet of sorrow. Because of his loss, he became even richer in words, even sweeter in melody. It was said that after losing Eurydice, Orpheus could now see into the hearts of gods and men with his music. But what good was that to him? He had lost the only woman he had ever or would ever love.

"He spent his remaining days, each as lonesome as the next, just playing his instrument in the woods, to whoever would listen, even to the birds and the rivers. Then, one day, a group of nymphs as horny as high schoolers huddled around the poet.

"They asked him to play them a happy song. He did. They asked him to play a sad song. He did. They asked him to play whatever he felt like playing, and he sang of eternal love lost. Half of the nymphs wept like they had never wept before. The other half fell madly in love with the poet.

"They told Orpheus to let go of this silly mortal girl, weaker than a snake, too delicate to hike back to reality, forget her. Instead, they suggested, marry one of us.

"But Orpheus didn't even have the courage to tell them No. He just walked way.

"The nymphs, so offended by his rejection, in great number held down the poet, and raped him."

"What?!"

"They raped him brutally and without mercy. Then they tore him from limb to limb, as easily as you would pick apart a boiled chicken, they stripped the very meat from his bones, and left his body mangled to shreds in that forest, those wretched nymphs!"

"Jesus!"

"Indeed. And not just that, my son, because of course this story has a happy ending. You know, the Greek gods had a funny way of ending things. You remember what happened next? Well, what happens to dead souls?"

"They go to the Underworld."

"That's right. Orpheus finally got to Eurydice. And they lived happily ever after, filling the Underworld with love and music. Now they can take walks, sometimes Eurydice in front, sometimes side by side. Other times Orpheus in the lead—only he can turn around and say I love you to his wife, as much as he wants."

Ilya sat on the stairs of a Brooklyn train station platform bound for Manhattan. He didn't want to end the phone call by going down and taking the train back home just yet. They chatted a bit more, about his roommate, about the apartment, about if Ilya had enough money. Then:

"Why did you ask about Orpheus?" asked the father, empathizing with this story of loss.

"I think Stacy might have been my Eurydice," said Ilya, feeling the same about the story as his father. "Although, I might have been her snake."

After humming in agreement, the father asked, "Did Stacy inspire you?"

"In a way, yeah. I'm writing again." He didn't mention the show, wanting to secure the date first, before inviting anyone, especially the guest of honor.

The father paused. "And are you seeing anybody?" he asked.

Ilya didn't want to say that either, not exactly, so he said, "No. Yes. Maybe. She's . . ."

"She's a nymph?" asked dad.

"I hope so."

Nikolai almost said, *Just like your mother*, but restrained himself.

ఎ

The skyscrapers at night shook and shambled, shimmied and shivered. Numbers, like sounds, when doubled are special, explained the mother, to her boys, the night she disappeared. The way things went occur to Ilya more this way than another.

David was insisting they go home. Maxine had gotten turned around. So she distracted him with numbers.

"You are 11 years old," she told David. "And you were born in '88. Now it's 1999, a special year for you, and a special number, which you should never forget."

"What about me, mom?" asked Ilya.

"You are 4, which is a cool number, too," explained Maxine. "4 is full of parallels, possibility, and one of the strongest numbers ever, because it can't be pushed around. Also, it's the number of steps in a—"

"What does 'pushed around' mean?"

"This, you dummy!" shouted David, knocking his younger sibling into the snow, leaving his face powdered in the icy cold, hardening, veins contracting, shifting red with pain and anger.

Still, Maxine didn't intervene. She didn't need to, watching as Ilya got up on his own, with a snow ball in his hand.

"Ow!" cried David, wiping the flakes from his face, turning towards their mother. Her look, however, said you had it coming.

"This is Central Park," said the mother. A little later, "And this is the Essex House—where Stravinsky lived and died."

She hoped they would ask her who Stravinsky was, since they had just watched *Fantasia*. But David wasn't having it. He insisted they go home. Then he remembered something.

"Why is my age special," asked David.

"If you multiply your age to any number something magical happens."

"What happens?" asked David. "What?"

"What is 'multiply'?" asked Ilya.

The mother patted Ilya's head. "Do you know my age?" asked the mother, to David.

"Да."

"And what number do you get when you add the two digits in my age?" Maxine was speaking like a teacher, David felt, but he was used to it from her. "What do you get?"

"9."

"When you multiply a double-digit number by 11 you add the two digits and put the sum in the middle. So, then, what do you get when you multiply your age with mine? What do you get?"

Ilya, who was quick to shout, shouted: "What do you get! What do you get!" not really understanding the logic of the conversation, but following the enthusiasm.

"11 times 36," said David, almost sure, "is 396."

"Excellent. Now, what about your brother's age?" asked the mother, testing him.

"What about my age!" shouted Ilya. "What about my age!"

David took his hands from his coat and exhaled into them. "Ilya is 4." Then he remembered something else. "I know, I know, when you multiply a single-digit by 11, you double the number: 44."

The mother kissed her big boy. "That's right. Do you know why? You can imagine the 4 has a 0 in front of it. You add 0 with 4 and you get 4. Which means you put 4 between 0-4, and get 0-4-4, or 44."

"I'm good at math, too, mom," said Ilya, jumping up and down in that brisk winter night. "Eleven, twenty-two, thirty-three, forty-four, fifty-five . . ." he paused. "Seexty-seex."

"No," jumped David. "Sixty-six. Seventy-seven, eighty-eight, ninety-nine." He inhaled the frosty air. "One-twenty-one, one-thirty-two, one-forty-three." He awaited confirmation. His mother laughed. He continued: "One-fifty-four, one-sixty-five, one-seventy-six . . ."

"Now let's flip our years," tested the mother. "What is 63 times 11?"

"693!" shouted David, absolutely sure. And, thinking quickly, he asked, "What about two digits that add up over nine?"

"That's easy," said the mother, about to explain it, when they were interrupted by the younger son.

"Where are we?" asked Ilya, who had been staring at the Essex House as they passed it, followed by Grand Army plaza full of tourists, then the middle of nowhere, where they were now.

Maxine looked around. The skyscrapers were aglow. The night cut through their winter coats.

"This is Second Avenue, Ma," cried David, not distracted anymore, now again deeply scared and worried. "We need to go back to Lexington."

Maxine knew that sounded right, but how to get there? "Let's go to Lexington. But first ice cream!" Sometime after the ice cold dessert, in the dead of night, was when Ilya saw his mother stare at another house, stare at it with intensity, as if she had been there before.

The door of the used book store chimed as it opened.

"I will be . . . right there," she said. "Be right back."

ఉ

The smell of cozonac perfumed the apartment that Wednesday. Light cut in from the outside, through the curtains, which divided Ilya's daily morning writing from Tiffany's weekly baking.

"My recipe is almost there," she said, when she saw Ilya coming in to the kitchen.

"What's missing?" he asked, wondering if he could bite into the tasty bread.

"I don't know," she confessed, smelling her new loaf come out of the oven. "It's missing home, I guess."

"I'm curious," said Ilya, "when do you work?"

"Why do you ask, because you only ever see me cooking? I work at night, just like you, in my bedroom."

"It isn't just work you're doing in there." Ilya wanted to pinch the new loaf, reaching for a pinch of the crust sprinkled with sugar, eager, hungry.

Tiffany slapped his hand.

"Ouch!" he yelped. "By the way, what kind of Romanian name is Tiffany?"

"We can't all have iconic ass names from our home countries like you," she replied, then smiled. "By the way, my real name is Rahela, super Romanian. But I like my American name more."

"Shouldn't it be Rachel?"

"Too bland.

Ilya paused. Then asked, "What should my American name be? I don't like Elijah."

"Elijah would suit you, actually, the prophet."

"What about . . ." Ilya chewed, ". . . what about Stevie?"

"Too bland."

"Why?"

"Oh," said Tiffany. "I meant my cozonac. I think I know what it needs." She gathered her spices, sugar, flour, and started putting them away.

"Aren't you going to make it now?" asked Ilya. "Since you know what's missing."

"Not now," she said. "It would take too long. Let's just eat what we have. Say, you have a new phone?"

It was ringing.

It was Julia. And the call lasted about an hour, as usually, just talking—about passports, travel bans, naturalization, other topics she was familiar with, as Ilya came to learn, like that bear riding president of a nation, Putin, his reelection with 76.69% of votes, the collage Ilya had made of him shot-gunning weed smoke into Ilya's other president's mouth, then about the director Tarkovsky and his debut film about a boy who dreams of his dead mother, and extermination camps, and Alexei Tolstoy, on to the totally different Tolstoy, the one who wrote one of literature's greatest love affairs, inspired by his fantasies and his wife, and did you know that Catherine the Great was actually German, on to a conversation about race with a small note on the Jim Crow laws, citing for example the group of workers who boycotted the Memphis Sanitation Company in 1968, where King had given one of his most moving speech, the day before his assassination, fifty years before the *Black Panther* movie release, which, having both liked the Kendrick Lamar original tracks, they agreed they should see, but only after coming over one day to try her Olivye salad and pork shoulder soaked in a saucy marinade, or homemade pickled anything, and a tall glass of her famous mint and berries квас, ending with talk about hopes and dreams, and about her son who started kindergarten last year, for whom she had to race back on Sundays—talking, essentially about everything and nothing, from that phone she had gotten him, both of them on their respective beds, naked.

ॐ*

---

* You know this by now. But if I don't write any comments, it is most likely because I like what I am reading so much that I get lost in your words, this world, the relationship blossoming.

By the way, you never liked my квас . . .

June 14th. Mix day, Thursday. Lost a day of job? Earned a day of work. Time to paw the DAW, finish cutting "Body Language," which I slowed down to 128 bpm, like the title to Diplo's *visual guide to music, culture, and everything in between: 128 Beats Per Minute*. Still a nice workout speed. Time and tempo, sound and music. Take a pinch of one, and stir the other. One exists on its own, the other in human form. The rest, everything, in between!

Speech, who knows, but music came about when one fool beat on rocks in a cave, while another fool in another chamber echoed the beats back. Strike one dweller with a lightning bolt, and you get the first electronic music artist. Rawr goes the leopard, and lol goes the hyena. I think a lot about Stacy still. The way she broke up with me over text, still. I remember the time she taught me about the different kinds of leaves at Fort Greene on the anniversary of the first battle fought between the British Navy and American soldiers, a defeat for the revolutionaries, lost was New York that day, so many years ago, and lost too is Stacy, when was that first date? Almost two years ago: elm leaves are serrated, she said. Gingko looks like a butterfly. What useful knowledge. As useful as learning another language. What is Julia doing right now? She has probably been awake for hours breast feeding her baby, how old is he, six? She seems like a morning person. The music industry is falling apart. Avicii's assisted-suicide finally hit me. Assisted by the world, apparently. "When I'm wiser and I'm older." All this time, I was mad at the industry, blaming it, but no one was at fault, we were all lost. Anyway, now I'm hit with a blow to my dream, the ego-mirage that any youngster can become a world-star producer. "Wake me up when it's all over." Those lines make me shiver now. I hope you are awake, in another world . . . Why write these entries? Just because in a book some lady named Julia like Julia said so? Or because Stacy did it and I want to copy her. Stacy. Julia. Where else am I going to blur from one romance to the next, but here, in my journals? Through song, maybe? I can't write, I can barely mix. I'll add a saw bassline, this track needs some grainy lows: F, F-sharp, F-E, F. Something to spiral towards, into, to, for: dissonance. No tonic note, is that possible? A pop track getting dark? Heh! There's only one thing left to do.

To be myself. Keep writing. Creative pop. There's still time. Like, what is the difference between creative music and popular music, anyway? Where do they overlap? Is the term popular synonymous with bad, and creative with good? Or are they two totally different metrics of music? These are the kind of questions Nikolai, his highness professor emeritus, used to ask me.

Dad's lectures on contemporary popular culture didn't end when he stepped off campus; they went on. Even now, away from home, he continues. I don't reply as quickly as I used to.

All DJs worth their salt—I said once, citing my second and third favorite artists, Diplo and Monatik—*straddle creativity and accessibility, call it innovation, call it seduction. Or, consider that the difference between creative and popular music is more complicated* than nerds make it out to be. Popularity and creativity are two not unlike cultures, with unlike motives, but overlapping cultures with similar objectives. Simply, they are two different languages.

What did he say? That I was all over the place, that I was a nerd. So I called him a nerd, and that was that. Like when another DJ tries to tell me how to do my job.

ౘ

"Remember?" Ilya would say to Rashad, if the two best friends ever meet again. "Remember how you were the fastest boy in class? You used to run around the playground during recess, tagging people, even if you weren't *it*? No one could catch you, so you had to slow down on purpose to become *it*." Sometimes Ilya would play tag, catch Rashad hiding in the bushes, squishing the little white balls that looked like bug eggs on the green leaves of the bush. It was the only way to tag him, when he was distracted by the bugs.

By the end of first grade both Rashad and Ilya knew one another well. Both knew that they lived in single-parent homes and had older siblings. This made each parent more relaxed. Thus, both had hosted sleepovers for the other, both boys had eaten one another's pepperonis on the other's pizzas, had watched Dragon Ball Z in its original Japanese, long into the night, screaming until their hair turned gold, or until a father or mother told them to shut up.

But after first grade, after second, into third grade, they would trade their last Pokémon cards. Rashad would start hanging out with band kids, which was fine, since Ilya started private piano lessons after school, but things turned cool between them. Split.

ౘ

He had asked to see her. She said she was busy. Then they talked, per usual, for an hour about everything and nothing.

"Have you ever tried drugs?"

Ilya asked if she was asking because she wanted some.

"I could get them if I wanted to. I'm just curious."

Ilya asked if she was curious because she wanted to try something new with him.

"I'm not offering, nor do I partake. I have a kid, remember?"

Ilya said she was a good mother, then asked if they could meet.

"This Sunday."

Light cut in from the outside, through the curtains, which divided Ilya from the rest of the world. He put on his pants. And tinkered with the EP.

ბ

A train passed overhead, clicking, clonking. Friday, just Friday.

And the front door of Zdras was open, the red one that from afar looked like a red stick of gum, long and skinny, with a hornet graffiti'd on the front and a round window like the eye of a bug.

At the door, slept the three triplet Dogo dogs, one yawning with its white jowls, before falling back asleep. Nothing new. But then, Ilya saw the homeless man, not sleeping.

"Can you spare any change?" he asked. "So I can buy a coffee and a bagel."

"Not this time," said Ilya, looking down, getting past.

"Not this time?" repeated the man. "What the fuck does that mean."

Ilya kept his eyes down, got past him, and entered Zdras without hearing what else the man had to say.

Through the door, then down the long staircase, on the other side of the dancefloor, behind the DJ booth, through a trapdoor, Ilya entered Tony's office.

"Can I have July 22nd?" he barged in saying. But to his surprise it wasn't just Tony at his desk and his wife sitting on his lap. Jonathan was in there, too.

"Ahem," the promoter said. "As I was explaining."

"What's all this?" Ilya asked, standing over the desk, and seeing there a few blue schematics.

"The new security system," said Tony, very much impressed by the presentation Jonathan was giving.

"I'll have the rig hammered up by the end of the week, and the software running by the weekend." He turned to Ilya. "Too bad there won't be any talent then."

Ilya scowled. "What's the promoter doing—"

"Could you be more specific about the timeline?" asked Tony, cutting Ilya off.

"Hammered up by Wednesday at the earliest."

Ilya felt the urge to say, though resisted saying, *I should be working that day, but you turned my night into a guest night.* He hated being in a social context where he felt his opinion had to wait. Part of why he loved playing music was precisely for this, he didn't have to care about others, or wait for them.

But then Jonathan turned his chin up to Ilya, as if responding to the thoughts in the air: "Last Wednesday, with the Moldovan, we saw record attendance." The weight of his voice was unbearable for Ilya, who shook, silently. "As I was saying," continued Jonathan, "Up by this Wednesday, a local deep house night." He stood up, stretched his hairy, bare arms, so full of tats and musculature that they almost took up the whole office and sprayed it with a douchey smell, before turning towards Ilya. "Which you're not playing." Laughing, stepping out, he left.

Quietly and tactfully, Josephine, on Tony's knee, spoke up. "He sure is ugly, but damn he's sexy."

Tony jerked his knee up, sending Josephine bouncing. "He doesn't have to be ugly or sexy, he does his job well." He then turned to Ilya, who had taken a seat where Jonathan had been, discovering with slight discomfort just how warm the promoter's ass had left the chair. Tony was about to say something important, but was interrupted.

"Tony, have you considered giving me the night I asked for? I've just released a teaser and got over 900,000 plays online." The DJ wasn't lying, yet he wasn't paying attention either.

"Ilya," said Tony, "You should know about the changes going on around here."

"What do you mean?"

Josephine looked sad, sad for Ilya and sad for Tony. "It isn't set in stone yet," she said.

"Basically it is," shot Tony. "Ilya, I'm selling Zdras."

"What!"

"Not yet," said Josephine, finding a place on Tony's lap again, caressing his knees.

Usually her affection helped, but now the boss looked irredeemably sad. Leaning back, he spoke: "Not yet, no. But after the summer, it's going to Jonathan. He has been with us ten years. Aside from me and that old fart who deejays after you, Robespierre, no one loves this place more than Jonathan."

Ilya lamented, *why, why*; and Tony almost answered the question.

But before he did he pulled a cardboard box from under his desk, and dumped hundreds of orange prescription pill bottles over the blue schematics on the table. "I'm going to rehab! Psychologist's orders."

"I'm so proud of you," said Josephine, rubbing herself against her man. "So, so proud of you, you, you!"

"That means . . ."

"That means," added the boss, "that it isn't up to me whether you get a show or not. It's Jonathan's call now."

"He hates me! I don't even know why!"

Josephine implored Tony to let Ilya have the Sunday.

"It isn't up to me," said her husband.

"Sure it is," his wife replied, "You're still the owner."

"True . . ." Tony faded into a daze, for a moment. He really did need help. Josephine noticed him starting to sweat and shake, so she asked Ilya to please go and get ready for his set, as she pressed her husband to her body, to soothe him a little, or at least stop the clattering of his teeth making an awful sound.

The DJ got up zombie-slow and began climbing the stairs that lead out the trapdoor, when it occurred to him that perhaps he should tell the truth. How about admitting that the show wasn't about releasing his EP, but about getting Stacy back. That the date wasn't his father's birthday, but actually his mother's birthday, Maxine's. Stacy knew this, and had pushed him to put it out there earlier, but it was never the right time. Then she left. Now what? He wanted to debut and in his mother's honor. Yes. Honor. Tell Josephine and tell Tony the truth. The truth would win him the date, just turn around.

But when he did, mouth opened, no words came out. He couldn't speak up, because his friend Tony looked too broken down on his wife's lap, the two of them in tears, hopeless.

ॐ

Enough. Time for business. A few people were already pouring into Zdras. And Ilya knew they didn't come here to stand against a wall. It was his job to make sure even the ones with two left feet got at least their booties bumping. That's right. Forget mom, forget art, don't even think about becoming a junkie like Tony. Get to work. Focus on money. Look, more people. It's time.

A drink on the dance floor was almost guaranteed to be drained, if not spilled. One can nurse a cocktail seated at a table, talking. But on the dance floor, listening to your favorite song, you will dance, not talk, drink and not, under any circumstance, have an empty hand. The smartest customers figured out the loophole around buying a drink was having another dancer in your hand, but again it was Ilya's job to inspire courage. It all revolved around the music. A bar without music is just clamor. And noise never sold alcohol. But Usher did. Lil Jon did. Garrix, 2 Chainz, Laidback Luke, and D-O-double-G did. Or does, or did. Compare the music from only fifty years ago with today's. Less instruments, fewer musicians. Take the lyrics. Mindless. University studies have put top forty tracks through machines, actually, and determined that there are fewer words in popular music today than ever before, fewer key changes, less dynamic range too. The kind of tunes that get played at Zdras, even by the likes of Ilya and his ilk, play simpler, chorus heavy tracks that remind the consumer of what they are buying: a night out, live drinks, cheap girls, or an excuse to goo the brain. Ignore the fact that live bands rarely perform at mid-sized night clubs anymore (with, say, a 500-person cap). People just don't care, and four guitarists in a shoegaze band with their drummer friend from Norway will always cost more to hire than a pushover twentysomething DJ. The last nail in the music-is-weaker-today coffin, is the loudness. The simple sound, noise, coming from these tracks: compressed, limited, overblown, mono-blasting anthems, one bass-fatter than the next, all clashing to be heard at supermarkets, malls, and as ringtones. We're a generation of listeners conditioned to content that competes on two industry standards: how loud the track is, and how many listeners spend money because of it (on drinks, tickets, merch; dare we say on recordings?). When a track is meant to be played in a stadium or through car stereos, few fans will shell out for the real experience. What most want is just a pirated sound bite of the chorus, which they will compress into a tiny crunch, to sound off during the punch line of a seven second meme. On the other hand, your average Joe music aficionado contents himself with renting music, saying, "No need to purchase, thanks," on the false pretense that with a concert ticket they will support the artist who can barely tour. Meanwhile, your run of the mill producer isn't always fighting the good fight, either. Most would rather torrent a glitchy version of professional audio software, which sucks. This causes beginners to clunker up the learning curve, to never produce an original track, and to give up too easily: having cost them little to start, anyway.

For now, any second now, Friday at Zdras would become only about the dancefloor. People wouldn't want to think too much, only goo-goo, gaa-gaa the brain, and let Ilya take them there. Knowing this, the good DJ would play them the hits, one after the other—everything except Stacy's song doing rounds on important online music magazines— maybe a little improv with keys, some ad-libs on the mic, but mostly songs the clientele had heard during the week, at the grocery store or the department store. Subtly, secretly sneaking in tracks that hopefully with a little luck they might discover the following week, should they seek them after thinking, "Oh, I've heard this before . . ." while breathlessly making out at Zdras, or pulling out a rubber in the restroom stall.

ठ

June 16th. Saturday, oh diary, now it's Saturday, Bloom's day, Boom day. I don't want to share all of me just yet. Yet, why write at all, if not to share, at least with myself? It's the summer: flow with the rising mirage of the city concrete from here to the end of the street. New York City. Where you is? A skyline of cocaine. Who you be? A purveyor of dreams. Yet what are we? Your consumers with a guarantor form. Hey, ну!* So what.

Beauty begs to be repeated.

In a handful of hours I will course my way to Zdras again for the Saturday set. 80s tonight, I can feel it. The people want throwbacks, so throwbacks they will get.

Right now, Tiffany works herself a breakfast in the kitchen. So boring how she drinks orange juice every day. Her neighborhood calls me, I don't know why. There is not a damn to do. Why don't I just type what's on my mind? What's all this looking out the window and imagining what I would write? Mixing is easier, because the music being mixed is being heard and improved instantaneously. Unlike with writing, where the word heard, begging to be written, isn't down on paper yet—and a whole minute can pass without you typing a damn, the page all blank, and your courage decreasing. Not to mention a track finished is a sick

---

* Phonetically: *"Hey, nu!"* calling for attention. Only in New York would you get such a mushy mix of languages. There are around 800 spoken in the city, according to the *Times.* I didn't even know there were that many languages in the world, let alone one city. "An island unto itself," wrote Woody Allen, of himself. A catchier phrase, if I may say so.

thing to behold, whereas what good is a diary page completed to you?

Or, this could be true too, I am a fraud and I don't know the first thing about writing, or music for that matter. How much time do I spend indoors? When was the last time my bare feet touched earth? That was the mind grenade Tiffany threw me from her yoga class: we rarely stand barefooted on earth anymore—note to self, go to the beach tomorrow—where my bare feet last touched the earth.

What's worse than being tired? The terrible side-effect of illicit and licit drugs, that they make you drowsy, drain your energy, make your wiener small, according to dad. Drugs. It isn't even the claw of the fish hook in my mouth anymore, that pain of addiction, the need for another hit—no! It's the always-tired that kills me, the bored drowsiness of our generation intensified by the lack of substances. Everyone around me is quitting. I did too, I can hold strong.

But the transition from Friday to Saturday is particularly tough. I haven't been able to sleep in since I quit dusting . . . coke, since Paris---No. I won't. I don't.

Those three "-"s by the way, I call, the W-dash. I've used it before. It signals a break: not a logical break, as in the period, or the comma, or paragraph break. But a writing time break: it means writing time has passed. It also isn't like the ellipses, which implies a vagrancy, a wondering of thought, or an omission. The W-dash, instead, is a breath, more in-line with dashes. You know N-dashes, they connect words and sounds (like the hyphen between "N" and "dashes"). M-dashes connect ideas with ideas, providing a moment's break between them—like a jazz musician, breathing between breaths of notes through his saxophone—from in, to release. M-dashes are fun—can't you tell? Though, like the W-dash, not as abrupt as the paragraph break, as shy as the comma, or as intense as the period. Notice. When. I. Forced myself. To use. Periods. Then. It. Sounds. Like. "Pretty. Boy. Swag." AKA the wheel-chaired best friend in *Malcolm in the Middle*. AKA Soulja Boy. In other news, what ever happened to Soulja Boy? Let me W-dash and find out real quick---damn that's an active ass twitter account. New shoes, new track, new look. "A trendsetter in rap circles." LOL. Who does PR for him? Some in the game do anything for that extra buck. And I? Why don't I? There's so much money out there. Yet I would rather mix.

Let me just put on my necklace, and get going.

ఁ

Commonly known as quicksilver, mercury has an atomic number of 80. It is the only metallic element that rolls around as a liquid at room temperature. Most often extracted from a reddish, vermillion crystal called cinnabar, mercury itself is used in thermometers, barometers, manometers, tilt switches and fluorescent lamps. Highly poisonous if ingested. Queen Elizabeth used it as make up, so did Mayan and Aztec rulers, ancient Egyptians and Romans too. Alchemists believed it was the primary metal from which all other metals sprung. Probably because it's so pretty. In Sanskrit the different names for alchemy usually include some form of "the way of mercury."

Most surprising of all, it's the only metal whose name derives from alchemy, or even a planet, itself named after the god of speed and mobility: Mercury. Or Hermes.

Most simple of all, it was the juice Ilya carried around his neck. The vial looked closer to a tube than anything, and hung from a metal chain, at all times. Though not to drink at a close moment of death, nor to help revive him as some emperors believed. He kept it because it had meant something to his father and that was enough for the boy. Certainly not because Ilya was volatile, capricious, fickle, variable, protean, fluid, whimsical, giddy or impulsive, which are synonyms of the beautiful 9-letter word:

M-e-r-c-u-r-i-a-l.

Saturday night, 4 AM. And a wedding party was coming to a close. A bride with her shoes in her hands, grinning so strong her earrings fell off. A husband with his tie on his head, dancing so hard his pants fell off. Genuine happiness. He could make it and not have it. Not bad, he thought, not bad, as Ilya was about to deejay his last 80s songs of the night. He spun right round, sweetly dreaming, relaxing into a love tainted. Not bad. That's when the old man DJ, with a mole between his eyebrows and gunmetal hair, appeared.

"Robespierre," he said, extending a hand.

"Ilya," said the young man, about to end his set.

"Have you heard about the change?" asked the old man.

"What does that mean for us DJs?" he asked, on purpose lumping his idol and himself into the same category.

"I have known Tony for longer than he has owned this place. Do not worry. You keep making music."

"Thank you."

"I liked the teaser. You are close to something, something worthwhile. Keep going."

Ilya could not hide his joy, his embarrassment, both contorting his face and trying to thank Robespierre. "How do you cast a spell, again?" asked Ilya. "Il y a une fois?"

"No, Il était une fois. Par example," said the old man, "il était une fois, I was born in France, fell in love with Chicago House, and came to New York."

"Not Chicago?"

"I would have, but when I got here I had too much fun. The rest is history."

"Woah."

"Enough apathy, young man, you must finish the EP. I can help you master it. But you must finish. I know you are not finished, but you must. No distractions. No excuses. Do not worry about mediocrity. Do not worry about what others think. Just push, Ilya, push. Get the work out there. It is your destiny."

"You think so?"

"Oui. Now watch how to flip an LP. You press the edges with your tips of fingers, see?"

ఓ

When all you have to base your new love on is the old one, how do you let go?

Under the Eiffel tower of Brooklyn—the Coney Island Parachute Jump—listening to the sounds of top forty radio, they danced. The loudspeakers were playing a remix of Camila Cabello's hot summer tune. Ilya imagined Julia looking like Cabello. Same smoldering eyes, but strawberry blonde hair. He purred, "Julieta," in her ear, as they stepped softly, slowly, now and then jabbing their hips, building up, swinging harder and harder: playing the bull and matador with their hips. Meanwhile families screamed in all directions. First, he would get close, work her pelvis. Next, she would spin, fan her fingers in his face, and laugh. Nearby, the rollercoaster zoomed by. Then, Julia tapped his shoulder. He grabbed and twisted her. Loudly, a wave broke on shore, leaving residue, washing back. That's when Julia articulated her way up, to Ilya's face, licked him, then sprinted off, to where the waves were. The rollercoaster ride was over. He chased her, to their bags, close to where she was squatting by the water, quiet, counting the number of shells in the sand.

As he squatted and kept silent, she mused: "Would you agree? There is no line between Coney Island and Brighton Beach, only one long beach. Any line you drew, the ocean would just wash it away."

Squatting even lower, Ilya replied, "I agree. Only, I don't think these apartments behind us all cost the same along this, so called, one beach." His pants got wet in the sand.

Julia took this as her cue to speak what was really on her mind: "Tell me, young knight, does a damsel wait for you back home?"

"My roommate," he said. "But it isn't what you think."

"You misunderstood the question."

"No one," said Ilya, feeling Julia look at him, but unable to return that look. "No one is waiting." He took a breath as deep as he could, and held it, comically, hoping to make Julia laugh. But she wasn't laughing. He exhaled. "I broke up with my girlfriend of two years last month."

"It hurts, doesn't it?

"Yes, yes it does."

"I'm getting divorced this week," said Julia.

Ilya could not *not* think about what that meant for him and her. "You're married?"

"Now you're asking?" Julia laid her back against the wet sand, and with both hands moved her hair from under her head. She could hear the crackling of the beach and the crashing of waves underneath her thoughts. "No, not for long."

"American?"

"Да, американец."[*]

---

[*] *"Da, americanetz."* You told me in a conversation once that Julia's ex was Puerto Rican, but now he's American? Or is he, like Ilya, "from neither there nor here"? This question of identity is so central to our story—I think it deserves more attention. Don't take it for granted. You are clearly complicating everyday assumptions about the concept of being FROM somewhere, by introducing these characters. Ilya says he is American, and he acts American, but doesn't he cover up the past

"Like me."

"You're not American. You're a blockhead."

"I was born here."

"But your parents were Russian. Николай и Максин!* I could hardly think of a more Russian upbringing."

"But my mother was American, only living in Moscow, a diplomat's daughter."

"She was born there," said Julia, feeling with her toes the tide approaching. "By your birth logic she's Russian. Not to mention she danced for the Bolshoi."

Ilya was already uncomfortable listening to Julia describe his family background, but to notice Julia's white top getting wet, together with the sand underneath, from the crawling water, was too much. He had to turn away and cover with his hands the growing feeling he wanted to share with her.

"I'm getting divorced," Julia repeated, turning toward Ilya and holding back one of her fruity smiles, seeing just how

---

just a little bit by saying so? Where is Julia *from*? Where are *we* from? New York City is the best place to situate this conversation, because where anyone is from is rarely from there. How many times have we heard a New Yorker brag about being "actually from New York," when really they were born in Long Island, or Jersey! Anyway, I like how Julia doesn't let Ilya get away with ignoring his past, that's for sure.

* *"Nikolai and Maxine!"* Exactly, where you are FROM has to do with how you were RAISED. Not just "from where," but also "how." Which reminds me of another fun fact. Did you know that the first US president actually born as a US citizen and not a British subject was Martin Van Buren, b. 1782. No relation to Armin Van Buuren. Thought you should know. Also, this chapter ends so *juicy*. More, more of this.

stiff she was making him, liking that. "And I'm having a party this Saturday. Care to join?"

Ilya felt his gut burst. "I work on Saturday."

"Another time then." Julia almost left it at that. But didn't. "What about Wednesdays, do you work on Wednesdays?"

"Not anymore."

"Perfect," she said. "Midnight on Wednesday is the equinox. I'm hosting a party."

ఠ

Half time:

A sooty cloud rolled in, bringing with it little silvery drops of rain. One, then two, hit the pages of the book the old woman was reading on the beach. A third and fourth drop awoke our old man, who stretched and yawned.

How grand, what glory, to reach the golden close of day, who some called the blue hour, when anything is possible, even silly. In one's life, too, there is a blue hour, where having accomplished much, it is time to play again. Or reminisce over a faded tune. Cut and clean infected wounds.

Behind them, a hundred and one naked boys and girls streaked down the sandy coast, doing cartwheels and high jumps, a stampede of youth.

The husband put a wrinkled palm over the folding tummy of his wife, as he watched the children drive a stake into the sand, then pile lumber together. They wanted a bon fire, to dance and to tempt the gray dizzying mass closer.

Suddenly, when a hundred and one minds transformed into colored balloons, which all floated upward, the old man was glad he had saved his young diaries, and not let them disappear.

June 19th. Tuesday Morning. And today will be right when I start and finish version three of Track Three, "Honey Beer," even if it sucks; the point is to show up, to push, to goddamn birth something new. It would be nice to come up with some new ideas I have never thought of before for "Honey Beer," but how can I, how can I create the most viscous sex song I've ever made, heard, if I haven't yet? I need inspiration!

In other news, David asked me to fly to San Fran next month and help him sell his app by playing music at his next conference: "Ты мне нужен." I was like, "No, you need a DJ." "Ты DJ!" How can I argue with that? But the last two weekends of July, plus the week in between? You know what that is? The show! Well, the chance for a show. Then afterwards we could travel to NY since he has another conference lined up. What about me? What am I going to say to my brother? He knows I might have this show, knows it is mom's birthday, but he thinks I don't take my life seriously, plus he knows we're not supposed to say *No* to family, so he asks. In fact, he only ever calls me when he needs something, never else. Maybe that's the ideal family situation, they leave you alone unless when necessary. What about fun? Good God. Tiff wants to hang out tomorrow. Tiff . . . let me work, Tiff. She will, and should, hear about Julia. Though, what if she jinxes things? How is it, damn, that I finally understand why Jack Nicolson went mad at the Overlook Hotel in that Kubrick Film: no one left him alone. He just wanted some peace and quiet to get his work done. And so do I, I just want to mix. My job already is spent with people, in front of people, performing sets they want to hear. The last thing I need is to spend my free time with the very same people I am trying to impress during working hours. Irony. Julia. I hate criticism, almost as much as I don't believe praise. There are laws in physics that describe vacuums; and the time I've carved out to mix is essentially free time, but as soon as it is made, the whole universe and its laws flood that vacuum. What do I have to complain about? That I want my free time? The world has bigger problems than that, but listen, they don't have the next song of the summer. I'm not the whole world, but I can give them what they want, a whole lotta tracks from the hole in my chest, which they can later fill with their opinions.

So, Stacy? Stacy! It's about time I stopped saying her name in my head like I were asking a question or calling her back. Why can't I stop thinking about her? When I used to have sex with her I used to roll a reel of other women in my imagination. Now when I have to jerk off I imagine old pictures of her that I used to have access to. Shit's weird. If I don't picture her, then I look at porn, just to not think of her, of her cony breasts, of the birthmark on her rib cage, that portrait of appetite. No tattoos on Stacy, but Julia? Internet killed the TV star.

All TV stars have tattoos, even porn stars. Maybe there's one without. Why is that?

My favorite porn, I have to admit is watching kinda older Russian ladies take advantage of much younger boys. Fourteen-year-old looking boys. Not real forceful like, since it's a production, you can tell. Russian production houses make young boy older lady combos by the thousands. While American production houses make incest spying on half-sisters or step-moms from the hallway videos. All these bent dicked American bros and small penised Russian teens just letting themselves be moved or taken.

What the hell! I didn't masturbate until late in the game, at 15. But before that I was definitely watching porn. All hentai. Folks, I have wasted a lot of time playing cartoon porn RPGs, especially this one with a little pixel bro who had to travel to various countries, and in each country complete a mission for a different woman around the world. You would either bring each woman a tool to fix her house, or perform some deviant sexual favor that involved running the mouse cursor over their pixel nipples, alternating key strokes to stroke them, or even send love letters from one lady to the other, sometimes answer multiple choice questions, what a waste of time, so much time.

Can I be honest? Of course, it's my journal. The hands down hottest hotty was the Russian, I remember to this day. Not my favorite, but the hottest. Rus. Why are they so hot? The Hot of the Slav: an Essay on Ass. They steal your heart away. Their eyes are devious, fierce and golden from hundreds of years of Mongol hordes, mixing genes, to put it lightly. Otherwise heavy, how they raise an eyebrow to ask you a piercing question without words. Their skin shines akin to Viking lore, as pale as pearl, and glory galore. While as tight as any landlocked central European country their spirit loves to dance. Have you ever seen a Slav dance, with each joint independent of the other, then spin? Admit that the most provincially hood of them is globally minded. They burp with a hand over their mouth. Good taste. Not a single lukewarm thing about a Russian, only hot and cold. And the Russian character in his game? As much a stereotype as the next. She only asked for money.

Meanwhile, the American character was ok looking by comparison, but was straight up the nastiest one, with the best mission, trivia: you had to tell her the capitals of various US states, and for each state you got right you got to take her in a different position. How do you think I learned about Helena, Concord, Juneau? Each state had its own maneuver, from disgusting to breathtaking. Don't ask what the Alaskan Pipeline is, or the New Hampshire Hump, or the Montana Milkshake.

And my favorite? Venezuela. She would recite motivational speeches and you had to guess who wrote them. It was great. It was pure.

Ask me what I'm going to do right now. Play.

ಠ

It was Wednesday, all of a sudden, and Ilya went to meet Tiffany and that guy she usually had hidden away in her room, the moaner, for brunch in the Lower East Side. Walking through Tompkins Sq Park, a stranger by the corner of the park asked if he wanted to go skiing, showing Ilya two half-gram bags of snow in purple bags with grease and fingerprints, black crust stuck to the zipping part, like the dirt under a longish nail. Ilya didn't say no, but kept walking, head down, and mind enflamed.

The chimes went off over his head when he got to the diner. Turned out that the two had already picked out a booth and were sitting side by side with their mouths together. Polar opposites, Tiff with her dreads in a bun, and this polo-shirted guy who looked like he would cut you in line at the grocery store. It wasn't until Ilya sat down that they even noticed he had entered. They chummed, ordered food, bantered, got desert, then digested.

Tiffany was explaining her last time at Zdras, trying to take a shot of this big group of drunks, when her date interrupted her.

"Simply dynamic," said Tiffany's date. "You know how to leverage the crowd. I love it." He turned to Ilya. "I keep asking her to photograph one of my networking events, but she said the subjects don't pose well."

"Your clients are there to exchange business cards," said Tiffany, "not to get wasted. You take a shot of two yuppies shaking hands once, and you've seen them all."

"I disagree," said he. "And I would even add that if you've seen one drunk person, you've seen them all."

Tiffany brightened up. "What if Ilya deejayed your next event, Jeremy?"

Jeremy turned to Ilya, who was playing with the crumbs on his plate. "Do you play R&B? R&B has been proven to raise endorphin levels and reduce cortisol, the stress hormone."

"Word," said Ilya, not looking up. "I got your endorphins right here." He squeezed a load of ketchup onto his plate, and started spreading it around, like he had seen Jeffrey Wright do with maple syrup in a movie once, as Basquiat. Oddly, after that, while sculpting something out of his food, he thought about how funny inspiration could be. Of course! What was missing from his Track Three was a little Rhythm and Blues, a little boogie, a small snap of the bra, the unbuckle of a belt, to add to his tasty, sweet, viscous, sexual, "Honey Beer."

Meanwhile, Jeremy turned to Tiffany. "Does he always do that, play with his food?"

Tiffany sighed. "He's solving something."

"Hey, Jason," said Ilya, tuning back in to the conversation. "You should drop by Zdras on Friday, I'm testing out a new track, and I can put some R&B in it for you, if you'd like."

The Foley artist roommate, always with a keen ear, caught Ilya's faux pas. "Yes, *Jeremy*, you should go, I know you work on Saturdays, but I promise you will have fun, plus, maybe, I will even go home with you that night and help you wake up in the morning."

Jeremy turned to Tiffany again, this time with a smirk, then turned to Ilya.

"My name's Jeremy," he says. "I've told you twice."

"We've met?" asked Ilya, looking up from his plate, with a half-smug, half-playful look.

"Yes, Ilya, you met Jeremy in Chelsea, at his rooftop party."

"You drunkenly asked me if you could change the music, all night. Excuse me," he said, holding back the tomato and sour cream gurgling in his stomach. "I must attend the facilities." He folded his napkin in three, then once more in half. Tiffany teased that he was a big boy and didn't need to excuse himself like that. He laughed like he knew that already. Ilya saw him put his hand on her neck, where her dread bun was, as he stepped over her, out of the booth, and into the restroom.

Ilya remembered the party at Julia's later that night, and wanted to ask Tiffany if she thought he should ask her out on a real date. But first, he had to catch her up on the story.

"You're dating Julia Simon!"

"Not dating. Seeing, talking to."

"Still, the morning news lady! The laundromat plays her show all the time."

"And Julia Simon is her TV name."

"She's so hot, Ilya. And I love her interviews. But damn, you two haven't kissed?!"

Tiffany was surprised to hear about this just now, almost two weeks after they first shared poetry to each other, wherein Ilya and Julia connected not so randomly at the beach, and talked every day since over a phone she had bought him, about whatever. Why didn't they meet up during the week, why hadn't he mentioned her earlier, what was her kid like? So many questions.

"I don't know," said Ilya.

"Do you like her?"

Ilya didn't reply.

"You love her?" she asked. "Don't you?"

Ilya replied, "She's different."

"You totally do. Is she coming to your show?"

"She can't. It's her dad's birthday that weekend."

"I get it."

"No, actually, he passed away, along with her mother. So she goes back to Cuba where they're buried, every year, to celebrate them."

"Oh . . . she's Cuban? I thought . . ." Tiffany looked down at her plate.

So did Ilya. "I guess you can say that."

"But what about tonight?"

"Tonight she's having a party. Equinox. Wanna come?"

Tiffany shook her head, as if to mix all the new information. As of now, Tiffany had understood and yet had not understood a damn. To Ilya's invitation, she said, "Can't," and then began explaining something about a passport, but then transitioned back to how crazy it was that this woman seemed to be all over him, yet Ilya wouldn't do anything, how she was getting divorced, how she had a six year old, how she was this famous news anchor for a local station, and yet Ilya didn't do anything, and . . .

Ilya interrupted her to ask why she was going to the consulate.

"To renew my passport," she explained, rubbing her bicep tattoos, the treble and bass clef. "The building is close by our house."

"Good luck," said Ilya.

"Luck? You never believed in luck," said Tiffany, smiling.

"I can't put it into words," he said, smiling himself, infected by her good humor, just one reason why they got along so well. Then he tried asking Tiffany why she was with this Jeremy guy. But without words.

The DJ jutted forward. He gave Tiffany a look that asked the question: Why him?

Tiffany had anticipated the question, so she pretended not to have understood Ilya. She bit her lips, and looked about the room as if clueless.

But Ilya leaned forward even more, as if repeating the question, nodding his head at her and in the direction of the restroom, waiting for an answer, raising his eyebrow as if to say, So, c'mon, tell me, why him?

Tiffany put her hands on the table, then simply said, "Because," rolling her eyes and pantomiming an orgasm.

ॐ

Julia's apartment was in Park Slope. This meant that the champagne was actual champagne. The hors d'oeuvres were catered. And there played a piano and harp player, looking like powdered doves in the corner—and not for tips or breadcrumbs, having been paid handsomely in advance. Ilya was dressed closer to a busboy than to the players on the elegance scale, moreover, couldn't help but notice the coat and tie attire all guests had on this weeknight soirée.

Being at a party blows sometimes. Especially one with blow, blow everywhere, but none to snort. Or when you don't know anyone. This is how Ilya felt at David's birthday parties, kid who would pull way more friends than his younger brother. It was in times like these that Ilya realized he spent too much time practicing instruments and too little time socializing. But the blow! He couldn't.

Because, of course, he saw Julia, elegant, elegantissima, the most beautiful woman in the city, first. What would she think? She kissed his cheek, and brushed his arm, with an "I'm glad you came" that sent his spit down his throat, started introducing him to folks. After a bit of this, she told him to go find her son, running around somewhere, before she herself ran along to greet other well-groomed guests, in many languages. Ilya thought he should find the son, until he went to the bar, and, knocking back a cocktail of some sorts, stood at attention before the musicians—attracted to what he knew best—assessing their chord progressions and counting their beats. Within a bar he knew exactly where they were in the song. It was a jazz standard.

Ilya snapped out of the trance the musicians had trapped him in, when behind him, above the average party decibel level, he tuned into, by accident, a pair of snide remarks made about his clothes. There was a stain on the back of his faded black button up, ketchup.

The bathroom smelled of boujee scented candles. By the sink was the soap. Underneath the soap was a seashell. Not the ones you buy in a store with a price tag stuck to it, but the kind you pick up in Jersey, big and colorful, with a chip on the side from the sea—he could tell by the smoothness of the chip. Turning up to the mirror, he almost saw past himself. Turning back down, continuing to finger the crack, then the grooves of the turned up shell, he pictured his Julia there naked. His—not the real—Julia, whose small but heavy foot would have shattered this old animal home, and probably almost did in real life before she noticed it and took it home, like she had taken Ilya's heart, he thought. That was the Julia he knew, his lovely and tan Julia, the one who was small enough to stand on this shell and just look beautiful. Ah.

Julia Simonovna Levina

Who were the guests at the party? And why were they all celebrating the equinox, the middle of, a high of, or low of, or both of something, depending? The time was near midnight. A kiss from Julia would be nice. How much more of the party would he have to bear? Just pretend to stick around. Have another mystery cocktail. Say hi to her son running around somewhere, then go upstairs to her bedroom. That's the plan, though Ilya. And he stepped out.

"There he is," said Julia when she saw Ilya. "That's the DJ I told you about."

She was kneeling down next to her kid, who had a toy bow and rubber arrow. Ilya was shot. The mother and son started laughing.

"He wants to be a hunter when he grows up," said the mother, "and a firefighter, and a lawyer, and a DJ." Julia stood up and stretched her hips. "Reminds me of someone." Meaning Ilya.

"What's your name, little guy," said Ilya, popping off the rubber arrow on his chest, and passing it back to the younger boy.

But the kid didn't take the arrow, instead he ran away, his arms dangling behind him, like some manga character would, off into the crowd. The crowd received him well, and offered him snacks. Ilya kept looking at the younger boy, saw him eating only the bread of what he was offered, not the tapenade nor spread on top, watched as the grownups took a liking to such a lollipop-stained kid. No one put him down.

"His name is Александр[*]," said Julia. "I wanted an international name."

Ilya was distracted, thinking, the way you pronounce it isn't international, but . . . then again . . .

"Do you know those twins, over there," said Ilya, revisiting the urge to point at these two women who looked like they had just gotten off the set of Red Bull's *Art of Flight*, with sunburned faces and flannel shirts.

"They own a music studio by the Cloisters," replied Julia. "And master sound for film scores. They owe me a favor, actually. Want me to introduce you?"

"I think I've read about them in a magazine," he said, not really answering the question, distracted. "*Tape Op*, or other. And, hey, I think they're playing pool in the bathroom."

One was pocketing a rolled $100 bill, caked in frisky powder, into the curve of her blue-jeans. While the other was pounding her flat chest, before looking around as if guilty of something she knew she shouldn't let everyone know about.[†]

"Playing pool with an 8-ball," said Ilya. "Get it?" But when he turned to Julia, he saw that she had been pulled away by someone in a zesty, orange toupee asking her about real estate in this part of town. So Ilya turned back to the twins, those short-haired, muscular, sinewy, loose flannel wearing, torn-up jeans sporting, coke-nosed twins with surely

---

[*] At last, the author's name finds its way into his own story.
[†] Poor kid! I hate these two. So irresponsible. The road to addiction passes through the vicious cycle of other people's problems.

androgynous names, and Ilya wondered if, why not, he could score from them, how much would they charge, would his headache finally go away? Would it be such a big deal? Shouldn't he celebrate? His temples drummed against the rest of his head.

"Hy!" Julia called, noticing the DJ distracted. She repeated herself, "Hy!!"

"Nu, what?"[*]

"I've been thinking about your possible show," she said, drawing the DJ away from those dark thoughts of white drugs. And he turned to her, not because of her words, but because of the warm sparkling breath coming on him, of her, Julia, all of her, smelling delicious, of apricots and ambrosia. "I've been thinking," she said, "of an idea."

"What is it?" Ilya managed to ask. "What is your idea?"

"The idea," she said, "that I've been thinking is . . ."

The time was very close to midnight.

Her son ran back, and jumped on his mother, into her arms, and nestled in there, a little too close, thought Ilya, for a six year old. Nonetheless, she picked him up and held him despite his weight and age. And he passed out right in her arms.

"He's very protective," said Julia. "And sleepy."

"What's your idea?" asked Ilya.

"You should perform with Stacy."

"I love Stacy," mumbled the little boy in Julia's arms, half-asleep. "Play with Stacy."

---

[*] Facepalm.

Ilya rubbed his forehead. Her music had finally reached the children of New York. It was over. Her presence would haunt him.

"You think?" mumbled Ilya. "You think that's a good idea?" It was like dating a girl and her telling you that she's still in love with her ex. It was like dating a guy and him telling you he's leaving because he needs to find himself. Something cheesy. Here was Julia, suggesting to Ilya his two biggest fears—reaching out to Stacy to ask her to play with him, and possibly bombing on stage while performing original tracks.

"I don't know much about the industry," said Julia, tapping her little boy's sleepy butt, as she propped him up higher on her shoulder. "But I think if you told Tony that she was going to play with you then he might be more . . . inclined."

"I would have to reach her somehow."

"It's 2018. You will find a way. Offer her to headline."

Ilya raised his arms and got red. "I don't think that's a good idea."

"I think it is." Julia propped up her son, but did it looking at Ilya's lips.

"She can't headline my own release party!"

"Tell me—"

"Because!"

"Илья," she said, as the music slowed down, and soft lighting faded in. "You're really close to my face."

Ilya was, he realized. He moved forward. She didn't back away. When he pressed his lips onto hers, she welcomed him.

Softly, slowly, the musicians stopped playing. "It's time," someone shouted. Soon everyone lowered their voice to a murmur. "You should meet my friends," said Julia, laying her son to rest on a couch nearby.

"I will," said Ilya, waking into a dream.

Julia nodded, then leaned towards his ear to let the following words leave her mouth with all the freshness of mint and sugar cane: "I hope you're ready." Half a minute later she stood where the musicians had been playing, and asked for everyone's attention. "Tonight," she said, "is a very special night. We would like to invite a very, very dear friend of mine, someone you should all meet, because, well, soon you will have to call his agent to make an appointment. Ladies and gentlemen, please welcome, *Ilya Nikolayevich Gagarin.*"

Light fell upon Ilya, while the piano, and everyone, waited.

III

A FAIRY TALE ALMOST BLUE / это утрата*

☉

---

* *Utrata*. It sounds pretty, but it stands for something terrible. It means "loss," as in the loss of a loved one. Very similar to the word *poterya*, потеря, which also means "loss," sometimes synonymously, other times with the loss of an object, such as a cell phone, a wallet, car keys, or one sock in a pair. Now, given that you are writing a story that began with the loss of a lover, and you link Ilya to Orpheus, the mythic poet who journeyed to the Underworld to get his lover back, only to lose her again . . . I expect this next section to deliver a blow. Sorry for the unintended drug pun, and my pessimism. It is just that I am feeling things: I feel anxious, worried, a little hopeful perhaps, but also for this loss. Such a word. Loss. Утрата.

Intermission:

A bottle of beer drifted in the ocean, in which a hermit crab had gotten inside. He enjoyed the view but found himself more often lost than thrilled. He couldn't break the glass, but at least the birds couldn't break in either.

A sauna of beer and sea in there. A sauna. So hot that it stopped floating on water and started floating in the air. It followed other rising particles of evaporation, into the clouds, until falling down with the cool rain over some remote mountain. Then it flowed downstream. Into the ocean once more. Wash, rinse, repeat.

Today, the crab could recite the water cycle forwards and backwards, were he able to speak.

Pop! went the sparkling wine, poured into the glass flutes with orange juice, both liquids swooshing with foam. Until it spilled over the rim top. That's when Julia gently ladled the pulp with the yolk of her fingertip, bringing it closer and closer to her mouth, between her lips Moulin rouge, helping it land quietly on her tongue, in her smile. Soon his glass would be filled too, and the whole movement repeat itself.

Lately, and daily, Ilya had been asking Julia if they could meet during the week. But every time she told him she was doing something that day or had to do something the next. This was a busy month, July, the month of her name, Julia, the anniversary of her parents' passing, the terrorism in southern Russia she had to cover, so much more. But did it matter what kept her away? Not exactly, not to the one wanting to see the other person. But didn't she want him too? Couldn't she want him just as much?

Only a handful of days had passed since their equinox kiss. With time passing as slowly as one sweats in the cold, that terrible waiting, wishing to be near someone you have gotten mixed up with, especially when that someone was this Julia. "Sunday," she had said, "same time, same place."

So Ilya, jobless and with his EP incomplete, hopped off his friend's couch and hobbled his way to Union Square Station, but much earlier than he needed to, because he had nothing else to do but kill time—and perhaps this was what kept his mind free enough to ponder the waste of his hours not spent on the laptop, or promoting his unfinished project, or inviting people to his show, et cetera—so he ambled far, and ambled good. Hearing the right train announcing it was about to depart the station, he jumped down a whole flight of stairs and slid in sideways between the closing doors.

"Next stop: City Hall." Anonymous faces, angry faces, faces that smelled of feces, in that crowded 4 train, which made him wonder even more: where were these dirty Sunday trippers going? Did they each, having donned their army boots, or having painted their fingernails rainbow colored, have their own Julia's? Their own boy toy Ilya's? Was everyone just like him, off to meet potential mates twice their age, or half their age? Or were they completely different than him, in that they were completely indifferent to anything around them, not even paying attention? And if not either of those extremes, then, could it possibly be, that these strangers on a crowded train headed to Brooklyn just had their own lives? (Ilya suddenly flared his nostrils. Oh God, how could that guy! Look at him pucker his lips, furrow his brow . . . wiggle his bottom!)

Fading out the crowd, the volume rose on his own "Live at Zdras" mix, soon to turn into Track Four, so that Ilya could check the audio quality on his headphones—the low end still a little muddy—as the train sped up and slowed down, the doors opening and closing, again and again, in fast forward, allowing throngs of beggars to step through the threshold which divided inside from out, while dancers also entered asking for money although for a bit longer than they had danced, and comedians cracked one liners, then left, plus everyone who seemed so normal minding their own business streaming drama shows on their phones with cellular data at each station, their grocery bags held up between their feet. Only when at an abrupt halt did the train car shake, making a paper bag of groceries tip over, sending apples and oranges sliding all along the unclean floor.

At Barclays, Ilya started getting nervous about meeting Julia—he hadn't reached the table yet where she would lick clean the rims of the glass flutes, no—he was still on his way. And at Barclays Ilya remembered the last time he saw a Nets game he had left during the third quarter because the Brooklyn Home team was ahead by fifty points, and counting, and he didn't like to watch games with no chance for the other team to win. Kind of like in real life, or in anything, concluded Ilya, not letting his hand run down the oily metal rail down the stairs to the B/Q platform, ignoring that hundreds of thousands of people coughed on that glossy, gleaming material every day.

Was that image of her at the beach real? It hadn't happened yet, and yet Ilya was sure it would, he could visualize it, in pieces. Would it be the yellow sundress, or a sleeveless striped button up? Hair up or down? In a good mood, or distracted? In a hurry to get home, or lazily able to watch the sunset for once? Would they talk about the present moment, or about the last time they shared each other's gaze? For now he was on the platform, waiting for that damn train to come already, the one that would take him to the beach.

He peered over the edge, head over the yellow line that reminded him "Don't become another number" like the accident statistics poster say inside every other train car. He saw only dark tunnel, no light at the end. But music, yes, a guitarist nearby. And who, who was that standing next to him? Standing, nervous, tapping his foot? It was him, for sure. What are the chances?

Ilya always thought that famous people did not ride the train, but then again, look, it's David Fricke. Not that most people knew who he was. Ilya only knew because he had watched a "Making of" the *Dark Side of the Moon* documentary on VH1, featuring this "writer for *Rolling Stones*," who explained the tempo change in that song "Money," whose narrow face and thin oval glasses between long rocker hair were hard to forget. Ilya didn't pause his music when he googled "rolling stones writers," just to double check the face, and remember the writer's name. But look at him, sad, exhausted, definitely not in any way on his way to meet a lover half his age. Just standing there, idly. While a guitarist, a cool jazz busker, did his thing far off, strumming a solid tune that made Ilya feel full of tears and nostalgic.

"Yes, I know him." Julia knew everybody, even David Fricke! "We crossed paths once at the station, when he was preparing notes for the band we were broadcasting."

Now, now, Julia and Ilya were sitting across from one another, at the beach, the Brighton side, under a scorching, midsummer sun, which left their skin as warm as the bottom end of a frittata. "Would you like to meet him?" Ilya didn't reply. Julia asked again, "Would you?" Still Ilya didn't say anything. So she huffed a little, and finally did that thing with the glass flutes, with her finger, as Ilya took a long, healthy hit of his mimosa.

"I saw him today," said Ilya, "transferring at Barclays. He seemed sad."

"You can't judge," said Julia, setting her glass down, "or you shouldn't. Maybe he was having a bad day, or maybe that's his normal face."

"I know but . . ." Ilya had nothing to add, thinking about how all he does on the train is judge others the way he would not want to be judged.

"On another note," said this woman, drawing the young man's attention like the riptide does a wave. "You need a job." And a wave crashed not far from where they sat.

"I know."

"I mean, you can't just walk around aimlessly day in and day out. It isn't good for your creativity."

"The show is three weeks away." Ilya finished his glass. Julia served him another. He thanked her, then continued: "Should I be looking for a job now?"

Julia shook her head, but only to undo a ponytail, letting her wavy, fruity hair come just to the tip of her shoulders, and waver in the wind, before she nodded, *yes*, meaning *you should*. "Remember the twins at the party? I helped them find that studio. They would be glad to meet you, if I recommended you."

"You could."

"And I will." This was going to be a short outing, Ilya could tell, just by her tone of voice. "But," she added, "promise me something."

"What?"

"Don't do anything stupid."

"What do you mean?"

Julia took off her sunglasses, and with the bottom of her blouse—it was the striped button up after all—wiped away the grease from the lenses, then slapped the frames back on. "I mean," she said, in her rich, low voice, "I mean don't do anything stupid with them."

"I promise not to embarrass you," he said.

"It's not for my sake," she said, knowing the story about his last interview. "I'm saying, don't embarrass yourself."

Ilya had a vague idea of what she was hinting at, based on what he saw them doing at her party, and how it made him feel. That party where he had stolen that merging of lips from Julia. Why was she going on about jobs and about celebrity writers, why had he traveled all this way, when now, now she was getting up, looking at her watch and putting things like her phone and her wallet back into her oversized bag?

"Wait."

"Ilya." Julia was standing up. "I've got to go."

"Why don't we watch the sunset?"

"That isn't for another two hours, and I've got to pick up my kid from camp."

Ilya stood up too. From a distance this pair looked so strange, yet so innocent, timeless, a well-dressed lady and a grungy looking youth, two chests facing like dancers. Someone watching might even say they were perfect for each other, like family, or more. There was something in the way he looked at her that revealed this, his sad eyes no longer ringed by bags, his freckled nose no longer red at the nostrils, and an overall healthy look save for his chapped lips. "Let me walk you to Brighton Beach Avenue," he offered.

"It's better if I catch a taxi from Neptune Ave, one block farther up."

She said it as if she wanted to go alone, felt Ilya. But he didn't care, he accompanied her away from the boardwalk, and then passed the train station he had gotten off at, one more block up, as she put it, to the avenue with the name of the god of the sea. There, Ilya noticed a sign in Chinese advertising a restaurant, a sign in Russian advertising a hookah bar, a pizza place named after an Italian family, a bodega run by Yeminis, a corner store with the Mexican flag outside, and a printing shop called "Printing Shop." Where in the world would you see anything like this? And how was Ilya holding Julia's hand, that wet, sweaty, plushy hand? Holding hands so intimately, rubbing his fingertips between the veiny knuckles of the woman who swung her arm as she strutted along the sidewalk full of cracks and bird droppings. His heart was racing, he didn't want to see her go. His heart was pounding, pounding. "When will I see you again?"

Julia turned to him and, tippy-toeing a little, planted a gentle reminder of the other day upon his lips. Ilya wrapped his arms around her striped bloused waist, letting the noise of car horns mix with the jangle of dog leashes, as he brought her closer to him. But then she pushed him away a bit.

"I'm going to be out of town for a few days," she mentioned, just before entering a taxi she called for. "Promise me you won't do anything silly."

"With who?" he said, although he remembered who.

"With the twins. I'll connect you, but you mustn't . . ."

He partly said yes, partly said no. It could go either way. Which, when undecided, is the worst thing to do.

Ο

In front of Ilya stood the two butch, ivory-cold, big eared, flat chested, audio engineering, wizard-like twins from the cover of the audio engineering magazine. They had invited the DJ to visit their studio up by the Cloisters, a museum in far northern Manhattan. Ilya had drooled over the shots of that space, back when he read the article about them. And now? He was in there, in that pristine acoustic heaven, as if living inside one of the photographs he had seen. And they were literally asking him, Ilya, about how they could work together.

"Jules recommends you highly," said one of the twins, just before having a cigarette in her mouth lit by her sister. "Highly." She puffed directly above herself, a motion that made her look like a choo-choo train.

"We trust her," said the other twin, who had a bit shorter hair than her sister, and two extra moles on the side of her nose. "Jules did us a huge favor by finding this place for us."

The young DJ observed the thick, wide windows along the top of the walls, the high ceilings with sound absorbing panels everywhere spaced an inch apart, the drum room in the corner next to the 48-channel mixing board, XLRs neatly rolled in crates of various colors, the red crate labeled for broken cables, the blue one for good cables, and the yellow one for maybe-broken-emergency cables; which seemed organized compared to the percussion closet, the only messy thing, really, about the studio, a place that hadn't been photographed. In there, Ilya noticed just how random and tossed about it had become over the years, with candy wrappers on the floor mixed with used condoms and piles of empty liquor bottoms, as if inside a grizzly bear had made love to a bronco and then thrown a party for college musicians.

"This will be your first project," said the sister with the moles, rubbing the back of her hands.

"Think you could start right away?" said the other, taking a long rip from the thing in her mouth.

"It's paid, right?" Ilya asked. "I mean the job. Julia must have mentioned I am a musician."

"We saw you play. You have talent. But unfortunately . . ." They looked at one another, for a long time actually, which was weird. ". . . we can't exactly pay you. But! If you bring musicians, you could record them."

"Do you take a cut of the—"

"Not a cut. All. We can show you the rates later. Consider this an internship, for experience. And if your college gives course credit . . ."

"I have studio experience." Ilya looked at his shoes, these beat up leather boots he had worn in and worn out. "You know," he added, "I was studying music theory in college, with a minor in audio engineering. I've clocked over a thousand hours at my mixer before senior year."

"Wait, did you say you graduated, or?"

"Didn't, I didn't." He felt himself uncomfortably honest in that moment. For what? He turned up. "I mean . . ."

"And where were you studying?" the twins asked, really slow, in unison. "Where?"

"A liberal arts college upstate. Say. What about a studio musician? I can be a studio musician."

"We already have—"

Suddenly, a band of thick bearded indie artists kicked open the door and piled in with their truck full of instrument cases, cases of beer, and a foul stench. "Twins!" they shouted. "WE'RE HERE!!"

Within a minute, the entire space was littered in stage equipment and drum heads. They were on tour and were best friends, crashing here for the night. They even brought cocaine and offered Ilya some.

"I guess we will talk about interning later," said one of the studio owners.

"Stay if you like," said the other. "If you've got nothing else going on."

The musicians ignored Ilya, which made him feel unwelcomed. But then they said something, which made him feel the opposite. It didn't matter, really, what they said. All he could think about was what he was staring at, the tapping of powder being cut with a metal, platinum credit card over the body of an acoustic Martin guitar. Because the guitar was missing a G string, it didn't take long for the roadie to make more lines than strings over the body of the instrument. And, soon, there were twice as many lines as strings. Each as evocative as the next, a crunchy white material honing in all of his attention, vibrating without vibrating, shaking without a pluck—Ilya even got this way with piano strings whenever he opened the hood of a new beast and examined its well-tuned insides, just his eyes could spark that feeling, that lust, that temptation to hit keys, to strike ten notes at once then sculpt a melody, since, having memorized many scales, he could hear the sounds, clearly, before even playing. And he stared, and he stared.

"Want a line?"

"Why not?"

Θ

Fireworks. More and more fireworks. All of the island of Manhattan with its fireworks, blew fireworks—crack, bang, pew went the fireworks—hissing long in Ilya's eyes and sustaining light in his ears. They were at The Lot Radio, his favorite bar with his favorite music, in Brooklyn.

Tiffany and her boyfriend Jeremiah or Jeremy had invited Ilya to the 4th of July dance party, in the Polish neighborhood of Greenpoint, by the Nassau stop of the G-line train. His roommate figured he needed to get out of the apartment, having noticed him obsessing over the bars of his digital audio workstation program—the gray one that lets you go into session view—looping the same dropped-in audio clip of him yelling into a microphone during a DJ session the weekend before.

"What you up to?" asked Tiffany, loud, but not loud enough for her roommate to hear. "I said . . ." She unplugged his headphones from his laptop.

"WE ARE LIVE AT ZDRAS, BABY!" roared his computer, but in loop: "WE ARE LIVE AT ZDRAS, BABY! WE ARE LIVE AT ZDRAS, BABY!"—shaken from his dizzying high, Ilya blinked back to consciousness, and his roommate. He was on the verge of a new idea.

"Want to come with—hey," said Tiffany, unable to get Ilya's full attention, because he started turning a knob on his program, modulating the looped audio track: "WE ARE LIVE AT ZDRAS, BABY! [higher pitch] *WE ARE LIVE AT ZDRAS, BABY!* [higher pitch still] *WE ARE LIVE AT ZDRAS, BABY!* [super low pitch] **WE ARE LIVE AT ZDRAS, BABY!** [less low pitch, sort of back in the middle] **WE ARE LIVE AT ZDRAS, BABY!** [half time playback] **~WWEE AARREE LLIIVVEE AATT ZZDDRRAASS, BBAABBYY~"**

"Ilya."

He kept modulating the track, this time splicing the last part to a loop, and then letting it trail off in a ping-pong delay: **"BBAABBYY, BBAABBYY, BBAABBY-Y, Y-Y-Y-Y-Y-Y-y-y."** "What?"

Tiffany invited Ilya out, and he said *Sure*.

And now the fireworks, in his eyes and ears. But all he could think about was editing Track Four of his EP. Boom! went a flash of red and green lights. Wooh! wooshed a Roman candle, and another, and . . . Pooh, Wooh, Wahh!

Meanwhile the dance party rocked on, girls in tank tops spooning and grinding, and boys with lightsabers fighting. Jeremy in a hoarse voice asking Tiffany why electronic music was all the same, all samples, all copies, and Tiffany saying no it wasn't, listen to the bassline, listen to the lyrics, while faded Ilya stared blankly straight through them, outside-in, realizing they were like brother and sister, before turning to the crowd and counting 50 people who didn't have drugs for him, 10 who maybe did, and another 50 too busy moshing by the DJ at this parking lot. Who to ask?

Ilya left and came back.

"Want any?" he offered Tiff and Jay a rock and a tab.

Tiffany moved her mouth but Ilya could not hear what she was saying. She slapped his hand down and stomped on the plastic baggies. Not losing sight of them, Ilya dropped down quick and went for the closer, pink one, which had spilled the tabs. About to pick it up, he locked in on the face of Disney's signature cartoon winking at the young man from the ground, as, on all fours, he crawled towards it.

But then, the metal toe on Tiffany's boot came down hard upon it, crushing and twisting everything Ilya felt in that moment mattered—except for the farther, turquoise baggie! After a lunge, which left him belly flat on the ground, Ilya managed to cup and protect, through tears in his eyes, his prized object.

Seeing him like that, Tiffany tried to talk him into getting up, only Ilya couldn't hear her—not past the popping of fireworks overheard, exploding into palm trees, or peace signs, those fireworks, blotting out the roommate's yelling—her mouth moving, as her boyfriend picked up the DJ from the ground, though a jingling, jangling pain hit against his ribs.

"Stop kicking!" yelling Jeremy, pushing back the moshing crowd from the damaged Ilya. "Let's get him home." He held on tight to Ilya, then held on tighter, because he could feel his girlfriend's roommate breaking free. "Damn!"

Ilya broke free and ran away from the guy holding him, ran far, in the direction of the fire and the works, the East River, towards the city on a rock.

He came to a pier, a nice long pier, where he could shiver alone, away from any crowds, safe from the warm dark summer night. Behind him, along a massive large brick wall, spray-painted there, was a mural of a young girl smelling a flower, which Ilya couldn't see. He only mimicked it, grabbing the flower of a lonely weed and hoping to fall asleep somewhere under the pier, after crawling up and over the railing, down and under it, like a roach, he thought, but not before rubbing the inside of the turquoise baggie into his upper gums.[*]

Celebrating and singing himself to sleep alright. Dialing Julia before passing out, reaching her voicemail, and leaving a long, uninterrupted silence on the call, until the line died, or he passed out.

Θ

---

[*] This is so sad. The relapse.

July 5th. Thursday morning, my journal. It's been a minute since that night at the Cloisters. And what a night last night. So much for being a studio musician. And I woke up under the Greenpoint pier today. My body aches from a dozen bruises, my eyes sting like I've been staring at the sun, but, at least, I got up before noon, and ran home. Before noon, in the AM. As it is written in the Gospel of Dre, chapter four, minute two, wherein he spake, saying: "Wake up in the AM, compose a beat." I'll write an entry then get back to Track Four. Damn, I look tattered like the security guard at Zdras, that hopeless homeless man.

Or, Robespierre. The dude spins records. Tells stories. He invited me to stay once—through hand gestures, pointing to his watch and fist bumping the air with short jabs like a T-Rex. He plays 4 to sometime after, so wild, on nights no touring act gets booked. That is when normal people sleep. For some reason Tony trusts him with the keys and with running the club during its after hours.

I can't believe I'm almost a year into writing a song a day; now time to do this the rest of my life: one new lyric or one new music track, every day, period. Most of these songs I would never play in a club. And the EP itself still needs a name. I can't call my first EP *Ilya Nikolayevich Gagarin*. That's corny. What if I change directions, later regret committing the *I.N.G.* artist name to a lame sound? My name is all I've got. Why would my EP be lame? I could always rebrand. What if I like it when I release it, but regret it later? Then I'll have to do an *I.N.G. 2* release, which is dumb. You can't have two releases with the same name. That's like having two white albums, or two black albums. Then again, two of anything sometimes sucks, sometimes rocks. In jazz if you make a mistake, all you have to do is change keys and pick up the fallen band member by playing the same notes. In visual arts, if you splatter some paint on accident on the left side of the canvas, all you have to do is repeat the splatter on the right side. Nothing like symmetry to justify a mistake in art. Call it license. But in business or in marketing? Repetition marks death. That's how you know naming albums, coining genres or marketing bands isn't art. You can't repeat. You can't make mistakes. I repeat mistakes, repeat my beats.[*] Now, aren't mass produced products just the same ole shit repackaged? Ok repetition in business is helpful, but monotonous. Whereas in electronic music repetition is unavoidable, in poetry it is instrumental, as in, optional, as in repetition can make noise sound beautiful, the language of angels: rhyme. Ode to rhyme: Rhyme, I give you time, you are mine, and my friends', to the end, O Rhyme, O Rhyme, you fine, fine dime, you are all mine, make my lines shine, from now to the end of time. Aren't beats repeated just sounds rhymed? Pulse. I remember the nursery rhymes growing up. Jack and Jill went up the hill . . . or Humpty Dumpty sat on the wall . . . even the names repeat sound. No one has sung those to me since grade school, and yet I remember them, because of how repetitive they are. I remember the first song Papa played in the car on the way to

---

[*] No kidding.

the Adirondacks: "ROXANNE / you don't have to put on the red light / those days are over / you don't have to sell your body to the night." Papa played Police. Alliteration, another form of repetition. How cute. Just what every kid wants, a playful dad, singing from the *Synchronicity* album.[*]

And yet, and yet, the one time mom sung to me the Russian bayu bayu song, I will never forget. That was just once, never repeated, but I remember.

Life can be repetitive. Especially life today. I believe that is why so many of us love electronic music.[†]

Going back to Russian, Julia wants me to improve. So I will. Starting by listing as many similar names in English and Russian as I can.

Alexander; Александр. Barbara; Барбара. Catherine; Екатерина. David; Давид. Eugene; Евгений. Theodore; Фёдор. George; Георг. Irene; Ирэн. Michael; Михаил. Natalia; Наталия. Nicholas; Николай. Paul; Павел. Peter; Питер. Olga; Ольга. Ok Olga is only Russian. Calling Olga an English name is like calling a блин a pancake, or a crêpe some French toast. Names are important. And words are important, too, as are their shades. You wouldn't use a blue heart emoji in place of a red one, any more than you would send a white fist-up emoji when you meant a black one. I guess what I'm trying to say is, I feel one thing when I hear

---

[*] *Outlandos D'Amour,* you nerd.

[†] I keep thinking about that drug scene in the last chapter. This kid needs a doctor, a professional. Can't he see the most repetitive thing in his life is his drug addiction? Will he ever quit? How can he write, let alone sit at his computer after a night like that?!

the word "Russia," and another when I hear "Россия," one thing hearing "Ilya," and another hearing "Илья," even if spoken by the same speaker.

Ah, there are also so many countries with the same name in both languages, too.

America; Америка. Bulgaria; Болгария. Great Britain; Великобритания. Germany; Германия. Egypt; Египет. India; Индия. Italy; Италия. Mexico; Мексика. Texas; Техас. I know Texas is not a country, but.

So many big words, three.

Absolutism; абсолютизм. Avant-garde; авангард. Aviation; авиации. Atmosphere; атмосфера. Ballad; баллада. Battery; батарея. Gladiator; гладиатор. Democracy; демократия. Dialect; диалект. Discipline; дисциплина. Idea; идея. Imitation; имитация. Individualism; индивидуализм. Instrument; инструмент. Kaleidoscope; калейдоскоп. Composer; композитор. Coda ; кода. Criticism; критика. Literature; литература. Marxism; марксизм. Opera; опера. Optimist; оптимист. Pyramid; пирамида. Popular; популярный. Overture; увертюра. University; университет. All words that resonate. And yes I used Google translate, but only to copy-paste the words here, swear. Distracted with distracting thoughts.

☉

Friday night at Zdras was pretty weak, not a lot of people showed up due to an unexpected flash flood warning, with kilotons of rain crashing down on the city. It would rain the next couple of days. So Ilya set his mix to shuffle and strolled to the restroom.

While at the urinal, three things crossed his mind in succession. The first was how weird it was that cartoon characters always wore the same clothes. But then again not just them, because Ilya always wore the same tight, torn, white jeans and the same beat up, black button up. The second was how strange it was that in stories characters never used the restroom. With the exception of Jack Black in *School of Rock*, this second idea was especially true, compared to how common it is to use restrooms in real life, as Ilya currently did, before that Duchamp shaped ceramic piece of art, his legs apart, unloading like one of the clouds outside. Giving him enough time to think about the third thing, which was this: how Ilya's third greatest fear, after bombing on stage and after playing with Stacy, was being hit from the back as he urinated.

Just as he was zipping up, someone pushed him against the wall.

"What the hell," shouted Ilya, his vial of mercury showing.

"Whuh duh hull," mimed Jonathan, shirt untucked, unbuttoned, so that one could see the US flag on his freckled chest.

"What the fuck's your problem!"

"Whuh duh fuhs yr pruhpruh!"

Ilya could have snapped. But he heard the last song repeat itself over the restroom monitors, so he didn't have time to deal with it. He ran past the head promoter, who was yelling, "Tony wants to talk to you!" before hissing under his breath, "Crackheads."

Ilya stepped down into Tony's office.

It was grimmer down there than usual. But Ilya didn't notice. He asked, "What do you need?" before adding, "And also, if your promotor pushes me again, I'm going to knock him out!"

Rather than listen to Ilya, Tony was more focused rolling a dollar bill over his desk, next to a bowl of lather on which a mirror and a razor lay cross.

When he finally did look at Ilya, he saw how roughed up his face was. Raising an eyebrow, he said: "Looks like you two have already been in a fight."

"Nah, this?"

"Then why are you tattletaling to me?" asked Tony, grunting, leaning over his desk. "I remember . . ."

"Are you shaving or getting high?" asked Ilya, seeing his friend relapse.

"Both." He continued: "I remember . . . the camp counselors telling us that if we had a problem with a bully, the first thing to do was to ignore them. The second thing was to move. Finally, if those two didn't work, then we should deal with it ourselves. Only as a last resort do we tattletale to the camp counselor." Tony coughed, went to go turn on the hot water in the restroom, and continued shaving in there. "You get it, Ilya? I'm your camp counselor."

"Yeah, but—" Ilya made his way to the seat at the desk and swooped a thumb into the white mixture like it were candy dip, then sucked his thumb to a pop. "What about rehab?"

"*I said, No, no, no.*"

"T, listen. I have an idea for the show. Do you have a second?"

Tony shook his razor at Ilya. "This better be a crazy idea, boy, a crazy idea!"

"What if I invited Stacy to play with me?"

"Stacy, your girlfriend Stacy?"

"My ex."

Tony raised his arms. "I.N.G. is official in the books for July 22nd!"

"Sweet."

"And Jonathan is going to help you promote."

"What the fuck!"

"Ilya, your social media has plateaued. You haven't published in weeks. Your people are unsubscribing." Tony stepped back in front of the sink.

Ilya got up from the desk. "I've been busy," he said.

"You, busy?" Tony almost laughed, but he was shaving.

"Yeah," said Ilya, pausing. "Busy. Working on the EP."

At that last word, Tony nicked a mole on his chin with the blade. He kept his cool, however, and brought the conversation back to the show, shouting: "Good. Since you're working so hard, tell me, when were you planning to invite your now less than 50,000 followers?"

Ilya hadn't thought about it. "I'll make the announcement last minute. It's more exciting that way."

After rolling his eyes, Tony whipped a wad of used lather into the sink, with a plop. "Jonathan's going to help you," he said, "and that's that."

"I can do my own invites!"

"Who are you going to invite, you don't know anybody!"

"I know you, my roommate . . . Josephine! Hey, where is she, by the way?"

She's with her dad, thought Tony, who, at the thought, cut himself again, deeper this time. Seeing blood, he started cursing Josephine, her dad, the DJ, everything outside of his control. "Boy, listen. Jonathan is going to help you promote, and that's *that*. So you two better go on a retreat and solve your issues."

Hobbling back to his desk, Tony stuck the rolled dollar bill into his nose and hovered over the mirror, dripping blood as he snorted, then got up and went back to shaving, gently touching up the space where his powdered nose met the lathered end of his upper lip. Meanwhile, he muttered, "Stacy . . . way to go," more to himself than to Ilya.

Now that the show was official, the first problem to solve was Ilya actually asking her to share the stage.

☉

Jules had been right, it wasn't that hard to reach Stacy. In fact, she had blocked Ilya on every possible level, except one that she had skipped on purpose, or had missed on accident, because Ilya never used it: Twitter.

After clicking the **[Forgot Password?]** button, Ilya searched for his ex.

There she was, after so long, that photo of her, in overalls, button undone, crumpled papers everywhere, and her looking up at Ilya's old camera phone, as she composed her hit blues single. "God damn," Ilya said outloud, "God damn." 13.3K tweets, 17.3K following, 2.6M followers, and 10.1K likes. (Compared to the 2 tweets, 5 following, 18 followers, and 0 likes, on his account.)

She had recently put out a series of music videos and behind-the-scenes clips of her cutting her upcoming album. Very cool stuff. But how to reach her, with a comment? Her tweets got 200-3k comments each. Fans flooded her with hashtags of themselves copying the dance moves of her music videos.

No way she would see Ilya's little call for help. He scrolled through. At last, he saw one tweet of hers with some 130 comments, an old one, about July 4th—telling people she was proud to be American, linking to a clip of many famous inventors from this great nation—if only she knew how he had celebrated and sang himself to sleep that night at the East River.

How sad, thought the DJ. Folks will like the videos of her dancing or comment on images of her body, but practically ignore her post sharing interesting facts about America. Ass comes before the mind, he figured. Anyway, this was his chance. After several rewrites, he posted a comment, specifically, about one of the inventors on that list.

Ilya Nikolayevich @inging 7m
Yo @StacyGi, wasn't Alexander G. Bell born in Scotland, inventing the telephone while living in Canada? <Link to the Canadian Encyclopedia.>

Within minutes, there was a reply.

Stacy Giacometti @StacyGi 2m
Sup @inging - seems you're right. thanks. how've you been?

This led to a series of private messages, and, after unblocking him, a call. Stacy answered right away. She knew why the date was important, that it was Maxine's birthday. So she said *Yes*, she would play on July 22nd. But on one condition: "Know this doesn't mean we are back together, don't try anything." Ilya agreed. All he needed now was to finish the

EP . . . maybe invite people to the show . . . but first a little line-ski . . . just one, to take the edge off after putting it on . . . a one-line meditation on how to have a little fun, nothing wrong with the tingling upper body, behind the coat of armor, that invincible feeling, and a rattling heart, and this damn restless leg . . . power, powder, cut, smack . . . like strumming guitar strings, the lower you go the higher you get—

_____

_____

_____MMMMMMMMMMMMEEEEEEEEEEEEEEEEEEEEEE

E_____

_____

_____

_____

__Weeeeeeeeeeeeeeeeeeeeeeeeeeeeeeeeeeeeeeeeeeeeeeeeeeeeeeee

e_____

_____

_____

_____

_____

_____heeeeeeeeee

e

_____

_____ damn.

Later that day, cooped up in his tiny curtained section of the living room, Ilya called his father Nikolai Ilyich. The dial tone was nice, the ringing beautiful.

"Привет, Илюша, как дела?" spoke Nikolai. A pause. "Привет? Илюша? Привет?"*

"Dad," he said, eventually, "what was the name of that song we would listen to with . . . that we would listen to with . . . *Mama*? I want to add strings to a track . . . Track Five . . . I'm working on, um, gotta sample it, you know?"

Nikolai asked if he son was *Ok.* Ilya replied *Yes*, then repeated his question, a little less slowly:

"What's the name?"

"The name of what? You are confusing me."

"The name of the song."

"I don't know the name of your song."

"The name of mom's song, the one she loved."

"Your mother loved Stravinsky. Perhaps . . ."

"Was it, 'The Rite of Spring'?" wondered Ilya, trying hard.

"Весна священная."

"Sacred Spring," Ilya repeated, snapping back. "I don't think it was Stravinsky, though, it was a pop song."

"Илюша," the father said, a little off tangent for the high Ilya, "remember how you used to watch фантазия every day on video cassette, until one day you broke the tape."

"Fantasia . . ."

"Да," mused Nikolai, "Fantayshuh."

---

* *Hello, Ilusha, what's up?* The father seems normal, then quickens, worried, unsure. *Hello? Ilusha? Hello?*

There was one last pause. Father and son said goodbye, one busy tending the backyard, the other totally тупой[*], as they hung up the phone, and did their own Monday afternoon thing.

What was that song? Ilya rubbed his sharp jaw and sparse stubble. He could not remember the name of the song, only that it had strings, and that his mother used to sing it. So not Stravinsky. He should have asked his father more directly, but talking about Maxine was about as hard as licking one's elbows for Ilya: you see it, you reach, but you always fail. Something that can only be accomplished by people who would inevitably brag about it. Still.

How did that song go?

"Blah, blah, blah / when I say softly, slowly..."

Chords? "Something, F, next C or E, then D-major."

But the name, what was the name?

"Softly, slowly."

No, the name!

"Softly, slowly."[†]

At this point, talking to himself, he got a call from Julia. But he let it go to voicemail. He felt ashamed. Too ashamed, even, to reply to her follow up text about how it went with Stacy.

He was getting a headache. And was hating himself, and hating his headache, and hating how there was only one way to stop it, the spinning. By riding the rollercoaster again, and

---

[*] *Tupoi*, blunt, dumb, or pointless.
[†] I know, I know, I know! It's my favorite song.

again. Hearing the skip of a broken record in his blood
clotted head, not too far off, not too far, not too, not.

Θ

Saturday at Zdras was insane. It still rained like crazy outside, but all the alcoholics and dance-oholics of the neighborhood couldn't go two nights without this club.

As anthropologists search for man's first language, biologists work to unlock the secrets of our genetic code. As taxmen whip citizens to remind them to pay for what they have already consumed, the Nepalese incense maker gathers herbs. Meanwhile an English teacher spends that extra hour grading essays, because she tells herself the student will care if she cares. And then, what, all those people who didn't go out during the week, show up to Zdras's throwbacks Saturday night, up and spend ten dollars on a shot of whiskey worth a dollar, because damn it all to hell. Every day people came to waste themselves away at places like Zdras. They tried hard to let go or be taken, sweat, or vom, so long as they danced en masse. That's why Ilya took his DJ job as seriously as the next professional contributing to society. Although, now . . . If only he promoted his brand more, the way his brother David did. If only Ilya could transition into producing full-time as easily as he did from electro beat to rock ballad. Then life might be easier. But never mind all that, everyone leaves his or her woes on the weekend. So much magic, so many combinations. Ilya could listen to a John Talabot track, say "Families," and cry. Would he overlap that sentiment with a Feist song ready to jerk him another tear? No, Ilya preferred to overlap yearning with ecstasy. In this pleasure dome of a club, walled in by his booth, the only space free of other junkies in the whole hellhole known as Zdras, he cued tracks that mixed Talabot to Kaskade, Feist to Fiona Apple, Cat Power to Morrissette, sometimes Four Tet to Feed Me, then TOKiMONSTA to Dua Lipa, Bjork to anyone, so long as the artists holding hands came from different continents, proved wild transitions were possible, that overlaps made sense. Yes, overlaps, my friends. Feed the people overlaps. Overlap two of anything, the old with the new, see what happens, maybe something terrible.

Or awesome. Ilya raised his arms, and so did a hundred people at Zdras, in tune with their DJ.

This obsession with overlaps? Again, it began in the living room at age 6. Ilya's progression as an artist had three stages. Stage one Ilya called the Imitation Stage. Rugrats theme song, but also the James Bond theme song, and some video game theme songs were the first. If you think those are light-weight, you're partly right, that's why it makes a good first step, consider Legend of Zelda or Super Mario as standards in the Imitation genre; but it can get more complicated, listen to anything by David Wise, and weep. Stage two, Ilya called the Journey of the Genre, and if it sounds like a Stravinsky composition, then you guessed right, because before hitting an age of double digits he had already started taking formal piano lessons and playing standards from babies like Mozart to dopey dudes like Satie to lovers like Pachelbel to godheads like Bach to freaks like Beethoven, Stravinsky and Enescu and Chopin and that excruciating six-month-to-learn "Gaspard de la Nuit" by

Ravel, which after he nailed in a competition the audience asked one another if the tyke wasn't, you know, autistic or something to have played it so well, but no way, because Ilya was too funny and too much of a braggart about it at the awards ceremony after—bragging is an excellent device to deceive audiences. Don't be confused though, classic and baroque and modern chamber music were only spring boards—the Journey of the Genre, remember? Ilya, as he grew up, grew to appreciate pop music's simplicity. If orchestral music was a missile, pop was an arrow, and Ilya became a sort of Robin Hood of stealing samples and making remixes for free. The Journey continued like this, around the time Ilya saw his first armpit hairs, David gifted him a mix CD with Alice DJ's "Better Off Alone," Robin S's "Show Me Love," and Moloko's "Sing it Back," and it was over. Dance music became something sexy and necessary. From 90s cheese, to 80s Chicago House, to 70s Soul, and their respective Rap remixes; or from curvy Italian Electro, to outer Space Disco, to sunny Trash Techno—you see what happened: the Journey—to savage Tech Techo, soft-spoken Minimalism, jazzy Acid House, rainy Jungle, brutal Drum & Bass, hard Hardcore, and god damn Booty Bass! Jpop and Kpop! To Trance itself, praise to the Cox, though to Ilya all music implied a certain trance. Without any planning or direction, like in a journey, he ventured into these genres— he loved everything—and if there was a problem it was that he couldn't stand still, or keep is leg from jerking when high.

The third stage, the one he wanted to break into, reminiscent of the masterpiece *Charlie Parker with Strings*, Ilya called the "Level Up"—when you break from the limitations of any one genre, electronic in his case—as did Daft Punk, Thievery Corporation, and even that sexy Argentine Santaolalla dude with electro-tango: adding live instruments to beats, beats to live music, what goes into what doesn't matter, not in orgies, nor orgiastic artistic creation. For Ilya, overlapping piano and beats was easy, check; blues and beats, with Stacy, check; but what more, what else? Overlap performance and producing, full-time? How? Overlap!

Just then Julia messaged him, asking what was up; when suddenly two girls overlapped with two boys near Ilya, legs straddling the DJ booth's railing. He ignored them as they wet one another's faces, dropping hands into jeans. Then all four asked if the DJ had any molly. He said go ask in the restroom. "And bring me some."

Needless to say, Ilya forgot to open Julia's message. Needful, however, would be to say how he felt the next morning. But not yet.

⊙

Around the time Ilya's shift was over, as always there he came, carrying a box of LPs, the man with silver hair, a big mole between his eye brows. He looked pissed, until he saw Ilya, then smirked wider than the Brooklyn Bridge.

"I have been thinking about you," said the old man.

A flash of having to work with Jonathan to organize the release party glared in his mind, as Ilya shivered and said something unintelligible to his idol.

"Hey," the old man put his hand on the young DJ's shoulder. "How is the EP going?"

"Going," said Ilya, jittery.

"You high?"

"A little."

"Better cut that out."

"Yes, sir."

"Will your EP be under your real name?"

"That's right."

"That's honest."

As the old DJ put a record on the Tech-12, Ilya started unplugging his things, and asked: "Martin Roth? Old School?"

"New school," said Robespierre, reading the track title, " 'An Analog Guy in a Digital World,' " said the DJ, scooting behind Ilya, fading the inputs of the dancefloor speakers from one device to another, showing Ilya how to do it gently, kindly, as opposed to how he'd seen the young DJ do it. The music died down a bit. Enough for Ilya to wake up a little.

"Yo," said Ilya, "I don't know how to talk to the promoter."

"There is another story you must know, from my Dominican baby-mama."

Ilya shook his head. "With all due respect, what I need isn't a story, when I need is help with—"

The man continued and out of respect Ilya paid attention.

"She told it like this:

"Three lions were arguing over which of them would be the next king of the jungle. They agreed that they should have a competition of strength. The first one to climb to the top of the highest mountain would become king.

"The first lion goes up the mountain, but halfway up yells 'This mountain is too strong,' and gives up.

"The second lion goes up the mountain, but halfway up yells 'This mountain is too high,' and gives up.

"The third lion goes up, but hallway up yells, 'This mountain is too high and too strong . . .' and hikes back.

"Who would become the king? It was still up for debate, until an eagle who had seen everything came down from the sky.

" 'I couldn't help but notice,' said the eagle. 'But the third lion should become king of the jungle.'

"When the lions asked why, the eagle replied, 'Because the first two lions tried but gave up. While the third lion went up and said, wisely, 'This mountain is too high and strong, but it is done growing, whereas I will continue to grow every day.'

"So he became the king of the jungle."*

The music was kicking so loud, so sweet, when Ilya stepped out of the DJ booth. Though it was a disgusting night.

---

* I have no idea what's going on. Nevertheless, this mini-story reminds me that I never finished the Ilya Muromets story.

So, this boy, he came from the river to the strong farmer and the beautiful wife. Luckily, they didn't care that he had come from a peach! They didn't ask silly questions. Instead they raised him, taught him to speak, sang songs to him, all in the hopes that he would grow strong and beautiful just like his parents.

Unfortunately, as the years rolled by, the boy never really learned to speak, never really learned to sing, having never ever learned to walk. He had been a gift from mother earth, yet, to his and his parents' dismay, he had been born cripple, a paraplegic, a good for nothing, who could barely cry for his mother's milk, let alone help his father sow—always reminding them of their mixed blessing, this peach boy.

Years go by, with the boy not so much as even lifting a finger, so paralyzed was he.

The parents, however, from the goodness of their hearts and from the love in their lives, fed him, bathed him, did all the things normal parents did, just without the pleasure of watching the child grow upright, or proud.

Again, years go by. The nearby village, in that time, started to decay. Neighboring raids had ravaged the land. Plague had devastated the crops and the remaining folk. Yearly fires left nothing in their wake. These were dire years.

After so much hoping, hoping for another miracle, only to receive nothing, hope died. Even the parents could barely support their magical son, let alone take care of themselves. Homes collapsed. Trees died heavy with thick, dry bark. Only rot and mushrooms covered the once fertile ground. Ash and disease were the only smells. And things went on like this for thirty years.

Thirty years, thirty years went by, like this, with nothing changing, nothing, except for the name of the day on the calendar.

"Are you suggesting that I just talk with Jonathan?"

"As many times as it takes." The old man DJ put on some sunglasses, then gave Ilya the thumbs up.

On his way out the back, Jonathan could be seen, along with the bouncers, kicking in the legs of a man that had been caught rubbing crystals into his date's drink, telling the man to never return or else they would end his life. Jonathan stood tall, a bat in his hand, his chest flag tattoo waving in the night, catching sight of Ilya.

The two locked eyes.

☉

They were far out from shore the Sunday after Independence Day. Sitting on a jetty of rocks. The taste of beach wind sweeping their sounds of making out. The sound of wet cotton shorts crinkling under the pressure of buttocks tightening. The feeling of swimming trunks tightening too, as hands met the other's arms, glistening in the light. Nibbling tender mouths. His and her chests pressed closed. Julia. Rubbing Ilya. Ilya tugging at Julia's bikini top. She was all he wanted, all he wanted. The knot came undone. And she giggled, already having reached behind herself, to hold the strings, and stop them from dropping. Not like this, she knew, not like this.

Still, in the heat of the outside world, Ilya lay his tongue on her neck, begging but an inch from her ear to let him in, let him in, like a big bad wolf boy lowly howling to be let in, growling to enter.

"Not here."

"Why?"

"Not now."

As Julia redid her knot, Ilya brought his hands to his own trunks, ready to pull them down. So now Julia reached in front and stopped him. Her hands there, Ilya went back to the knot at her back and held on to the line, wondering what he would make her say when he pulled the string this time.

"Тихо..."

"Alright." He stopped short.

"Хорошо," echoed Julia, wanting to switch registers, as a way to change the subject of undressing, and return to their kissing. "Почему мы не практикуем наш русский язык? Или наши русские языки?"[*] She leaned in, but Ilya turned away.

"I need to practice," he said, facing the horizon. "But I get awkward."

"Don't beat yourself up," she said, laying her hand back on his trunks. "Я помогу тебе."[†]

"You will help me . . . yes, I need practice."

Repeating his words, Julia said, "Мне нужно практиковать," offering him the phrase, petting his tight abdominals.

He repeated her words, which were his words first, but sarcastically. "Mehnye nujnah practice maya pa-russkie."

She frowned, sincerely. "Мне нужно практиковать русский язык," she said, less patient this time, who still planned on taking seriously the conversation.

"Mehnie nujen practice my pa russkie," Ilya said, exaggerating his accent, scooting away from her, making it a point to upset her, overcome with tension.[‡]

"Молодец," Julia said, with equal sarcasm now. "Молодец, мальчонка."[§]

Ilya watched her dive into the water and stroke away, swim away.

---

[*] *"Why don't we practice our Russian? Or our Russian tongues?"*
[†] *"I will help you."*
[‡] You mean, blue balled.
[§] *"Well done,"* she said, surely sneering, *"well done, you big baby."*

"Смотри," said Ilya, standing up, "неплохо!"[*] He dove in after her. They tussled between the waves and the floating seashells, under the single cloud blotching the blue sky of the day, a pale gray. "I need you—your help. You've helped me so much already."

"Не за что," called Julia, going up for air, kicking the water and getting the boy wet with a whip of her leg. "Nyeh zah shto."[†] After sticking her tongue out at him, she swam farther away. But Ilya quickly caught up. They could barely stand on the sand floor, this far out from shore.

"Da, da," said Ilya, "ya nie plajoii."[‡]

Julia was just about to ask why he didn't practice, why he didn't take it seriously. Then she remembered his age. She rolled her eyes and tried to swim away even farther, but Ilya grabbed her by the wrist, making her swallow a bit of water. She spit it out at him. He splashed her. And, after rubbing her eyes, Julia noticed something odd and unfamiliar about his look, like he was someone else in that moment, someone unrecognizable.

Letting herself be drawn in to his musculature, within his grip and his embrace, she peddled with her legs and with her feet to stay afloat, asking, "And this?" She was rubbing Ilya's

---

[*] *"See,"* he said, probably banging his chest, *"not bad!"* This reminds me of the piano scene way back.

[†] *"My pleasure,"* shouted the woman, first naturally, then in a fake American accent, *"my pleasure."* The subtext is pulling me under. What's going on!

[‡] *"Yes, yes,"* he said, in his signature accent, forcibly. *"I am not bad."*

chest, the one with the long, pink scar from his heart to his ear.

"It's a long story."

"I like long stories."

Ilya shook his head.

"That's ok," she said, "I can wait."

Ilya swam around behind Julia and, with his toes finding a sandbar to stand on, he hugged her tightly, palms on the warmest parts of her. "And you?" he asked. "Where are your scars?"

Julia turned around, unable to stand, using his arms to stay afloat, causing ripples in a balancing act that jostled her body in a way Ilya could not ignore. "I certainly have my own."

"Like your ex-husband."

"What about him?"

"Why didn't it work out?"

Julia smiled. Then she jumped backwards and swam away in a back stroke, yelling, "I'll tell you some day!"

☉

The year before, while still enrolled in college, Ilya had decided to study abroad in Paris. It was the spring, and graduation wouldn't be until December for him. So it should have been fun. But, as it turned out, Paris is when and where he got the scar on his chest, that grizzly thing from his heart to his ear, from the tip of a knife that wounded him in the yellowish light of a long underground pedestrian tunnel. This is how it went, that night irreversible.

His interest in the culture began with the French films he had seen for a cinema class, then grew with the records he flipped through in the antique stores of the Latin Quarter, grew even more with the bare number of hours bumming around the city of love between his three classes a week. He also went to parties, quite a bit. This was around the time Ilya realized being a DJ wasn't half-bad. On weeknights he would go out to strip clubs with his roommates. On weekends he was hired by friends of friends to DJ some cousin's house party. Why did they ask him? Because he had won his first mixer, earned in for a hundred volunteer hours at one of the music stores he frequented, plus whenever he got to a house he would immediately jump on the piano and play for people. There was always a group of girls who could sing along to Randy Newman or to Sam Smith, though he preferred Harry Nilsson and Serge Gainsbourg; or Ilya might have even improvised the pop songs on radio stations Cherie FM, Mouv', or Fun Radio, those which he had just heard the chords to, letting the native ladies do the singing. Some hosts would, in that French faux amis polite way of speaking to strangers, ask him to please get off the piano, whereas others would ask him to DJ the music instead. He gladly did, as long as he was helping people have a good time.

There was one party, a fateful one, which ended particularly sweaty. It was the party (and night) that later on Ilya would reference as the reason he got into powdered drugs, because that night there were plenty to go around. Plus Stacy had broken up with him over text, the first time, but anyway. It was a completely barren house with no furniture. The windows wouldn't open. The fridge was locked. And if you wanted a beer you had to ask one of the roommates who would invite you into their bedroom, close the door, and open a mini cooler with beers to the very brink, so many that one or two would fall out as the mini-door was opened. Ilya found this part especially dangerous. Especially for the women. When, sooner rather than later, he was being serenaded to by a racist Erasmus girl with strabismus, in a bathtub, both twentysomethings drunk out of their minds and sunk into misery, neither seeing straight. But the most random part was that someone else was on music duty.

Fast forward. In yet a different bathroom of the house, during the small hours of the morning, Ilya woke up alone with maybe drool or pre-cum on his jacket sleeve. He remembered thinking, no one is a saint.

When he left the party, the few remaining guests were still banging the floor with their fists, or swinging side to side. The music had taken a deep, deep techno turn and the kid deejaying wasn't older than fourteen, with sunflower shells in piles around his feet, and a terrible tic attacking his neck.

Ilya stepped outside and there were early morning taxis, but he decided to save money by walking back to his mouse-infested attic of a home. The image of trapping a certain mouse that had been bugging him for weeks kept coming to his mind on that walk. He imagined seeing it nibbling away at a box of cereal, when, wham! Ilya would leap on it like a panther, and snap its head, flinging him with a whirl from his tail out the skylight. So much aggression directed toward such a small animal.

But Ilya was a peaceful young man of twenty, why be violent. Tiredness overtook him, as well as tenderness. Just make it home, thought Ilya, pass out and let the mouse live.

The smell of yeast and dirty ovens, cooked seeds and rotten eggs, entered his body, as he stepped down the pedestrian tunnel.

A woman screamed. A fist shut her up. A moment later, she screamed again. Then skull met wall. Ilya stepped down, unguided, unsure, forward. It was a red tunnel, full of mosquitos. Down the way a man held the woman to the ground. He lay on top of her. Undoing his belt. A knife held to her throat. Him talking dirty. Ilya stepping forward. The lights flickering. The smell unbearable, yeast, rotten egg, pre-cum, all mixed. The echo of a heartbeat. When the man turned around and yelled some French bullshit, Ilya sprinted and kicked the man in the jaw like a penalty kick, which sent him rolling. His knife also spun away. Ilya helped the woman up, who had almost gone unconscious but was now swinging her arms at Ilya with her newly found freedom, attacking him. Ilya tried holding her, telling her in English that she was fine, but she struggled and fought back with all her might, scared as she was, her eyes closed, finding Ilya's neck, then crying into his chest, while still banging her fists against him, though slower and slower.

Until, getting up, the man pulled Ilya down to the floor in one swoop, drops of spit and blood dripping from his face, followed by a swift hook to Ilya's nose, then another, then another, each a bullseye. Ilya crossed his arms over his face, while the lady pulled at the man's hair, but he turned around and head-butted her, then delivered a straight jab to her stomach, reducing her to a fetus on the ground. This, however, gave Ilya time to leap for the knife. He leaped, fingertips touching the blade, but the man had already started pounding Ilya's back like dough. Ilya kicked the man in the jaw he had broken, but the man was possessed, adrenaline and amphetamine making him invulnerable.

Finally, Ilya grabbed hold of the weapon, but as soon as he did, the man elbowed Ilya's back. Ilya dropped the knife. The man lunged for it. He grabbed it. Both men stood up, with Ilya wrapping his jacket around his left arm, like a shield.

Taking turns, they pump-faked one other, stepping in a circle. Both sweating blood. The man, his teeth mashed and crumbled, eyes wide as clocks. Ilya feinting with his body, the man flinching. The man feinting with the knife, Ilya not flinching. Stepping. Stepping.

Sirens. The man sprang at Ilya. Ilya took the first blow with his arm wrapped well in his shirt, which did a good job of absorbing the blow, but the man pulled back and delivered two more thrusts as fast as he did the first one. Ilya couldn't block the third hit, meaning his gut took the sharp end of the blade. Then a fourth stab sent the thing in, out, and up his chest, with the blunt side clipping him over the left nipple, cutting flesh, slicing meat, rolling upwards, over the heart, to the ear, but not quite reaching the ear, yet off the top of the neck. And then the man ran, ran. He ran, while Ilya fell there, on his knees, watching the motherfucker hold his belt and sprint faster and faster, never to be caught, losing breath.

Some days later, Ilya woke up in bright room, surprisingly alert, and safe, although it hurt to crunch his abs, or twist his body. That same morning he called his father back in New York, and by evening the father was in Paris.

Nikolai was surprisingly calm, as if he were just happy to see his son alive. This made Ilya happy too, but not as much as something else. In a vague yet sure way, at least he felt this way every day for the next few months, it were as if he had avenged his mother's passing.

It was while unconscious, recovering in the hospital, that the family of the other victim had sent balloons and kept an eye on him. Marya was her name. Wrapped in the Iranian style, with a garment covering her ears and hair over her bandaged head, showing the gauze a little in the front. The first questions the family of Marya asked were for his name, where he was from, and he replied, in English, and they were not surprised. An uncle said that if Ilya had been French he would have walked right out, but the sisters and aunts told him to shut up. The father meanwhile was silent and asked if there was anything, absolutely anything, that he needed, he would help.

The father, who happened to be the head of a small gang that mattered, would see to it personally that that neighborhood stayed predator free for the next fifteen years, until his eventual passing, for which a funeral would be held and Ilya would be invited. So he could have and would have given him anything, and felt he should have too. But all the boy asked, all the boy requested from Marya's father, was for a phone, so he could call his father.

☉

"EE-LEE-YA. EE-LEE-YA."

They chanted, "EE-LEE-YA. EE-LEE-YA."[*]

The beat sped up, they kept chanting, "IL-YA. IL-YA. IL-YA. IL-YA." And. Yet. But. Ay Be, Ah y Be, Au Be Yn. Dan Tubtey. Yun et yand. Yeah. Fame.

And Ilya knew by now what was happening, three artists who had borrowed from one another fought on center stage for the iron heart of the audience tossed there for only one to grab. But none would win. Bon Iver wrestled James Blake who hog tied Sam Smith who himself locked the first musician in a choke. And between them lay the heart. Yet why only one could hold it and not all three share it is the same reason why we have only ever thought of one at a time. But what is this mash-up? The three musty-tears made out, then argued who was brighter, who was darker, who was phater, who had the best mids. Recall the reverb. Delay the satisfaction, drop everything and dance, as you condense audio and hit tubular bells with Shure mics.

Above, though, neither name nor flame burned, no nothing, only fame, the silent truth, the nameless, the voweless, the YHWH. The urge suppressed to move unleashed itself and Ilya freed himself from time into the infinity of infinities, onward, boyod, voivode!

---

[*] I'm waiting for them to chant my name next time: EE-LOW-NA. EE-LOW-NA. Wouldn't that be a mindfuck.

Feeling like a true Girl Talk this mute boy lassoed the three musicians and whipped them into single-file, then politely asked them in Indian style to sit rudely, before rude boy was a thing. Before words lost their weight. After they dropped dead, done for, turned around, tuned in, dropped out. Timothy Lorax. Parcel Most. Pebbles of Madeline crumbled into a Mary Flintstone. Das Effecks.

Delete. Push. Enter. MIDI boxes. Hot laptops. Ear Aches. Bobbing heads. Sweaty pits, sweaty tits. Neon wristbands. Suicide scars hidden by festival bands. Zippable bags, marks of the trade, aids of bands, plastic generation. Clean-ex, ex-clean, Stacy-ex., Ecstasy! Mofo, the copyright mouse! Mighty Mikey Mousy. Aristotle Chipotle, Chipotle Aristotle. Beer can, bacon. Downshift, upgrade. Shaved heads. Booty pimple popper. Status symbols. Saturnalia regalia, carnival systems, divided by one: lines upon lines upon lines in time. And yet but not a damn thing funny, got to have a con, or be gone, in the land of milf and honey bees. Those creatures who dance to communicate where the treasure at. Grandfather flash.

Inside the bag, blue meanie-whiles, a white Ilya inhales exhalations from within in a nightmare of biblical proportions, the reign of rains, a song full of gongs, making you groove to prove how smooth the criminal in you will be right back, the time of times, fractal-ly malfunctioned, maleficent fratboys, since the time of last, paste past passé. Terrance Malchik, Terry Macintosh, M.I.A-missing you, I am, Cut, Copy, and paste "Far Away," Jeff Marshall

Airplane's 80s body moves, while Larry heard you say Deep, then Yesus took you to Chi-Raq, in a sermon of sirens busty, saving days. A tale with tail, a story with beat, a bribe with breasts, a plot with chest hair, and the rest. A trick. È only a trucco.

My heart, sexy heart, cuz music's gunna set you free. Move your pumping sexy heart. Shake your booty body, sexy central nervous system body toosh. Rock a mind, my mind, nacho mind, but mine. As I yours do. As yours I do. As I do yours, Stan. Kazakh!

Before now and then Ilya got on stage, back then, right now. He put his hands on the laptop, his mixer cueing two incoming tracks that were spinning on either side, a pedal on the floor for whammy crunch, his hands firm on the laptop for a chord. They asked for a happy song. He played it. They asked for a sad song. He obliged them. They asked for a third and he played the most beautiful composition of his own, like Orpheus Rex.

After that, they pulled him off the stage. But before that, he hit the E-key, the key of his name. So into shreds he was made, passively, though the most violent act it was, actually.

Down with the clown, down, down. Drop.[*]

Ο

---

[*] Got to have a nightmare, in a book about a dream.

"Eurasia!" shouted Ilya, in the dead of day, in his quiet apartment living room so calm.

"What?" replied Tiffany.

"Tiff, Tiff!" shouted Ilya. "I have an idea!"

"Aren't you supposed to yell *Eureka!* when you have an idea?"

"What's the fun in that?" asked Ilya, before asking for a favor. "Can I borrow your microphone again? I want to record vocals for Track Five."

They both knew he meant the good one, the ribbon mic Tiffany had bought using an entire month's worth of income.

"Sure," she says, for the tenth time. "I'm getting a producer credit on your EP, right?"

"Track Four is for you," he said.

"It better be 80s inspired," she said.

"Yes!" He wasn't lying. "You heard a clip the other day, Track Four, titled 'Live at Zdras,' from a Saturday night throwback night earlier in the summer." He stood up. "Just absolutely full of Dub, reverby, wet, delayed, reggae-ful, a Peter Tosh sampled mish mash mix over Diplo beats and Sean Paul rhythm, transitioning into a 2005-M.I.A. sunshower of galang-galangs."

"Galang-galangs, huh?" exclaimed Tiff. "Purple haze!"[*]

---

[*] I love how I have to hit the "References" tab on Word every time I add a footnote about your references. Now, M.I.A. did date Diplo, as mentioned in the opening scene. Horrible break up, according to *Billboard*, just before Interscope Records released her *Arular* album in

"But I'm working on Track Five now," concluded Ilya. "Wanna add some backing vocals." Dedicated to someone else.

The purpose of the microphone came from an idea that was planted in him the previous night, when he re-listened to an old Animal Collective track that sampled a bit of The Grateful Dead, the first ever official sample of a Dead track, and AC blew it up, inside out. The seed of that idea had germinated that very night, while he slept, because sometimes that's what the brain does when you sleep. Most of the time it does some weird playback loop, but other times it does something useful. Therefore, that very morning— germinated, incubated, watered—the idea of recording backup vocals with the mic spouted. So Ilya went back to his curtained-off room and booted his computer. On the floor was his inspiration, the CD for the Animal Collective EP that was inspiring this next song with no name yet. On the track the cymbals crash alone, then crash with snare. Under the CD was a copy of the book, *Mixerman*, Ilya's foremost superhero, who also started playing piano at 6. Ilya remembered reading in that book about the funny fact,

---

2005—that night her ex apparently trashed their hotel room and called her a "sell out." Real abusive stuff, scary too. On both sides. Yet they seem to have made up a bit and been friendly enough to post about it online ten years later. Lastly, on *Rolling Stone*, she said something in an interview that reminded me of this project, about creating *Arular*: "It was to break boundaries and it connected with people who had the same sort of philosophy in life—that boundaries don't exist." Though she doubts this is possible in today's NYC. What do you think? Neat, no? Many, many connections.

among many, that the genre of a track is determined by the snare drum. Back to the CD. Not that snare. Back to the book. "Always bring a good six-pack of beer, when getting to know your artist." It also states that it's preferable to have an album of 10 great tracks than an album of 12 with two filler tracks and 10 great ones. Cut! The Pharcyde? Far-side from dab, bad, in rewind-to-review, phew: Rick Rubin takes the track back on Beastie Boys, then Jay Dee takes it back to the track on "The Drop."[*] So Ilya worked hard to make sure that this next track meant something. So far he had "Здравствуйте (Be Healthy)," "Body Language," "Honey Beer," and the "Live at Zdras (June 2018)" from a session earlier in the summer. Although he was at over 30 minutes, he still wanted to add a magical Fifth Track. The last track, the title track.

But Ilya needed more EP inspiration. So much inspiration. Animal Collective's "What Would I Want? Sky" would inspire the depth and backup vocals. Télépopmusik's "Breathe" would soundtrack the vulnerability. And the lyrics and chorus . . . the lyrics and chorus . . . the lyrics and the chorus needed some other inspiration. "Softly, Slowly," what was that song! It was on the tip of his twisted tongue! So Ilya searched. He opened his old playlists. And he scoured.[†]

---

[*] You need *Genius.com* to make sense of this sentence.
[†] According to *Mixmag* Electronic Dance Music (EDM) is the third most listened to genre of music, with 1.5 billion listeners world-wide, behind pop and rock, but ahead of hip-hop. "Techno is played in 40 percent of Berlin clubs, where clubbers spend €200 euros a day according to

The producer who had the greatest impact on Ilya wasn't Tiesto, Armin Van Buuren, or even Avicii, R.I.P. These artists made Ilya dance, but not mix. The music maker who most affected Ilya, who first inseminated his wildest aspirations was Aphex Twin. Aphex Twin is this DJ's DJ out in the middle of nowhere, England, whose hour long sets on BBC Radio One, and the fan uploads on *mix.dj* influenced Ilya, fueled Ilya, revved that little boy's engine to a hundred miles per hour, if not to mix then at least to listen endlessly to the soundscapes that obscure ass dude was painting. "I make a song a day," Aphex Twin said in an interview, or maybe Ilya made that up, in a dream about Aphex Twin spinning at a rap battle final match, between Black Dante and Black Thought. Following in his idol's footsteps, Ilya trained himself for hours at his dad's home, after Paris, every day, even into what would have been his final semester of college, to achieve his ultimate dream—what he was doing at this

---

another study." Also, judging by another article on *Complex,* called "An Idiot's Guide to EDM Genres" the genre shows the potential for countless subgenres, with so much variety that the only conclusion possible is that what distinguishes this repetitive, hypnotic, addictive, cult-like class of beats and bloops comes down to one thing: fusion. If I have learned anything about the strange world of EDM is that it mixes everything it comes into contact with: DJs are the bottom feeders, the sea sponges of music, sucking up everything, and spitting it back out for the fish with bioluminescent faces to dance to, in the oxygenated underworld of deep sea life.

Enough facts and diary rambles, though, give us a story!

very moment, on his own, over the computer, but with an angel on his shoulder—producing the EP of the summer, 2018. He just needed to complete one final track. This untitled track. Maybe leave it untitled, thought Ilya, before dismissing the idea as dead. He recorded the backup vocals as intended, inverted them, blew them up, inside out.

Then continued his journey.

$\odot$

In high school[*] he had been shown Ishkur's "Guide to Electronic Dance Music," with every possible genre of electronic music, turning Ilya into that annoying kid in high school who got upset when you called jungle music techno music, or house music electronica.

"Aphex Twin?" the librarian had asked, looking over Ilya's shoulder at the music video he was watching at school, via a proxy, because this video was banned on public school computers. Ilya was fifteen.

" 'Rubber Johnny,' " he said, proud, when asked the title of the track. "By Chris Cunningham. Do you know him?"

"That means condom in England," the hook-nosed librarian replied, referring to the title. "Play the video."

At minute 1:30, after some grotesque mutant in a dark room moaned and crooned, the video showed something that could in no way be mistaken for a water balloon rolling off of a big kid's finger, the title shot, because it was, in naked reality, a condom being tugged off a British man's genital member—not quite the image to be watching with your snoopy high school librarian.

"Office."

Nikolai, who had been called by the vice principal, alleging Ilya was homosexual, scolded his son, for watching this ровно[†] at school, what kind of kid did I raise, stuff like that. But Ilya explained that he wasn't fixated on the images

---

[*] Thank you!

[†] Makes me wonder, what would my father say to me if he caught me watching this in high school, what word would he use to describe it . . .

of the video, so much as on the rhythm and the composition of the song. The father, curious, asked to watch the video. So they watched it, then another video that Ilya liked even better: called "Window Licker," which is ten times as pornographic, with actresses in tight bikinis, hula-hoops, Miami, and everybody morphing into grotesque replicas of the artist, dancing under a rain of champagne. The father only got up and told his son to do his homework, no response. But he continued, filling his mental database with material, his brain firing as fast as possible to remember the stringed song.

Around the time of that powerful mix CD with Alice DJ and Moloko, which his brother had given him, Ilya finally made the transition from classical to electronic music with the free starter pack of drum samples on a program called Fruity Loops. Ilya became fascinated with the software's interface, which displayed rhythm as a visual set of beats. One of the first masters of the beat, electronically speaking, were the Germans: Kraftwerk, the original robots, who on the remastered version of "Home Computer" broke down a steady drum groove at minute 3:39 so nasty that it made Ilya squirm in goosebumps the second time he heard it at minute 6:04. Boards of Canada are the second coming of Kraftwerk, that is, if you mixed in some Tangerine Dream and some RjD2 for good measure and lit an opium stick from the opposite end of where your mouth goes. Following the yarn, Boards of Canada's intro to "Olson," Track 13 on their LP *Music Has the Right to Children*, must have inspired Dead

Mau5's "Raise Your Weapon" song. And the whammy from The Smith's "How Soon is Now" song sounds a lot like the guitar in BoC's "Dayvan Cowboy"; but then again maybe BoC can't be compared to The Smiths or to the Mau5 because their music changed so much during their careers; for example *Campfire Headphase* sounds less like Kraftwerk and more like Radiohead; but, again, it's wrong to compare bands that are as disparate as the lives their artists lived; and yet even the most absurd connections still exist; because these types of artists did do one thing the same: they always changed, always evolved, always. Connected to this faith in innovation, to the first drum hit on the wall of the cave in that allegory about man's ascent from grunting beast to expressive artist, these bands rocked forward, in unison, each a heraldic voice in the choir for victory over discord, mayhem. All else is illusion, labels, the separation of two badass musicians; any act of art against the void can be juxtaposed, because in doing so we remember the connective tissue of creation, this fight against chaos. To categorize is to divide, to divide is to judge, to judge is the opposite of creation. Creation is the primordial act. David was right. But Nikolai was right too. The EP needed a name, needed a single: Track Five. C'mon!

And here—on his computer, mixing, writing lyrics, listening to music—Ilya thought up some more old news: the listener wants to enjoy good music, period. The artist wants to birth good music, period—asterisk, hopefully music other people think is good. But again, it is all a chain, and it all begins with Kraftwerk, who probably got their inspiration from some place, call it aliens or psychoactive entheogenic particles, i.e. mushies, if you don't have an answer yet. Anyway, Coldplay sampled Kraftwerk's "Computer Love," so why couldn't Ilya sample Coldplay's "Life in Technicolor" in his song that flowed from "cool jazz" to "free jazz" to "smooth jazz," by way of a Thelonious Monk piano solo to Anthony Braxton's tuba improv to a Medeski Martin and Wood piano finale, and tail-end it with the glimmer, just a glimmer, of a two second sample of Jethro Tull's flute for the coda, in a composition that marked Ilya's musical coming of age in 2007 forever—seven years after Maxine's disappearance. That was Ilya's first song in the late 2000s that gained popularity on the up and coming social media. Ilya uploaded his track, titled "Jazz Trip in Technicolor," on any website that allowed him to sign up with just his Yahoo email: Bandcamp, Soundcloud, even Myspace, which was making a comeback thanks to Timberlake. Anything for that search optimization. The first photo of Ilya, with the same rose-colored glasses he has had for over ten years, became the cover art of that track, and how strangers pictured the track on their computer. With his early taste of validation, Ilya quit playing video games, quit computer games, quit school (emotionally at least), and spent all his free hours in his bedroom, full of his father's classical music CDs with the white band and red and blue stripes up top, making music that helped him escape the real world, and elevated him to a realm of uncompromising bliss.

The song? Sometimes he felt as if he were on autopilot, turning the pixels designed to look like knobs on his laptop's monitor, back and forth, other times he felt he were a skipper, not of tracks, but in the driver's seat of a boat cutting across a quadrillion cubic inches of water. He did a set of jumping jacks to get blood flowing up to his head. And it hit him! After so many references and cross references, his brain nodes had hit gold: "Tiny Dancer," this was the song he had been trying to remember; this is the choir, the angelic voices; thank you, Paul Buckmaster, your immortal strings live on.[*]

The producer felt something like hot waxy fingers scurry up his back, as he looked down at the verse he has written. He decided that this time, out loud, that this, "Yes," this, will be the single, his mother's eulogy. He called his brother.

"Just in time for ma's birthday," David said, over the phone, as he appreciated how it took Ilya sixteen years to talk about her with mumbling. "By the way, have you talked to dad recently?"

He called his father, to finally invite him to Zdras, since the show was set in stone, and he had a direction for the single, therefore the EP. But, to the boy's dismay, the father said he had other plans. "I'm going to San Francisco to help your brother on that weekend."

---

[*] My favorite song!

"I . . ." Ilya was suddenly delirious. "I wanted to surprise you. With a party for mom. A single for her with her favorite song."

"A birthday party?" said the father, moved. "Her favorite song? We can celebrate when I come back. Send me the song when it is ready."[*]

☉

---

[*] Loss.

They were breathing, they were being, inside a cheap-o pawn shop full of broken toys and stained glass works of art. Wouldn't it be crazy if they had his amps and keys from the day he passed out on the beach? Unfortunately the store didn't have them. Anyway, by the time Julia and Ilya were done discussing meaningless topics, Ilya took it upon himself to speak his mind.

"My dad can't make it to the show next week."

"I'm sorry to hear."

"And you won't be coming either."

"I'm flying to Cuba, remember." Julia was surprisingly calm. Then Ilya remembered how she was going there to honor her father and mother's passing, where they were buried, thousands of miles from where they were born, tens of years before.

"I remember."

"Be patient with your family," she said. "And yourself."

Ilya wanted to say something related, but instead, putting down a fake Fabergé egg, back into a basket of other fake Fabergé eggs, he spoke up: "The EP isn't even done."

"I thought you made a breakthrough yesterday?"

"I did, and I have all five songs tracked, cut, and mixed."

"What's missing?"

"They don't sound right together. They need to be mastered."

Julia headed towards the back of the pawn shop, where the boxy TV monitors were stacked, collecting dust. She blew the dust away. "Really?" she said, not really sure what she was replying to, her eyes moving from one stand of junk to the other. "Wasn't Robespierre going to help you?"

Ilya brought his eyebrows close. "How do you know Robespierre?"

Julia turned around, speaking. "My son loves him."

Ilya stepped towards her. "How is Alexander?" he asked.

"He's fine," Julia replied.

"At camp?"

"Every Sunday."

How long did they have to meet like this, these two? Why not during the week? Why did so much time have to pass? Ilya pressed Julia's shoulders, right around the furniture section. But Julia hushed Ilya with a classic, "Тихо," and told him something like, "People might see us."

Ilya looked over his shoulder and, down the narrow space between shelves, through to the cash register, he didn't see anyone, except for pedestrians walking perpendicular to his line of sight, like actors crossing a stage, but far, far away from him. "So?" But Julia was gone when he turned around.

She was outside now, back in the full swing of noisy southern Brooklyn. Ambulances zipping by, trying to save a life, Doppler effects sounding tinny, red, blue, and white lights blaring. Key chains being dropped, without bass. And a thundercloud approaching, roaring in the distance.

"It's going to rain, isn't it?"

Julia didn't say anything. Nor did she back away, as she had been doing all day, when Ilya wrapped his arm around her waist.

"Sagan and Tara told me about the other day," said Julia.

"Who?" Ilya knew who. His mouth got dry. He was prepared to say anything to keep Julia. Julia. Tan skin with the littlest hairs. Dark eyes. Her hair. Wrinkles. The wind at her chest, then his, then hers again, when she spoke.

"The twins, Ilya. They told me you partied with them and that you didn't even stay to clean up. I thought you quit powdered drugs."

"They had work, but they couldn't pay—"

"Isn't that the way it goes? You help until they have money to pay you?" She stomped her foot against the payment. "How could you!"

"I don't get it, Julia, you want me to go back, but you don't want me there; you don't want me here, and yet you meet me every week."

She made fists out of her hands and shoved Ilya away with all of her weight, which wasn't much. He stepped back then back forward. Again, she pushed him away, leaning her weight again his chest, that chest she had longed for and still longed for, which he would have given her, but they weren't going to, not here, not yet.

The pink scar thumping against the vial chained around his neck. The story. She remembered the story he told her. She wanted to know more.

But instead of asking she stormed off. And then it rained. Leaving Ilya standing there, wet, alone, waiting, watching.

☉

The skyscrapers towered ominous, ambient, smashing any peace. The mother looked for Fourth Avenue on the east side of Midtown, where there was no Fourth Avenue. The older brother moaned and groaned that they were lost, that the way was south. There was ice cream, then the used book store. And that's the part where the mother disappeared, leaving David and Ilya alone.

"Let's go," said David, getting up off the carpeted floor of that yellow smelling store.

"Mom said she was there and would be right back."

"Mom lied," said David. "You see the owner turning off the lights? Let's go."

It was zero hour, December 18th 1999.

"Where are we going?" asked Ilya, snot frozen under his nose.

"Where do you think we're going?" said David, squinting his eyes at the high street signs near the traffic lights. "We are going home."

"Do you know how?" said Ilya, sniffling ice cubes.

They turned down Lexington. "Easy," said David. "Papa bought me a map for my birthday, remember? I've practically looked at it every day since."

When they reached Grand Central Station, the two boys experienced what anyone seeing the building for the first time experiences, awe. Add to that the feeling of being one minor and one toddler, separated from a mother, and having to use the restroom, but holding it in—and you have what David and Ilya were feeling that night.

"What do we do?" asked Ilya, watching his older brother approach the information desk. He was talking in what felt like another language, the language of adults, not the play voice of their childhood games. It seemed David was the new mommy, grabbing Ilya by his hand, and leading him down one corridor to the next, his other hand holding two tickets, which he hadn't paid for, but of which the ticket office representative had handed him after a long discussion. It felt like David could solve any problem.

The train zipped past Harlem, which looked photographed, framed by the train window, each light from each window a view into a wholly different world with its own story and poetry; any number doubled, like David's age, very important and special. As soon as they got north enough to both be in the train car all to themselves, they cried. Mostly David, for Ilya had cried nearly all the walk through Midtown and through the cave-like concourses of Grand Central and on the trashed platform above ground waiting for that exact train they were now on, zipping by. But, David, he was unleashing a torrent of frosted flaked tears that landed on the sleeve of his coat, soaking the very rash and skin under his nose, and choking him.

"I love you," Ilya told David.

David straightened himself up. He inhaled his snot. "We'll be home soon, Ilya." Then a ticket inspector walked by.

Whenever the boys went to a museum or a concert with their mother, they practiced being different ages. Usually younger, to give David a discount and Ilya a free pass. Now, with that practice, David pretended to be older, and told the ticket inspector his brother was older. The tired, old inspector, though very suspicious of the dubious youth, couldn't help but be engaged by David's high vocabulary, ignoring their bloodshot eyes and coats covered in snot.

"Perhaps the chill has gotten the better of us," mused David, receiving his ticket back. "Sir."

The sir, not having heard that form of address in years, and less from a youngster, recalled some advice he had received once as a school boy: if you ever wanted something, you could get it with the right vocabulary and attitude. In other words, it wasn't his job to corral every little snot-nosed kid running around, especially if those snot-nosed kids could find the right train, keep quiet, mind their own business.

"Your ticket, son?" he asked of Ilya, whose opened mouth dropped drool. After checking the ticket, he looked again at David. "The chill, huh?"

"Yes, sir, the chill. Aren't we glad to make it home! Our father shall be expecting us soon. You see, our regrettable tardiness is due to a most guilty indulgence: we absolutely had to have ice cream on the way to the station."

"Ice cream? In December?"

"Yes, sir."

"And your mother? Isn't she expecting you?"

Ilya put his nose to the window, didn't reply. David, holding back tears that were welling up in his throat, also didn't reply.

☉

First grade, penultimate week. With a parent miles away, Ilya sat curbside in the tardy section, feeling tardy, feeling lonesome. He and Rashad had agreed to swap some holographic cards at carpool. But Rashad was still inside the school. So Ilya sat with some different kids, showing off their collections to one another.

A tall boy from one of the older grades sat in the circle with Ilya and the others.

"I heard you have a holographic Blastoise," said the tall boy.

"Yes, look!" said Ilya, proud.

"Can I see?" asked the tall boy.

"Yes!" Ilya was more than happy to tell him all about when and where he got it.

As soon as the older boy got hold of the card binder, though, he pushed Ilya down, and dashed.

Ilya tried running after him. But wasn't fast enough. He lost the boy, the cards, and hit the ground after slipping on some pebbles.

All was lost.

Until, darting from the front door of the school, was Rashad. He sprinted and caught up with the bully, and tapped the back of his back running leg just enough for it crash into his front running leg, sending the bully tripping face first to the ground, dropping, then running away.

"Where did you learn to trip people like that?" asked one of the classmates.

"My older sister."

Ilya couldn't say a word. Except: "Thank you, Rashad."

The two friends moved away from the crowd, to better console one another.

"Do you know what he is?" asked the fastest boy in school, of the loser who had disappeared.

"A bad egg," mused Ilya, having heard that phrase earlier that week.

"Worse," said Rashad, with terrible gravity. "Worse. You know what he is?" Rashad leaned in to whisper it in Ilya's ear.

"What's that?" asked Ilya.

Rashad looked around, anxious and trembling almost. He whispered the bad word another time in Ilya's ear.

"I don't understand."

"It's the badest word in English," said Rashad, with the look of someone about to teach his friend something. He leaned in, whispered it again.

"Maddahfuhkah?" asked Ilya.

"Mud-da-fuh-kah!"

"Muddafuhkah?"

"Yeah, faster, mudda-fuhkah!"

"Muddafuhkah!"

"The badest word!"

"Let me guess, your older sister teached you," said Ilya. "I mean, taught you."

"Yeah, she calls her boyfriend that when she gets mad at him."

"Is she mad a lot?"

"No. Sometimes she calls him muddafuhkah when she is happy too."

"Am I a muddafuhkah?" asked Ilya.

Rashad got very serious, as he put a hand on his best friend's shoulder. "If you a muddafuhkah, then I'm a muddafuhkah."

Θ

Double time:

The wife untied the knot holding her swimsuit together. And pulled the one-piece down to a snap, before tossing it on the beach in a clump. Her untanned, sagging chest met the sky. It rained heavily, biblically. The husband counted her steps before diving into the water, swinging her arm in freestyle. The beach bid him farewell too, as he chased her.

Both were dark, the sea and the sky. Whirlpools made waves and thunder claimed the air. Flying fish flew. Seals sank silly. And the couple who had been and had lived at the beach was stroking immeasurable lengths out from shore. Dolphins kept them company. A shrimping boat blew its horn. And the couple who had married an invaluable amount of time ago was fighting the currents fighting to drown them apart. Lightning struck the wife. Thunder masked the husband's calls. As a wave finally did them in, folding them in like marine debris.

Only then did the weather clear.

Wherefore from above, glinting in moonlight, one could clearly see the vial of mercury around his neck, pulling him down, to drown.

Ilya didn't like how last Sunday ended with Julia. So he asked her out that week, to meet Wednesday, the day before her flight. She said yes. They should meet at Brighton Beach.

But she wasn't there when Ilya arrived that day. Before losing his mind, coincidentally, she texted him to come over to her place, and he replied that he would.

Julia lived in Park Slope, we know, a skip and a boogie from the beach, the kind of neighborhood where if you were a woman without a stroller you were shunned as a potential robber of the few men who stuck around: the way the anonymous neighbors treated Julia. At first when her son was a baby in a stroller they stopped to chat and laugh. But as the years carried on and the other women had second and third children, whereas Julia did not, eventually walking around the hood without a baby, the women resumed their disdain for this strange foreign gal. Why? Those horrible neighbors! They once saw Julia drop her driver's license on the floor, while fumbling for her big bumble bee phone, and they didn't even bother to let Julia know. They just picked it up and stared at everything they were jealous of, until realizing whose card it was, then they kept it to stare at it some more, that driver's license.

Her eyes? They were as dark as the eyes of birch bark.

Her height? Not tall, not short.

Her hair? Among the richest things about her: rich, shiny, like cake, strawberry, orange, blonde, yellow, everywhere.

Her skin? Between hot translucent honey and refrigerated milk, depending.

Her voice? Always the same, no oscillation, unless affected: Ilya learned to tell when Julia was being silly, playful, earnest, worried, excited, et cetera—all by the sound of her voice. Its consistency rested in its always being honest, always speaking from Julia's immediate feelings. This made for a lush, wise, resonant articulation. And, crazy coincidence, Ilya's favorite things about Julia went in order, of least favorite to most favorite, from toe to head. He didn't like her long toe nails. He found her knees chalky and stubbly. But he adored her tummy, couldn't stop staring at her Cuban raised behind, found sanctuary along the straight curve of her back, idolized her Slavic breasts, and would make love to her voice box, given the chance, would kiss her zealously whenever he had the chance, and could suck at her high hereditary cheek muscles three times a day, whereas on top of it all lay her crown and her jewels: her brain and her thoughts, her hair in waves.

Patience.

Yes, he texted her before ringing the bell. Yes, she opened the door. Yes, she was about to ask him how he got there so fast from so far. But Ilya dived in. He swam inside her mouth for a breathless instant, then came up for breaths as if stroking through water. It was maddening, this making out. They fell to the floor of what was her first floor landing.

I don't care if this comes off poorly, Ilya thought. He grabbed what he could, it was borderline insanity. Julia let herself be taken, there, on the floor she had vacuumed for so long without ever imagining, but maybe hoping, this young buck would do what he was doing now, squeezing her; he knew and she knew this would happen. So much tension had built up, need it be said? Hair got tugged. Lips met and parted. Slip and slide, he glided right in. Julia moaned, pornographically, like she imagined Ilya liked. She was right. He squeezed her wrists and did everything in his power to hold back the full rage within or without him. He would have broken her, he could have bruised her and hurt her, something begged and ached to be damaged, and it was Julia's very voice inside his ear, entering him the way he entered her, scratching and gnawing in bits, putting his mouth to her nose, pulling with his breath hers and making her moan again, though she gave herself completely, and felt it was still not enough, the bang of the war drum inside of her, entering in circles the way a South African boy in St Petersburg had told him to do once, no ecstasy surging through except as in a blind dream.

The clocks ran backwards. Her chest looked like two spinning records on two turntables. How could he have missed it before? How sexual. Elsewhere midgets and giants applauded, and Ilya screamed for his life, orgasming with many kilowatts of nuclear energy. Dust clouds. Slowing down to a halt. But Julia wasn't having that, it was her turn, and she threw him back, spun her record breaking breasts, and grinded him like she owned the remaining minute of his swollen passion inside of her, grinding herself into a fit, plugged in and gasping, because she would not have been enough for Ilya, galloping towards the root of her partner's pelvic bone, which she did with a soldier's determination to drill herself. To not hear them, one needed to be outside the building *and* wearing noise-canceling headphones. But, as this wasn't the case for many, Park Slope, with its poorly laid women complaining about their husbands who masturbate too much, swelling with jealousy, as Ilya the DJ let himself go inside Julia a second time, no need to hold himself from total catastrophe, Julia's frantic, spasmodic, matron grating of this young man, until he flipped her over, and for a third march to glory felt nothing go to waste. And a great sound.

The chirping of birds, where her sun tan stopped and her white warmth began, on her waist the tattoo of a tiny bird—because there was a tattoo after all—flapping, stretching, relaxed.

☉

"How was it?" he asked.

Julia was on her back, both of them still on the floor, she looking at the man who had just given her the first deep orgasm since the birth of her son. "It was really good," she said.

Ilya leaned back, into her, and closed his eyes under the spinning ceiling, the ticking of a grandfather clock tick-tocking at sixty beats per minute. "I hope your kid didn't hear us."

Julia turned on her stomach, to lay on top of Ilya, her warmth almost unbearable, to a normal person that is, but Ilya liked her hot heat, he didn't see anything odd about it. She laughed.

"Александр," she said, getting up. "He's at his father's while I'm gone these next few days."

"What does he do, for a job I mean, will you tell me?"

Julia smiled. "He's a taxi driver."

"So the other day . . ."

She didn't reply. She got up. Meanwhile, Ilya looked around at the toy trucks tossed around on the ground around where they lay, suitcases everywhere, unzipped and empty, not ready yet for her flight the following day. All the while, the TV was switched to a cartoon channel, and Ilya figured Julia must have not turned it off when the boy left.

"I sometimes sit and watch a show, no matter how bad it is, because it makes me feel like he is close to me."

Ilya said, Word, or Huh, or something that proved to Julia that he had absolutely no idea how to respond after copulation, to the fact that this woman was in fact a mother. Ilya, all of a sudden, like a dog who had just vomited, started inspecting the pie he had left inside Julia. Then asked:

"Are you ... on the ..."

She slapped him with her foot, lightly, laughing. "Shoot first, ask questions later, huh?" she said.

"Well?"

"Yes, I'm on the pill."

After unloading a bit of her and her guest in the bathroom, Julia turned on the lights in the kitchen. There, she cracked some eggs in a frying pan, and lit the stove. Soon, a beautiful fragrance filled the room, of olive oil and oven gas, crushed black pepper over yolk. Battering the eggs, she spoke: "On. The. Pill. By the way ..." She smiled. "How old are you?"

"Didn't you ask me on our first date?" Ilya recalled. "I don't answer questions like that."

"26, 27?"

"No."

"28?"

Ilya pressed the vial of mercury on his chest, which he hadn't taken off. "I'm 22."

Julia then said, Word, or Huh, or something that indicated to Ilya that he was sexy as hell and looked older than he was, something he never took for granted.

"I'm 44," she said, a little casually, a little smiling.

"You're too young for me," joked Ilya, only about to realize the significance of her age.

The eggs were almost done.

Then it hit him. "You're 44, I'm 22, and we're 22 years apart. That's amazing, like planets aligning or something." He didn't mention the part about his mother, who taught him the math. Instead he just tested Julia, asking what 44 times 11 was. When she couldn't crunch it quick enough, Ilya gave her the answer.

The eggs were done.

Julia made it rain parsley and red pepper flakes. She asked Ilya if he liked garlic, and loved his answer: a resounding yes. So she minced two cloves and sprinkled that over the midday snack.

"Is this lunch?" Ilya asked. "Are we dating now?"

"We can't date. And no, this is a midday snack, don't you pay attention?" She used a wooden spatula to divide the scrambled eggs into thirds: one third for her, two for Ilya, who ate greedily, as she watched generously.

"Pay attention to what?" he asked, after swallowing his last bite, holding his arms together so they wouldn't shake, though they did. "And why can't we date?"

"That's your problem," she said, as she rubbed his quivering arms, like she had done with his legs not so long ago, feeling nothing in that moment, now, but sorry for him. "We need different things."

"What?"

She calmed him, but only a little. "You should . . ." She couldn't say the words, she couldn't tell him the things he needed to hear. Meanwhile Ilya's eyes, baggy and red with rings, made her sad. She was sorry for him, sorry for a lot a reasons, sorry she would miss his show. Sorry he had relapsed. No words of advice will help him, she figured, deciding to *do* something for him upon her return. For now, speak only facts, as she said: "I'm leaving tomorrow."

"So? Long distance is easy."

"No way. Plus, you have your show on Sunday."

"So? You inspire me."

"But I might get back with my ex."

"Your ex-husband? I thought you got divorced."

"No, my ex-boyfriend after my ex-husband."

"?"

"Not you, someone else."

☉

Together with Jonathan, Ilya had come up with a hell of a promotional program, even Tony congratulated the duo.

"You two make a yin yang," Tony said, cupping his hands together.

Ilya shivered. "Look, T, just get us the posters like you said."

"They're right here," said Tony, surprising the yin yang before him. Unrolled on the table, clearing some jewel cases and mirrors, lay the poster, which read:

I.N.G.
At Zdras
(22 July 2018)
Extended Play \/ \/ Release Party
with STACY

< then his face, a little smudgy, square; and Stacy's triangular white face >

~7 PM Doors~
8 – 9 PM Free Import Beer with each
purchase of EP (Go ahead, buy two)
9 PM Stacy Giacometti (DJ set)
11 PM I.N.G. (Live set)
~To MIDNIGHT~

"Stacy looks good," added Jonathan Murphey, the head promoter, always metallic with his sarcasm. "His baby face came out ugly, though."

"Check this out," said Tony, as they stepped out of the office into the DJ booth. There was a box under the table under the Tech-12s. Inside the bottom box was a pair of gloves.

When Tony put them on they lit up in neon rainbow.

"Freaky," said Ilya, his pupils dilating in the dark, then suddenly shrunk by the vibrating lights of the gloves.

Tony wiggled his fingers a bit, warming up, then performing a hand dance as fluid as oxygen in blood. Ilya was amused, until he leaned back and pressed a latch under the DJ booth.

The ceiling seemed to give in, when a net dropped and released dozens of old balloons of various colors, causing them to drop.

"Don't touch those balloons," Tony explained. "They had nitrous oxide in them, I think."

"Laughing gas?"

"They're probably expired. Anyway how's the EP?"

"It's not done . . ."

"The show's in two days! We should be focused on promoting now . . ."

Tony led Ilya out. As he did, the DJ asked, "By the way, what's gotten into Jon?"

"He got back with his ex,' said Tony, smiling a dopey ass smile. "Look at him."

He really was happier now. Back with his loved one.

☉

That Friday, hours later, during the heat of the moment, at the climax of the night, the decade's top twenty count down: Ilya laid down Dua Lipa's 2018 "New Rules" so he could somewhat pretend to be a bootlegged version of Marshmallo's 2018 "Happier," before slipping into Calvin Harris's 2017 "Slide" to become Kendrick Lamar's 2017 "HUMBLE," which no one was; rather, "Bad and Boujee," dialing the "Hotline Bling," to create a 2016 vignette, into 2015 from some "Uptown Funk," until he "Can't Feel My Face," or anyone's, which the crowd loved, before going even further back, to 2014 with Nicki Minaj going sort of "Bang Bang" on Sia's "Chandelier"; to 2013, even, swinging on a "Wrecking Ball" straight into everybody's "F**kin' Problems," featuring Ilya's problems; thinking he was "Born This Way," "Gangnam Style," somehow; wishing Julia would say "We Found Love" "On the Floor," where he threw her; because, with the pre-chorus of "OMG," he realized, he was giving up his "Pursuit of Happiness" for it, before he and "I Kissed a Girl," "So What," what up; because this week Ilya skimmed his greatest-shits folder on his computer for tracks to go all Girl Talk on the people, better yet, Kids & Explosions, back in time: to this monumental music video from 2003, which projected behind Ilya—"Act like you got some sense, you might get *a little bit* of this here money"— Ilya had sampled the intro—"Performing their smash hit, 'Hey Ya,' one two three four: My baby don't mess around . . ." And Ilya didn't even trick up the song, didn't cut it, just let it play, and the crowd did their thing, and "If what they say is nothing is forever / then what makes, then what makes, then what makes, what makes, what makes, what makes / Love the exception?" And after the hook Ilya turned up his instrument, improved with the high end of his keys, inspiration filling him, frustrated that he couldn't bring the notes to light fast enough, but here he was sweating, his finale, Ilya getting some vocals in and harmonizing with the "Hey Yaaa"s while the thought at the back of his throat, which he ignored but felt, erupted as this: he didn't want to make popular music, but to make music popular, this kind of music, universal, deep, meaningful, with a message, something people will enjoy, because it is for them, of course; and of course, he wasn't just a DJ or a producer, but a musician. Someone somewhat popular, too, might one add.

"We love your channel!" said a fan. "I.N.G.!"

"Are you coming to the show tomorrow?" he asked.

And they looked confused, walking away.

That's when the old-timer DJ came up to the booth.

Ilya thumbed up, but was pulled asunder by a couple of ladies, then slapped.

Meanwhile the old man shook his head. *"Il était une fois,"* he howled, "How is the EP?"

"Almost done . . ." Just ask him to master! But Ilya didn't.

"Do not get distracted." Then, the master handed the boy an LP, and asked him to put it on the table for him.

The boy did, just as the old man had taught him.

⊙

July 22th. Sunday. The calm before the . . . you know. What else?

When I think about how there are folks who don't like electronic music because it's repetitive, when I hear people say they don't like reggae for "some reason," when out of towners complain about how dirty and noisy New York is, when it occurs to me that there are actual real life individuals who with a grin exclaim they don't like *The Little Prince*, because it's "boring," then I know everyone, not just me, blows air out of their ass.

Adults only care about numbers,* reminds us Saint-Ex. Only numbers:

> If you were to say to the grown–ups: "I saw a beautiful house made of rosy brick, with geraniums in the windows and doves on the roof," they would not be able to get any idea of that house at all. You would have to say to them: "I saw a house that cost $20,000." Then they would exclaim: "Oh, what a pretty house that is!"

The same with music, with art, with anything, even *The Little Prince* itself, they just look at the number of pages and assume it's for children, without reading the text, which isn't simple, especially in French, where it is *passé simple*—don't let the name fool you.

---

* Lol . . . me? You're lucky to have me.

They want numbers? Fine! Where's my growth as an artist in numbers? Where's my growth as an individual in numbers? Let's message Majestic Casual, STEEZYASFUCK, let's message somebody who's somebody with numbers! Invite last minute to the show, remember.

So many deejays. So many producers. Those are some numbers! We are the only industry so crowded. Am I wrong? Probably---according to *Quora*, one out of every hundred people on the planet are music producers. So 75 million. Not bad. It's hard to be like everyone else, when you are the exception. Not to mention, it's boring to fit in.

"Just be the best you can be," commented an employee from CBS. How, sir? How? It's 11:11 am, make a wish.

I don't wish for numbers, I don't wish for money, or math. I don't wish for fame or fortune.

I wish only for the feeling of accomplishment. I want to produce a song and feel good about it. I want to feel good. How can I make others feel good if I don't appreciate my own work? My own biggest critic syndrome taken to the veritable extreme, because I feel like I swallow so much negativity.

Soundcloud works its algorithm. Listeners trickle to my page. But listeners who are producers themselves. We congratulate one another. 1,000 followers. Tracks, 80, my live sets and remixes.

On the other hand, YouTube plays a part. I have from 300 to 3000 listeners at any given hour of the day. Joined 2008, over 100,000,000 views. Today, 49,988 subscribers. Almost a thousand videos. My tracks and experiments and mashes. My favorite artists have a tenth of my numbers.[*]

Apple muzhik, I forgot my password. Spoty-potty, it lets you label your product the way you want, but I never made an account. I like platforms where you can comment. Simple as.

"Simple as that for your simple ass," who said that? Kidd Cudi---homie. Just got on a long binge listening to him. I can't concentrate. I can't focus. Noise on deck, Beck blast, bruh. And that's the name of the sound, my word. Hola. For the blessed of my Priviet. With a bless and a horn, horde. Btw, it just occurred to me the W-dash will never take off. Writers are on a mission to hide the effort of their labor— "The key must turn once, but not twice." Isaac Babel babbles on like David Gray sings in his song, no relation to Alex Grey the psychedelic body emperor, himself no Repin, though he reppin the shrooms, picking em like Levin does at the end of the book that Levina loves, the Mrs Love I love.

New music: Avoure – "Aura." Jan Blomqvist – "the Space in Between." Shingo Nakamura. Mixes by YouTube's Firstperson. Some by Houseum Records.

---

[*] I must admit I did not see Ilya as popular until this page . . . with the numbers I "see" it better. Guilty. And yet, you know what I think about it, numbers serve as a sign post, since they quantify how *much* people dance and how *many* make out to his music, the details you've given until now. Numbers and memory give order to the impressions and sensation. Otherwise this all, becomes . . . well, this blabbering.

Last thought before falling to bed: "Get out of the way!" people tell me. "I'm walking here!" Imma start saying. Or else keep spinning my wheels.

---back. Both the dash and myself, back for a second. It has either been a few hours or a few days since I wrote in here, the nap killed me. So much noise, so much. So many distractions, so many. I can't even focus, or begin to focus.

---nervous about the show. Invite people last minute, don't forget.

---she texted me not to try anything, *anything*. These women are so similar.

Θ

Show day.

A train passed overhead, clocking and croaking. The front door was open, always a red one that from afar looked ajar, full of gum, long and skinny, with a hornet graffitied on it, with the round window for an eye. Ilya carried with him a big flat square cardboard box.

"Hold it." It was the homeless man. His hair gelled and slicked back. He wore a green suit with moth holes in it. "What's that you got there?"

Ilya replied automatically. "A large thin crust pepperoni pizza."

"Hmm," said the man. "Would you mind giving my pups a slice each? They're awfully hungry."

Ilya looked at the pups all sitting at attention, their noses pointed, and their white ears cocked. The DJ tore a slice per pup.

"Thank you," said the man.

Ilya moved to get inside.

"Not so fast."

"Dude, I've got a set to play."

"It's your release party," said the old, homeless, twisted-beard man. "I'll let you in if you make me laugh."

It was 3 PM, Sunday.

"Have you heard the one about the hipster burning his tongue?" ask Ilya.

"What."

"Why did the hipster burn his tongue eating pizza?"

"Why?"

"Because he tried to eat it before it was cool."

After a slap on his shoulder, the night's talent stepped down.

Down, down, to the lit-up dancefloor platform, which had been converted into a little café lounge style stage, with a stool and a guitar stand. Who was on it, in white short-shorts, red crop top, and a beat up jean jacket, under a star-striking spotlight? None other than the booming blonde, her life in young blossom, with a voice like a volcano, and a face like a flower:

Stacy Giacometti

Already, taking up the whole stage, the whole space. Her fingers were loosely holding the microphone. Her stance dominated. There was already a small group of fangirls and fanboys. A handful of producers Ilya had never seen before. A photographer. A merch table with keychains and paper fans, signed by her, and a stack of CDs next to a cardboard QR code that read "Download." DJ set my ass! Her smoky voice was singing, testing. Busy, so no one saw Ilya. He walked past. Down, further down, down the trapdoor.

"I brought pizza," said Ilya, putting it on Tony's desk. The boss looked tired, which was unusual.

"Put it there." Tony didn't say where. There was extra nastiness in his voice. "These pro-douchers have been here since noon," raved Tony, almost to no one. "They're asking for sound, want to have their own booth, want a VIP section, but the show is in five hours, door in four, I don't know who they think they are."

"It's called selling out," sneered Ilya. "Don't get mad."

"I need to retire."

Josephine came out of the restroom. "Papi," she said. "I booked our hotel for tomorrow."

"Hotel?" Ilya opened his eyes wider in that dark, damp, underground office.

"Ilya, you should know about some changes going on around here."

"Again?"

"Jo and I are going to DR for the rest of the summer."

"Is that a good idea?"

"Hell yes it is."

"I mean, is it a good idea to leave Zdras . . . so soon . . . What the fuck!"

"Jonathan's got it." Tony put a hat on. That's when Ilya noticed a suitcase on the floor next to the desk.

"But tonight's the big night!"

Tony shook his head. "What's this? Pizza?"

"Yeah."

"Honey, you hungry? I'm not hungry."

"No, baby."

Ilya was confused. He put his hands on his cheeks. And collapsed on the couch.

"Ilya," said Tony, picking up the suitcase. "Where is the EP? It isn't done, is it?"

"I brought my laptop," he said. "I was going to put some finishing touches on it now before the show."

"You should be relaxing, resting." This was ironic coming from Tony, but also sad, seeing him leave like this.

"Let's go, baby."

"Yes, Tony." Josephine got up. She kissed Ilya on the cheek and bounced along after her husband. "Good luck, Ilya."

Upstairs, one could hear the sound board operator pushing the vocal gain just a little too hard, and causing some horrendous feedback.

Tony shook his head. "What's going on . . ."

"You, bro!" shouted Ilya, standing up. "You! Why are you leaving, you know how important this show was to me, how important Zdras was to you, this could have been something!"

"You're telling me?" Tony laughed. "You didn't even finish the god damn project. Now your ex is up there, with a whole room full of people and it isn't even 4 PM. She's going to pack the house. It's her night. You are auxiliary, extra, icing, nothing."

Josephine had water in her eyes. "Don't be so hard on him." Then, turning to Ilya. "Can you finish before the show?" Everyone in the room knew he could have, maybe, but he wouldn't.

"So long, kid," said Tony, putting his hand on the rail of the staircase out of there. Just then, the trapdoor went, *wham*!

⊙

"Tony, son of Giuseppe!" It was Robespierre.

Tony carefully lay his suitcase on a stair step. "R.P.! What a pleasant surprise. I haven't heard you speak at all, let alone to me in, let's see, how long?"

Josephine shook in place, looking down, taking a step closer to Ilya. Then, taking a deep breath, spoke: "Salut, Pa."

Robespierre acknowledged his daughter's address with a light nod, then turned to his ex-best friend turned son-in-law. "Less than a year."

"Since the wedding!" shouted Josephine.

Ilya sunk in his seat, quietly.

"I did not speak up then," said the gunmetal haired man, rubbing his forehead. "But I speak up now. You must stay for your DJ's show."

"Sorry, R.P., no can do." Tony picked up the suitcase, nodded to his wife to come along.

She didn't move, clenching her fists instead. "T . . . we should."

Tony, in place of getting angry, pleaded. "Baby, please, you said and I thought that it was best to go together somewhere nice, relax, get away from all the stress."

Josephine raised an eyebrow, crossed her arms, and shrugged. Tony knew that meant she had changed her mind. He sighed.

The suitcase made a thump, against the ground.

"We'll be upstairs."

Drops of sewer water hit the keys of the laptop, his shoulder. He thought he saw his mother for a second. His neck itched. A quarter of the time was spent cleaning those drops, looking around, lamely mastering the whole EP into one track to upload, at least for free, there wasn't enough time to learn how to sign up on ASCAP and BMI, for iTunes, to license his music. Robespierre told him not to worry, he could help him later, just chill and get into the right headspace, but Ilya was losing it. He hadn't slept in two days, staying up working on this thing. There still weren't main vocals on the track he loved the most, nor did it have an instrumental solo like it deserved; only his backup choir and strings. It could therefore come out for free, as one big mix. Maybe upload a live-stream . . . but forget it, no camera. Mix.

Though his brother couldn't come, though his father wouldn't make it, even though it was his mother's birthday, although movers were setting up a photo booth near the bar loudly, though his ex-girlfriend was passing the guitar around to her friends, and even considering that his friend and boss almost ran out on him, the silver lining of this was it allowed Ilya time to focus, which was just what he needed.

Tiffany entered. "Stacy says she hasn't seen or heard from you all day."

Ilya didn't respond.

"I guess that was the agreement?"

Ilya hit save on his laptop, then grabbed a half-eaten chocolate bar lying around. Chewing, he asked, "How's it looking like up there?"

"It's crazy." She was referring to the line outside. "I've never seen anything like it here." She looked at her watch. "And it's not even 7 yet and she's already decided to start early and play a longer set. She's creative."

Ilya leaned back, chewing more of the chocolate. "What if I went up? Think she would be pissed?"

"Better not to risk it," said Tiffany. Sitting next to Ilya. They were both on a couch. "Are you nervous?"

"It's a total failure."

Tiffany folded her arms. "It's not a failure until you bomb on stage! And even then, you'll survive."

"I'm not good enough, I don't know anything."

"Shut the fuck up, you don't know anything? You're the jukebox nerd, the know it all, the smart ass, the . . . what's gotten into you?"

Ilya chewed some more chocolate, saying, "The whole summer has been leading up to this, and I messed it up."

Tiffany didn't have to image how Ilya felt. She could hear it in his cracked voice, in his watery eyes, in his lack of friends, in his reduced to dust and ashes confidence, stuffing himself with another bit of that chocolate. Tiffany took it away, ate a piece, and then spit it out into her hand.

"Gross. Weed treats, really? I'm going back upstairs."

"When should I go up?"

"I'll come get you."

⊙

What was he supposed to do? He twiddled and twaddled. He scratched the walls and could see the dust sparkle in his nail. He opened Tony's drawers and saw what he knew he would see. Just one hit. Just one won't kill ya.

The trapdoor swung open.

"Yo!" It was Tiffany. She was sweating. "It's crazy, it's crazy!"

"What happened?"

"The line, the line!"

"What happened?"

"There was a huge line of fifteen year olds outside. None of them could get inside."

"And?"

"And a car ran over a teen. There are cops everywhere, snooping around outside, asking to go inside, and Jonathan is talking to them now."

"Am I still on in thirty minutes?"

"Are you hearing me, Ilya?" Tiffany looked at him like one does a stranger who just touched you the wrong way. "Fool, there might not be any show!"

This was officially the worst night of his life, worse than the incident at the beach, almost as bad as the night in midtown, practically the same as his nightmares, because now, after so much build up, Ilya was dropping darkly, falling hard, with someone ending damaged. Not to mention he was forced to wait in that crack den office, his EP unfinished, his ex up there, and that does it, that does it.

"I'm going up."

Tiffany just saw him get up, move up the staircase, and exit.

Stacy was on stage, guitar on the stand, mic in her hand. "Our hearts go out to our friend," she was saying. "This is a reminder to not text and drive, please, we have to stop that."

Everybody in the crowd cheered, jeered, agreed. Then asked her to sing, sing, sing! Stacy glanced around and the consensus was affirmative. She replied, "No, show's over," but they wouldn't let her, c'mon, please they begged. That's when Stacy saw him, her ex-boy, and everything about her changed, as if the glow that had surrounded her suddenly dimmed, while her eyes opened wide and her jaws tightened. "Fine," she said. It was around 11 PM when she walked and talked to each member of her backing band, full of famous people, telling them to just follow her, she would do one more, before turning towards the crowd, yelling, "Fine!"

Her six-string was slung over her and tightly tuned, when Stacy strummed a loud, proud, open E-chord. "Here's a short, little song called, 'A Long, Long Time' ":

Something tells me that for a long, long time
You're gunna be on my, my mind
I think about you now and then
I wish we would have just been friends

Today we've grown apart
Torn apart our hearts
In two parts, then into pieces
For the better? Is this better?

No, I don't know what it's like
Not to know you, not to want you
Because I never tried, I never learned
To love you or how to lose

I just did, I just did

Right then the cops busted in, shut the show down, took Zdras's liquor license and called it a night.

Ilya ran up to Stacy in the confusion. He complimented her playing. She didn't have time to say thank you. She was rushed out. While Ilya stayed there.

In a now empty bar. With only Tiff, T, Joe, Jon, R.P., and a handful of nerd DJs, the few fans of Ilya who showed up, including one particular surprise: the waitress from Brighton Beach, holding in her hand a compilation of her favorite songs by him—ripped from YouTube and burned on a CD—for him to sign.

IV

SERAPH / вечеринка воссоединения[*]

[*] *Vechelinka Vossoyedineniya*. Sounds like a name, doesn't it? Say that five times, really fast. Although, *Seraph* is nice, could also be a better title for this book—how about for the movie?

On another note, something I've noticed is we transliterate the Russian O letter into the English O letter, when really it would be better spelled A, or Uh, to maintain its phonetic equivalency. A similar thing happens with the Es. The Russian E should become Ye, since it is almost always a long vowel—I just turned the page—I guess you get into all this in the next part of the book. Parts, or movements you call them. Anyway, enough. Let's get this *reunion party* going.

Sunlight flattered visitors today, riding the sea faring tide, like rays on the water's back, with clouds far yet nearing. For now, so bright it was outside that the entire beach took on the same hue, especially when wearing shades. Julia sported the same oversized glasses as always, yellow lensed, which she claimed let her see things clearly. Ilya had on his glasses, rose-colored, which he claimed made life look a whole lot better. The two of them swapped glasses, and held on to the other's pair for longer than the joke of swapping was meant to last: so they could see how the other looks in the way the other sees. All the while, Ilya slid a little closer to Julia on the bench.

"How did it go" Julia had gotten back and agreed to meet Ilya, though she had a million other things on her mind. "The show?"

"Terrible."

"I heard." Julia really had to say it, but the confession wouldn't come out, she still needed to hear Ilya talk it out. After a while, she spoke up, "I'm glad you came. I want to tell you something."

Ilya shook his head. He looked terrible. And he couldn't even bring himself to ask, what?

"We can't be together."

"No?"

"I'm seeing someone. My ex. I told you about him. And you know him. He has a big American flag tattooed on his chest. He works at Zdras. He's the promoter."

"No!!!"

"Yes. And I told him about you."

"That's why . . ."

"Sorry. He's jealous, you can imagine."

"Ok, but why wasn't he at your equinox party?"

"He was working."

"Right."

Julia hugged Ilya. "You could get back with Stacy."

Ilya winced. "It wouldn't work out."

"Don't you still . . ."

"Yes, but she told me not to try anything."

"Best to do as the lady says."

Abruptly, Ilya hugged her, he couldn't help it. Julia hugged him back. It was so hot outside, however, that Ilya could not help but hold on tighter than the weather allowed. Sweat and confusion befitted the two. Until Julia stepped back. And changed the subject. "You don't have any tattoos, do you?"

"Not one. I don't like tattoos." Ilya folded his arms, and brought the subject back up. "What the hell are we?"

Ignoring the question, Julia said, "I have a tattoo."

"What?"

"You don't remember?" She got up, tugged down her skirt waist a touch, and revealed her tiny, tiny bird, a hummingbird smaller than a penny, perched on the eraser end of a pencil, on the part of her where the hot tan ended and the smooth white began. "A zunzuncito," she said. "A hummingbird the size of a honey bee, native to Cuba. My Tía used to call me that." Julia let her skirt fall back down.

"Wait, show me again."

"Sorry, you don't like tattoos." Julia had no further comment. "Let's walk."

It started to drizzle, faintly, finally, clouds overhead.

Julia saw Ilya looking at her. She watched him thinking. Drops of rain fell on their heads, and on their shirts.

But then the drizzle became rain. Ilya suggested they walk around, but Julia said, "No, thank you," her hair shouldn't get too wet. She suggested the restaurant, but Ilya grabbed her by the hand and took her to another spot down the boardwalk. Julia let herself be taken; though her hand felt stiff, the rest of her body glided. When they reached the entrance canopy of a public restroom, they stood there for what felt like another hour, watching the rain turn even heavier.

"Know what," Ilya spoke. "I've never sampled Alan Watts. I should. He was this great thinker from the 70s." Julia wasn't paying attention, so Ilya continued. "You probably know him. He said if you have no idea what to do, just wait, watch."

Julia ignored the comment all together, not having the slightest idea what he was talking about. She drew a pack of cigarettes. "Tell me," she said, "now that the show came and went, what haunts you now, what are you . . ." she lit up. "What are you going to do?"

"I didn't know you smoked."

It was a pack of *Romeo y Julieta* cigarettes she had brought back from her trip abroad. She crossed her arms. "Tell me," she said, still expecting an answer, though she had plenty else on her mind. She felt cold. She missed her kid. Her kid's dad sucked. Meanwhile, what did Ilya know? Ilya could only imagine one thing, amid all the drama and all the heartache and all the accidents, the one thing he wanted most in this moment was a damn kiss. She knew it. He knew it. And there it came, without pause, him swooping in. But again she turned away, not caught by surprise. Ilya went numb, and crossed his arms like her. She felt like she was making a mistake in ending things, but was just unsure enough to not distinguish the parts she liked or the parts she didn't like about Ilya. It was all one big mess, and time to move on. Which is when her phone buzzed, luckily. So she replied. And ignored him for a minute. Until right before she had to go.

"Young knight, have you ever seen *Kingdom of Heaven*?"

"A long time ago."

Julia turned to him, and with her bumblebee cell phone tapped his shoulders one at a time, her chin high, and he eyes upon him. "On your knee." He dropped one, as she spoke: "Swear the knight's oath."

"What's that?" He looked up.

She spoke again: *"Tell the truth, even if it leads to your death."*

"The whole truth and nothing but?"

"Tell the truth," she repeated, *"even if it leads to your death."*

Ilya's eyes watered. He wrapped his arms around the navel of his gold breasted queen, calmly upright and so lovely, while crying, saying, "What do I do?" He tried to breath. "What do I do? I'm still in love with Stacy. And she probably thinks about me too. You're right, we could get together, but for what. She has other things on her plate, like PR, a tour. And me . . . I don't know . . ."

Julia sighed, hugged him back as she brought him up. "I know," she said, holding him tightly, staring at him with closed eyes, looking away as she opened them, and taking in the rain falling on them. "I know. I know." His leg started shaking as he stood. So she caressed that part of him, tears in her eyes now as well, with Ilya's gaze drifting away, sad and broken, his nose welling too, with blood.

Julia, anybody, could have guessed why he bled from his nose, bled from everywhere, just look at the poor DJ, and you would know, you would know.

"You'll find somebody, watch." Then, pulling out that same pen with the insignia of the television station, she drew on his arm in big bold letters the word: **NO.** "And you don't have to have a tattoo, but it would be nice to have a reminder . . . of what's important. Know what I mean?"

"I know what you mean." He stared, and stared at the word, meant to help him quit.

August 6th. Happy Monday morning, pimp, can you hear me? Why make music? Why make another album. People love the music they love. People are satisfied with the old. Why add more. You know why?

Because you'll never know who shows up out of the blue with a mix of your random tracks, asking you to sign it.

Last night, I saw the video of Led Zeppelin in the mid-sixties, after their Yardbyrds days with the *Blow Up* movie*, playing for a Danish Radio. But for real. What trips me is to see them go as mad as they would do at a big concert but for this small intimate show.

The greatest thing about seeing these old dogs is twofold: to see how powerful they are in front of fifty stone-faced kids in a small studio, killing it, absolutely killin it, as they would be in a massive stadium of five digit ticket paying madmen and madwomen and madtrans and madpersons and madstags and maddoe. See them on a groove. They, the rockers, grooved. They were the product of their time as in they are the musicians of their era as in they played what they had to play at the time that they played it. Meanwhile I am a magician, the product of my age and day. Turned 22 last Nov, will turn 23 the next. I am loving this end of Julia, end of July, end of Julie, end of Jules, end of John, end of Joe, end of Jon, end of Eli Jenkins Junior. Zdras down, but I am moving and correcting and making love and sickly singing. I

---

* By Antonioni. I liked it, though I know you didn't. Experimental Italian cinema is a nice lens to frame this story with, in my opinion. The influence is clear to me.

am moving and bouncing and I am loving and making beats. Are you over there on the other side of a monitor, dancing? I am dancing with you. We are the angels on the head of a pin called the collective unconscious. Or the pin is God and we are through its eye. Isn't it possible? You want to believe? I don't. But I'll ill-humor you. Let's assume God exists, then what is all this? Somebody's voice.

I will tell you a secret—and I am making this up as I go— the voice you hear as you read this line is the voice of the devil as heard in the Book of Job. But the dance you dance on the head of a pin is the result of the music you heard, the energy of God. And the pin is a line.

But back to Led Zeppelin, back to genius. They conquered the crowd because they had mastered the line.

Let's talk about *line*, not the coke shit I am learning to lose, but that opera-singing concept so fascinating. A singer needs, above all, line. Of course it can be broken and there are exceptions but let's not break, let's talk about the line. The line is a single breath of singing. It should be loud, it should be direct, it should have a single intention. Line is what seduces a listener. Line is what brings the audience into the palm of the singer's hand. Bad singers don't have line, they sing with indie mimicry, all falsetto, fake and broken. They aren't even staccato, just copying the last 15 year old one hit wonder. Real staccato is hard because you have to bridge a line with silences and breaks, which I think is possible, but let's look at the extreme (other) which's legato: legato is the line par excellence. A singular line. The beauty of the line is in its simplicity. A single line. It isn't so easy. You can use a ruler. But we don't want electronic lines, but we want a brush stroke. Whoooosh. That's a line. It's powerful. Juan Diego Flórez, an opera master, sings 'Una Furtive Lagrima' on YT: that's how you should start understanding line: like that guy's voice, making one shiver. It's line on crack without the crack and without the break.

After that sneaky furtive tear, I wondered once if pop music had the line. Of course! It originated pop. But now pop music is stylized and fake. Musical pop. It isn't classical. Classical is honest and from the chest. Pop is airy and wha-wha. Think Lorde, think Billie Eyelash, or Eilish. These singers act tough on camera. Who knows what they are like in person. Insecure, like most of us, so high. On the ground, however, the earth grovels beneath our feet, and then heaves us up into the air. Pop singers these days sound affected, as in they affect their voice for sound effects: and it's terrible for your vocal cords. You sing like that, all airy, not letting that pussy in the throat, your vocal cords (it looks like a pussy, sorry, it's true, just google image that shit: "vocal cords gif") chill out. Well if you sing like that it's bad for your throat. That black hole. I don't want to get into the technical aspects of that, but what I can say is these syncopated (even that word is too generous, I love syncopation) artists rely on amplification and limited condensers. Fuckers! They couldn't fill a Carnegie Hall with their voice even if they tried. Which is fine, as a teen we act fake to be real.

We hear Freddie Mercury, on the other hand, sing "Don't Stop Me Now" and that dude is the king of lines, even in rock. What about Led Zeppelin, I ask, and we see that radio station video of them in some random Nordic country, no one knew what they were experiences, but felt it sure enough, line after line: DDDAAAZZZEEE AND CONFUSED I'VE BEEN SO LOST . . . a single breath, a single intention, a single come-hither of the singer luring us, the listeners, in, into the palm of his hand. And I want to be there. I want to be seduced. And of course, I think about singers in electronic outfits.

So lines. Electronic music is all about the line. My story for example(s). Isn't that a line?

It's time to quit New York. Go on tour. Live.

If you don't stop to smell the roses, life will pass you by. Although, if you *do* stop to smell the roses, it will pass you by anyway. Time sucks, and yet it's what we most need to get anything done, to become anything. Ilya's biggest most important missing ingredient.

David had texted Ilya that he was in town, the conference went well without him, now he was landing today, attending a tech conference the next, and then flying out the following night for another conference across the country.

"They do it on purpose," he wrote, over text. "Tripping across the country like that." He meant it figuratively as well as literally.

Ilya approached the hotel in the Upper West Side, as his brother was stepping out, dressed up and in a hurry. Knocking into Ilya, on purpose, and rushing past him.

"Bro?"

"Hi," said David, turning around then turning back to walk away.

"Aren't we hanging out?" Ilya caught up. "Hey!"

They were a block down now from the hotel. "I told you I had a meeting at 8, and that we should hang out before."

"It's still before."

"It's 7:05."

"Like I said, before."

"You told me you would get here 'closer to 6,' and that's after we had agreed on 5."

"Well, well, I could have planned better if you had told me—I don't know—not the day *of* that you'd be in town."

"I found out today we had an extra ticket."

"Aren't you the boss? Why didn't you buy a ticket for the conference?"

David looked at his watch, his fancy graduation present from their father, a thing Ilya noticed, but never mentioned.

"It's 7:08," David said, rubbing his forehead. "How the hell does time go by so fast?"

"It's New York."

"7:09, my god. Ilya, where are we?" He looked around. "80th street and Broadway. I need to be in Greenwich in an hour and twenty-one minutes. I can walk there. And I want to talk. Shall we?"

The brothers were on Broadway in broad daylight. Sometime later, the older brother spoke up. "What do you call these?" David pulled out a sandwich bag of shriveled, bruised, blue and brown mushroom heads and stems.

Ilya slowly drew his hands out of his pockets, quickly snatching the bag. "Since when do you trip?"

"That's why I had asked you to come earlier. So you could tell me how to use these."

"You don't use them, you eat them."

"Do you want them? I don't do this shit."

Ilya smelled the contents. "I'm trying to quit drugs," he said, reaching for one of the mushies. "Again." They were stopped at a red light near Trader Joes at 72nd.

"That's good to hear." David grabbed the bag like it were a toy he actually now wanted. "I suppose you don't want them, then."

"Psychedelics aren't drugs," Ilya said, snatching it back. They started walking again. "There are so many. Say, if we each eat half now, then we'll be inside-out by the time we reach Washington Square Park."

"They're not just for me. I'm supposed to pass these out a cap and stem per person at the conference tomorrow."

"Says who?"

"The investors. Have you heard of microdosing?"

"Yeah. It's lame, dude."

"I'll share if you promise, but really, really promise to quit, for good."

Ilya could have said no, could have said yes, straddling the line in between, unsure . . . until he decided. Straight up decided. Done.

They passed Lincoln center. It was crowded with tourists in dazzling colors. The intersection bent and curved. The roar of car engines zoomed by in oscillated waves. The tall, tall buildings greeted people with towering wobbles. The underground shook with thousands of years of geology and thermo-energy. This city was alive and would never die.

Suddenly, without covering his mouth, with his head upright, a stranger in a suit they would never see again sneezed in the brothers' faces. They rubbed their eyes.

"Damn, dude . . ." said David. "Anyway, I don't feel anything,"

"It takes a little longer," said Ilya, coughing a bit. "And it takes more than one tiny mushie to feel it." He asked for the bag. David pulled it out and handed his brother another cap. Then he flicked one up into the air and caught it with his mouth.

"How's the deejaying."

"I blew the show the other night."

"You told me. But I thought the cops busted it?"

"I blame myself."

"What happened after?"

"I still played a bit, to like two or three people. But when I got home all my social media accounts had gotten hacked."

"Word." Just then, distracted, David pointed out a half-eaten—not even; a quarter-eaten—bagel on the ground and wondered how long it had been lying there on the sidewalk. Ilya squatted near. It was covered in sesame seeds and dog hair. Whoever had taken a bite into it had a small mouth, maybe a child. Judging by the amount of cream cheese, which first of all was so low one could tell the bagel had come from one of those cheap street carts, it must have been hours baking in the hot summer sun.

"Did you eat dinner yet?" Ilya asked, poking the thing.

"Gross, man, get off from that. Let someone else have it."

As the brothers disengaged from the forgotten bagel, and made it halfway down the block to the upper fifties, a skinny bloated man in a pink tank top, sparkling skirt, and curly blond hair, put his arms down and frolicked towards the bagel, picked it up with a single finger through the hole, and casted it into the air, catching it in his mouth. "Not too hot, not too cold, not too dirty, not too clean," said the Goldie Locks bastard, before he danced away. It reminded David of how he had eaten his flicked mushie. The boys ate more mushies.

"What time is it?" asked David.

"You have the watch," said Ilya.

"I know, I just want you to tell me."

Ilya grabbed his dumb older brother's arm and put the watch to his face. "You tell me what time is it."

The older, taller, stronger brother laughed. He looked at his watch. "Damn, it's only 7:40. And we're already at Times Square."

It was as bright out as noon. Throngs of people snapped photos. Billboards melted. Models posed. Mobs mingled. Parents toured. Rappers flowed. Cars zipped. Hotdog stands sold. Doors chimed. Pamphlets decried minimum wage. Soldiers smiled. Officers policed. Thugs buffaloed. Buffoons monkeyed. Idiots horsed around. Ladies asked for directions. Gentlemen abided. Abbots gently moaned. Directions asked for ladies. Buffalo Bills hugged. Police-people offered ice cream. Smiles sold ears. Mages cried mini-tantrums. Wind chimes adored hot dogs on sidewalks. Zippers cared. Flows were rapped. Tours parented. Singles sobbed. Posses modeled. Bill's board melted. Photographs popped out people from throngs of Kodaks. Noon was never as bright as Times Square.

"The Square of Times!" shouted Ilya, unheard by all except his brother.

"It's so loud here," replied the brother.

"How do you say what I said in Russian?"

"Площадь Времени."

"Ploshits Vremeny."

"Not shits, man, PLO-SHEETS. Площадь Времени. I don't get you, you never wanted to learn."

"Let's get out of here."

The brothers headed further south, past $(Times^2 - (d))$.

A young lady in the back seat of an SUV yelled something happy to the boys who were still walking, themselves a little silent and bored, until this young screaming lady stuck out her booty and spanked it in the air.

"You don't see that every day," said David.

"Word."

"Say, time's speeding up again. It's 7:50. We're barely at Penn Station."

"It would have taken longer by train," said Ilya. "It would have . . . have, would have had, would had had have . . . by—"

"No, it wouldn't have had . . . have taken, it would have taken three minutes at the platform, one minute on express from Times Square to Pennsation."

"Penn Station?"

"Pencil Station, yes."

"Pennsylvania State, Pennsylvania Saint." Ilya felt the greatest revelation was coming on, rubbing his chest, and hitting his brother. "Saint Satie, Erik Satie!"

"Ilya," said David, "are you seeing anybody?"

"I see all of New York before me!"

"I meant, are you dating anyone?"

"I've been seeing a Julia . . . the Julia."

"Where is she from?"

"Russia, but grew up in Cuba."

"Does she speak Spanish?"

"Perfectly."

"How old is she?"

"44."

David bit his lips. "Nice."

"But we broke up, I think."

"Damn."

"Are you . . ." Ilya asked, "seeing anybody?"

But David deflected. "All things considered, you should find someone closer to your age, with your interests. It would be good for you. For both of you."

Destination reached. David was distracted, and early to the meeting in Greenwich, at least it felt that way. So the brothers sat in the twilight of a park that was not square but yes named after the first president of the United States who led troops through this city in defense and defiance of a tyrannical monarch with the same name as him, coincidentally, but for winning earned himself a pretty arch of triumph. Elsewhere jazz musicians filled the air. Trinket salesmen did no one a favor. Chalk artists painted new dimensions on the ground. And the brothers sat on a bench and stared outwardly.

"What time was your meeting?"

"Everyone's late," said David, who was never late, locking his phone. "We're going to a comedy basement."

"Comedy Cellar? It's super famous."

"That's the one. But first we're getting pizza at a vegetarian place next door."

"Artichoke Pizza? Sort of vegetarian."

"Yup."

"I thought you said this was a meeting."

"I was stressed about being late, wasn't I? By the way . . ." David stretched. "What's the name of that song for mom, again?"

"Untitled. . ."

"Lame. And it's really not finished? I thought—"

"It isn't . . . needs one more . . . guitar lick, or something."

David's phone buzzed like it were getting a call. But it was really just a fat text chat group of techies all of a sudden sharing porn memes and telling one another they were here and there, but mostly at the "sort of vegetarian" place.

"C'mon just release it already."

"Unfinished?"

"At least with a name. And I bet you have one for it, what is it?"

"The name?"

"Yes."

"You really wanna know?"

"Yes."

Ilya whispered the title: "Seraph."

Swing time:

Music excites you, ignites you, ennobles you, delights you; you are slowly falling into a trance, you are the recipient of my love, you are falling deeper and deeper into the beak a hummingbird. You continue to fall, you are Alice, you are Eve, you are every girl in between and after, then you turn into a man, and you sign with your left hand the contract of our mutual alliance, between prophet and soul, and then you are lifted up and no longer fall, and then what matters is one thing: that you dance; dance. How many angels can dance on the head of a pin? It isn't a riddle, it isn't a thought experiment. The question is an image. That's all it is. An image. And once you envision this image you unlock its mystery. Just picture it. Three genderless angels holding hands, long hair, and long dresses, traditional, doesn't matter from where all traditional clothes are similar in that it is loose and comfortable and passed down from generation to generation endlessly before and after. And now zoom out, their smiles getting smaller and their dance getting wilder. They are on a head of a pin. And that pin stitches you to the present moment. You are tethered to the infinite, the pin bends. You smile. You smile and you dance. You shake off your genitals. You become the fourth angel, a sexless genderless angel, bouncing to and fro.

Facing Ilya was the head of the world music showcases. She organized shows for the late summer sound festival in Queens, a project organized by a council of community leaders. Last minute they needed volunteers. Naturally, Julia made the email introductions, and then left Ilya and her friend, this show producer, to set up the actual interview.

The café by the north-south W train smelled exuberantly of roasted coffee, and grounded beans, clanking espresso machines, and the sweet sweat of a jazz guitarist humming coolly at the daytime open mic.

"I haven't heard a guitar in-tune at an open mic," said Ilya, "in like ever."

The interviewer laughed. "I really like your energy, Ilya," she said. "Really."

"Really?" Ilya had been feeling extra good lately, and he wasn't sure why, he felt especially smooth that day. "Thank you." He rubbed dust off his shoulders.

The woman laughed again. "Julia was right about you. It would be great if you can help out."

"How can I help?"

"We have boxes and boxes of flyers."

"Consider them passed."

"And we have hours of video footage that need organizing and uploading."

"Consider them posted."

"And you know how to DJ?"

"I'm the best."

"Good," said the organizer, smiling, remembering how nice it was to be young and cocky herself, not so long ago, mind you! "Good, good. We had a sponsor join us this week, and there's no one to keep their clients happy. We need some of that Russian instrumental music I heard on your channel."

Ilya was endlessly flattered when someone said that to him. He held himself back from saying any more words. Instead he just smiled, nodded, and shook the woman's hand when she put it out for him.

As Ilya left, the organizer stayed to order a second cup of coffee. For some strange reason, only thinking about it did it start to make sense, this was a particularly beautiful day. She enjoyed her talk with this young kid. He didn't finish college, just like her, not in four years anyway. But he was bright, and had told her he wanted to go back, just like her, eventually. This youth was so happy, at that age, surely for no reason. Just young and free, she kept thinking.

The cream in her cup felt extra smooth, tasted extra sweet, the brew traveled down her throat extra sensuously. Just as unexpectedly as life had presented her with the pair of hands that would help distribute the remaining promotional materials cluttering her office, she was receiving a message on her phone. This from an ex-boyfriend of hers. Technically a boy two ex-boyfriends ago.

She didn't even get to read the preview, so lost was she in the scrambled dizziness that the wild combination of letters in his first and last name evoked in her, before he called.

"How've you been?" he asked, with a voice so rich and deep it melted her like it were the very first or very last time she would hear a real man's voice.

"Good," she said. "I mean fine, I've been fine." There existed some mandatory small talk, before executing the next necessary line.

"I miss you, you know," he said, leaving the ensuing silence to fill in the blanks of why he had called. "I do."

"I miss you too . . ." she said, holding back the baby name that almost slipped out of her, the one she had used for him their entire relationship past, before choking up a little, all on her own, in what were about to be tears, had the man on the other end of the phone not said what he said next.

"Want to meet?"

"I'm at the coffee shop."

"The same one as always?" he asked, a little slower than his normal pace for speaking, she noticed.

"Yes, I'm there now," she replied, thinking herself bold for suggesting a meeting as impetuous as his phone call.

"I know," he said.

"What?"

"I know you are there," he replied. "I'm outside."

Could he, could he really be? She turned and saw his beautiful face through the sidewalk window, just as the guitarist was concluding his solo, and welcoming a musician up to the stage.

August 7-12th. I took a look at the Cyrillic alphabet again, those thirty-three characters, and I think I came up with a solid grouping. It isn't that they spell out a code or anything. But learning them by heart might demystify my past.[*]

А Е О К М Т

The first six letters to learn are the cognates with English. A, E, O, K, M, T. Together they spell a cognate, too: Комета. But more on that in a second.

First, a praise to letter A, what a glorious letter. In English my name has it, Ilya. But not my name in Русский язык. The alpha, the first. Aum. A seed. A vowel. Azul, like Julia's favorite color, and lapis lazuli, her favorite rock.

Next, the letter E. A pretty important letter, if I had to guess, in English, given it's the first letter in the word "English." But in Russian, it's pronounced a bit differently. It's a long sound, and the reverse sound that "a" makes, "ey." So crazy. "Yeh." Saying "e" in Russian feels like rolling bubble gum along the roof of your mouth with your tongue.[†]

Ah, then the letter O. Crazy O. Let's write about O later.

---

[*] What a coincidence you were practicing the letters right before we finally, and really, got to talk for the first time. Practicing, and coming up with silly, pointless text just before you followed me back to Moscow! It impressed me very much, coming with me, and making me think you knew the alphabet . . . Julia Cameron would call it Synchronicity, I suppose.
[†] Probably the most important sound in the book, yes?

Next? K. K is the rim shot. K, k-k, k, k. K, k-k, k, k. Such a harsh sound. It cuts. It kills. It coordinates. It conflates. It conquers. And Cools. Cats.* Koalas and kangaroos, and Nikolais. Some draw it differently, note: K.

The letter M? Em. My whole chest a palette of sound. M&M like the candy or like Eminem or like my mashup of Post Malone's "Candy Paint" with Eminem's "Walk On Water." M like money. M in Музыка. M for Mama. M as movement. M the wave, the upside-down W, M.

T? Simple. Tony.

And all together? Комета. Did you guess? Comet (+) uh.

В Н Р С У Х

The next set of Cyrillic letters: В, Н, Р, С, У, Х. These are the ones to learn next because they look like English letters, though they make different sounds.†

В in Russian is not the English Beta, but the Greek Veta, the "vee" sound. Bunnies have Vs. Vuh.

Н in Russian? The "n" sound, like "n" in nose. Looks like a nose, a Russian nose (Н) doesn't it?

The next letter is easy if you sound an "R," but in writing tucked back the wiener, so it looks like Р, but makes the same sound. Like a Pirate, "A-r-r." Or a leopard, "r-r-r." The name

---

* My favorite animal.
† If you hadn't been a DJ, you could have been a dorky teacher, wiping chalk on your tattered blazer, as you asked your students to come up to the board and draw connections where there appeared none, like your father.

of the boy in the Shakespeare play about star-crossed lovers: Ромео.

The next letter is a quiet little fellow. He isn't cool like K, but he's super like S. It's the Russian C, the "es" sound. Like the "c" in façade, only you get rid of the reflection in the lower half of the line. Cyborg. Century. C-men.

Next the Russian Y, which in русский is the "oo" sound, as in "fool" or "food." It's in the word "Русский" itself, see the second letter? An important one, because Russia is always making other countries ask, Why? Why? Julia's on TV, asking why, why?

Last, Russian X. The equivalent of English H. When I see X, I hear a sigh. Sigh on the dotted line. The wrong answer on a test. Julia's hard sigh. She's so open.*

Б Г Ж З П Д

The next set of six letters are the ones that look different, but sound like letters in English: the sounds are beh, like bunny. Gue, like get. Jeh, like James. Zee, like zoo. Peh, like Penelope. And deh like da dead don't dance, dork.

"Zoo" in Russian is zoo-park, but pronounced zah-park: зоопарк. Did you know animals make different sounds in Russia than in America? No, one isn't better than the other. The animals are the same, as are the people that raise them. But the noises we assign them are different. Any six year old in America can tell you what noise a pig makes: "oink-oink!"

---

* Would we have met without her?

And I don't even have to spell out what animal goes "bzzz," "meow," "woof-woof," "cock-a-doodle-do!" and freaky "craw-craw" or "chirp-chirp." Respectively, the Russian pig goes: "хрю-хрю" (khryoo-khryoo). The bee in Russian does "ж-ж-ж." The koshka, she goes "мяу- мяу." The dog, "гав-гав," hah! The cock? "Ку-ка-ре-ку!" The sparrow, "кар-кар." The chick, "пи-пи-пи-пи." (I don't know what noise turkeys make in Russian. We will have to ring that old muzhik, Старый Макдональд, on his farm and ask him, e-i-e-i-o.)

Б kind of looks like a "b," but with a hoodie.

Г looks like gamma, easy, physics.

Ж (which sounds like "jeh," but gets the "zh" spelling in transliterations, like in "muzhik") is my favorite letter in the Cyrillic alphabet. It looks like a butterfly, or a bee. So remember!

And З, well, it makes sense if you write z's in cursive.

П, I know, looks like an "n," but you're just going to have to put "peh" in your head for the п sign, or just remember what mathematicians use for 3.14.[*]

And Д? Looks like fangs on a beast, doesn't it? Or consider, disk-jockey: диск-жокей. D. Deh. Д. It's almost

---

[*] This recalls the section about pi, two hundred pages ago, with your earliest memory regarding God. To me, spelling, math, religion, and philosophy are the most boring subjects imaginable. But, I know how much they mean to you, as well as how important they are for this book. Creation, beginnings, prophecy. Dreams, nightmares, reality. Music gods, and the One. The love of your life, and happy endings. Like ours that will hang over this whole tale when you reach me at the end.

silent in the name: Джульетта, which just sounds the hard "ж," like the soft bee, ж-ж-ж . . .

И Й Л Ф Я Ю

This set I'm writing now is the most difficult. That means the next and last two will be easier. But maybe these are easy, too; they are found in English as sounds. I think it's hard because the characters look way different than anything Americans are used to, almost "made up" one could say. Well, all characters are made up. So buckle up. Here it goes: И, Й, Л, Ф, Я, Ю.

I hope you recognize two of these. They're in my name, Илья. This first one, И, the backwards N. The "ee" sound, same as in English, "И-nglish." See?

The next one you see a lot at the end of words and names, like Andrei and hockey, and even in "Russian Language" as: Русский язык. It's pronounced "yih." A funky И with a cap to limit it, shorten it. It's why I wear hats, to keep me restrained.

And what's up with this pi with the broken foot looking thing, Л? Well, think of an LP: its jet black grooves, its funk, its turntable-ability, and you have an LP, or Л-П. Ah, no? Yeah, that's weak. Not worth a lol. Lol. Or Love? Or Levina?*

---

* Sometimes, while reading, I wondered if changing her last name even made sense. Wouldn't people figure out who she was? Maybe not. No one could call this a memoir, not a straight-forward one anyway. It mixes journal entries, dreams, myth, on top of the real struggles you

L-oser? Loser. L-user. That "u" is important. It's the next letter: Ю. It'll become madly important.

You, Ю, you, Ю. When did she adopt the name "Julia?" Should I call her Юлия, по-русски? And when you get mad at someone, F you! Ф-Ю. That's the next letter, Ф. Yes, Greek comes in handy here. For real. Last, but not . . . as they say . . . YA! Я, Я, Я. The funky R. Я. I think therefore Я.

Ц, Ч Ш Щ, ь ъ

The next six characters form the percussion of the Russian language, a language that otherwise sneezes and purrs.[*]

Think of a pizza: the delicious smell, the savory cheese, warm marinara sauce and sliced tomato and, hmm, garlic. Yes. Now look at this letter: Ц. That's the "zz" sound in pizza. As in пицца. And everyone likes pizza. And cheese, the "ch" in cheese. Yes. Чиз человек. Yum. Ч, cha, Ч, cha, like stepping down on a hit hat.

The next is a shy sound, the same "sh" in shy, and "shush," the Ш. You say shy, "shai." Drop the last sound and you have the Ш.

The next one looks similar and is pronounced similarly, only I find my tongue is up higher and closer to the roof of

---

had releasing your unsuccessful debut. The world would have to wait for the next one, which would make a splash. You're welcome, btw.

[*] Random, but I haven't seen not one of my favorite animal this whole time.

my mouth when I say it: Щ. The same letter in borsch, борщ. The sound is like the one between the end of "fish" and the start of "chips," like part "-sh," part "-ch." SHCH. Щ.

The soundless signs are next, ь and ъ. Just Wikipedia it— like Stacy used to say, whenever she didn't know something. I could never get her interested enough to learn this language, even type a single character as small as ь to find out what it means, or where it comes from. Now I'm trying to relearn what I once knew. Why? For Julia. For myself.

Ё Ы Э

My favorite toy as a kid was the yo-yo. And to spell that in Russian, I thought it was "ё-ё." So simple. But it's actually spelled Йо-Йо, which looks ugly and complicated. If only life were as simple as ё-ё. "What would happen if you gave a yo-yo to a flock of flamingos?" asked James Earl Jones in *Fantasia 2000*. Russians sometimes don't put the dots over the ё, which complicates the matter. Like, is the name Левин or Лёвин? I only own the Pevear and Volokhonsky translation. Complicated.*

As complicated as the second to last letter, Ы. It's so common, and it sounds like the "i" in "sift," different and more guttural than a regular "i." Most plurals end in Ы.

---

* But worth it. These pages only make sense when considering the audience for this book is American, your one half, to understand your other half. Through symbols, or through the thing itself, both in story.

Last is another wild one. It's so simple: Э. It looks like the "E," but backwards, and sounds like the short vowel version of it too, just "eh." And that's how this whole exploration in letters will end: on a big ole short ole EH. Julia's on TV.

O

But wait, come back, the O! O say can you see. Ou. Au. Om. Aum.

So strange, sounds and letters, and there is absolutely no consistency, which is all I want, which suggests something like languages are made up, big surprise, or languages are yet evolving, hopefully getting better like a band we love even after they put out a bad album, because if I have to read another O when I need to say "uh" in English or in Russian, then I am going to bend my laptop backwards unto itself. I must double check this, but I think Cyrillic had four more Os than today. Today we have the cognate O, which I wrote long ago about (O the circle of life) O. But that's only the normal O. There's the monocular O, with a dot in it, looking like an eye or a breast. There's the binocular O, which looks like a face with no nose or mouth. There's the dual monocular O, which looks like a monocular O after it doubled itself as a germ, but before it divided into two singles. And then finally there's the rarest of Os of yore: the multiocular O! which looks like a multi-eyed seraph. My version of MS Word can't even type these characters unto the page. Lord knows how one should pronounce them, but I bet you it would cause some magic to happen. Like being there for Julia's O, my favorite.

Know what, my next EP will be titled *Multiocular O*, or spelled as its unpronounceable symbol, like the "love symbol" Prince had for a minute. We'll see. You'll see. I'll see. O say can you see, Seraph: *I.N.G.* By the dawn's early light. U.S. Us. We. Rus. Мы . . .

Rewind to June 3rd, 2018. Julia was sitting at a table alone with a birthday cake. Stuck to the creamy icing were six wax candles and a red letter A. She had spent the morning mixing chocolate and eggs for her son, to see him enjoy the three or four slices he was capable of devouring, as he would tell her about his weekend with his father. Unfortunately, the boy ended up not meeting his mother at the beach, as agreed, because his father wouldn't drive him there after all. This left Julia, on that warm miserable day, realizing that they, the already separated couple, should divorce.

Now, go back fifty years, to Yekaterinburg, where Julia's father, Simon, ran an auto-repair enterprise. He had modernized the shop after taking it from his father, who couldn't run a profit without making noise. The old way of thinking was to open a second shop, work longer hours, and hire party members, yet all these initiatives, the grandfather's, remained in vain. So, he had to take what he could, hitting the bottle and the wife pretty good. Hit the children too. And the couch, where he slept away the daylight.

On his eighteenth birthday, in July, Simon stepped into the repair shop and told the employees that he was the new boss. Next, he went home, where his mother prepared peas and mayonnaise in chipped ceramic bowls, and told her that he was ready to take care of the family. Last, he stepped into the living room where his father dozed. A slight nudge shook him awake.

"What, what?" called the grandfather, the dim light of the room made his sleepy eyes hurt. He was barefoot.

"What," said Simon. "You forgot today's my birthday?"

The grandfather rubbed his feet. "Eighteen, huh?" He offered his son a glass. "Drink with your old man."

"It's empty," replied Simon, keeping his eyes fixed on his father's half-shut ones. The old man smacked his lips as he made his way over to a cabinet in the corner. Opening a cabinet, he gently lifted a black cat that was inside.* There, the bottles were also empty.

"We'll go to the bar," exclaimed the grandfather, "to celebrate my eldest son!"

Snuffling towards the door, the old man stumbled over a still warm samovar on the floor—spilling tea and staining the carpet with a little toe blood. The son had to lift him up.

"Let go of me," said the old man. "Let me go . . ." Luckily, he passed out, into a snore, without a fight. Together with the siblings, the children loaded their father onto a train car headed for Moscow, leaving him with nothing but the rag they had used to wipe his toe wound. They assumed that, at best, he would vanish somewhere along those 1,600 kilometers and no one would hear from him again.

It wasn't until four years later, after Simon had saved the business, and placed his siblings in universities across the country, that a letter arrived to the old house, detailing their

---

* Well.

father's unfortunate end. Apparently, he had gone past Moscow, all the way to Riga, in Latvia: where he fell into the Baltic Sea some chilly day. Local cobblers, who had come to know him as a street rambler, confirmed the frozen body.

"A touch of irony," Simon hummed to his wife that night, the night they conceived Julia. "He did love the ocean."

Malenka, the mother of Julia, was known as a quiet woman, easy to get along with, easy to catch a cold from, yet always kind enough to hold your place in the bread line. Otherwise she held her head down, whether she sneezed in public or spoke to government officials. It was surprising, then, just how much and just how long she insisted the family visit Cuba. It seemed her only wish was to see her expatriate sister in Habana. After sharing 200 letters in six years, in which each sister lamented the distance, Malenka secured the visas and set her yearling daughter and husband aboard the month long voyage—departing from Riga. The trip was a birthday gift to her husband.

By a bend in fate, however, while out on the bow of the ship to view the same water his father had drowned in, the top of Simon's head met the end of a lightning bolt. Tumbling overboard, he was swallowed by the ship's break in the sea. For many reasons, the ship continued.

The mother, Malenka, always of weak health, now a widow, even caught tuberculosis before she and her baby landed in Habana. When they did reach it, her health had too far deteriorated. She could barely hold her child in her arms, during the funeral service for her husband. No body of course, but she had a small tombstone built anyway, with a vacant spot next to it. It would be easier for the kid this way.

Candles, unpracticed prayer, and palms to a gray stone with frankincense.

About the meaning of her husband's death, or about how she blamed herself for it, she only had her sister to tell. Her last dying word was a solemn promise asked: "Take care of Julia." Her sister, the expatriate, used to a bohemian style of independent single lady, gladly adjusted her life to take in the child. She would be a blessing to her.

But there was more. Melenka kept a diary, for Julia to one day read. In it, her last dying sentence was a promise asked seldom: "Remember your father." So everywhere, no matter where in the world she ended up, she would bake a cake for the father she never knew—all chocolate, according to the diary—as soon as she was old enough to bake.

2018. Beach. Those six candles. That red letter A, unlit. Salt in the air, dissolving. Divorce, decisions, dividing the kid's time, Christmas, school responsibilities. He was turning six today. But his dad didn't want to bring him, as he had said he would. Any minute and the last-straw text would enter, the one that said he wasn't coming, that taxi driver dad, he wouldn't make it to the beach. He and their son were still go-carting.

So Julia sat at the table, sat still, thinking thoughts. What a sweet cut to remember memories. She sliced a piece and ate, although she didn't quite enjoy chocolate cake, the only kind she ever learned to make well. But her son did, just like her father. The mushy sponge, and decadent flavor, made her mouth water. And chew. Swallow.

1970s Cuba. Because of her white skin, Julia had to stand out as humble, yet also had to fit in the best. At recess, Julia did all the things her friends did, pick on boys, try cat food once by an empty soccer stadium, and sneak out at night to go dancing. When it came to dancing, she pretended to be terrible, until pulled by the wrist, then she flowered into the most stunning salsera. Never wilting, always blossoming, her life developed roots where no one expected her to. She kept an eye on the ground, and an eye out to sea.

It was a pair of old ladies across the street who started calling her "Love," though her name was Levina. "Julia Love," which in Spanish sounds like, "Who do ya love." They had a terrible sense of humor, too, and Julia loved to complain with them when coming home from school—miserable women always grouchy, only happy when this youth came and encouraged their bitterness and bickering, until becoming happy again.

In a country fascinated by automobiles, paired with the diary entries, she had reminders of her father everywhere. The bohemian aunt, who insisted on being called "Tía," would remind her niece of her past, as well. Although, it wasn't difficult to conjure a memory. Julia had only to see a ship out on the water and imagine the long ago voyage.

One part outsider, two parts curious, and three parts gifted: Julia earned a master in journalism at the University of Habana, after studying oil painting and art history at the Superior Institute of Arts—her undergraduate thesis being a single canvas which she had hung at the entrance of a friend's apartment that got renovated over the course of nine months, beginning with an dilapidated living room, next a gutted living room, until finally a renovated apartment, each passing month Julia adding the details that were added in real life. Thanks to her professors' and peers' expectations, even in her late teenage years, she became the one to ask about the fall of the USSR at any dinner or hallway conversation. Later, by her mid-20s she integrated into a broadcasting career that she and Tía could be proud of. They moved to a new home. There, newspapers were stacked so high they could serve for furniture. The number of novels to review, too, got so high that the women had to sacrifice the bathtub for storage. Her work lead her mind to travel around the world, and to understand it enough to be able to write cunning reportage. Yet her real eyes and her real feet never left the island.

Until on impulse, in 2008, at 34, she flew to Mexico City, for fun. She had never left Cuba before this trip, and after it she would never return. It seemed every day in the new capital gave her a fresh reason to stay, even Tía thought it was good for her niece, the career woman, to consider other possibilities. They couldn't live together forever.

Many birthdays later, after having acquired a new residency, a posh job as a television anchor, and a habit of going out on weeknights, she at last met the man who would sweep her off her feet, a Brooklynite. It was on the dance floor of an annual salsa congress—with beads of sweat on her chest like pearls, his hair gelled and greasy conducing the electricity in the air, as he twirled her—that they fell in love.

He knocked her up. The pregnancy was aborted. And they agreed to try again in the US, after getting married. Ten months later, she moved to NY, to live with this guy.

His name, Andrés Domingo Juarez. A taxi driver, who was exceptional at salsa, and believed that a summer holiday in Mexico City would change his life. He felt proud when his intuition turned out to be true, meeting the woman who would become his wife, and who, like him, agreed to terminate. His family would never have considered the option, so he didn't tell them. He just returned to NY at the end of summer with a wedding ring on, and told them only the good news. The family still slapped their youngest boy, but then congratulated him. Ten months later, once the spousal visa came through, they embraced Julia.

Julia Love, as everyone called her in Mexico, soon learned the hard way that having the wrong combination of great features could turn against you. A great job, great hobbies, and good looks led a single woman of 36 to do wonderful, silly things. So what, she and Andrés had lost the token of their first summer together. They could try again. What mattered was that she had a man, a man interested in cars and dancing, and showed himself to stick by her side, even virtually, through the trying long distance relationship.

Plus, the idea of going to NY, of a new destination, thrilled her. She knew she could bring something to the table. Maybe she could interest her husband in oils other than car oil. After all, they were moving to New York. She would have the right to work, and had only to renew her residency, by applying for a permanent green card, after two years.

Unfortunately, by the time Julia's two-year conditional residency was ending, so was the passion.

Death in the family (a father on his side, Tía on hers) and financial straits mired the newlyweds' first two dozen months in misery. All that work to be together felt like a waste.

They never went to museums. They never did anything fun. Andrés did dabble with various carpooling apps. And Julia did struggle to land a job even remotely comparable to what she was doing in Mexico or Cuba. It seemed New York only counted "native" years in the industry as experience, meaning years in journalism spent in the United States. All her time covering Russian relations for Cuban media, or reporting on Cuban affairs for a major Mexican news channel, didn't mean much to the towers in the big apple.

Eventually, Andrés wiggled into Yellow Cab. Most rookies fill and file the paperwork in a few weeks, but it took him twice as long. Side note: the couple made love only four and a half times, since settling together in the newest of new cities.

Two years, with such little change, and such few moments of true intimacy. Soon came the time for the interview to change her status from conditional to permanent residency. That's why she had an interview. The date happened to land on her birthday. And all she could think about was how she didn't want to go through with it. Disappointment hit hard. She could end things, go back to Mexico. Or she could start an affair. For once, she went with the easier option. That's when she met Jonathan.

But then, just before turning 38, she got pregnant again. And Andrés was definitely the father, from that fourth and a half ejaculation in her, how romantic. So then, on her birthday, conflicted, jobless, with nothing to fill her but a fizzled out love and the product of a failed relationship, she entered the interview, and told them she wanted to stay. The government accepted her petition. And everything changed.

She got a job as an intern at a local news station. It would turn into something valuable, yes, while pregnant with Alex. Meanwhile, she kicked out Andrés, but kept seeing Jonathan. He was happy to be with her, while the other was happy to be gone.

June 3rd, again. And the taxi driving father sent her the text that he was still out with their boy. Julia stood up and was set. She would end things. Fill herself elsewhere.

Julia's most frequently used emoji:

Ilya's:

David's:

Tiffany's:

Tony's:

Stacy's:

Unknown number

12:01

Come to Zdras.

It was Jonathan Murphey. Of course Zdras wasn't there, only the train above it crackling and crooning. The homeless man. The three dogs. Nothing changed. Except the hornet. Gone. Now just a door, repainted green. And above it a massive sign, which read, "Dos."

"Welcome to Dos," said Jonathan, holding out his hand.

Ilya stopped walking towards the door. He looked at the hand, then up at the man holding it out.

"You're supposed to shake someone's hand," said Jonathan, "when he puts it out."

Ilya grabbed hold of that steel vice grip. The two men descended together.

"I had bought the place just before the accident," explained Jon, "but after the terrible show is when I really got to work." He told the story of how he had put in the paperwork for a second bar, the bar of his dreams, dedicated to local, independent producer-DJs, just like he had always wanted. "The future is local," he said, "we sell coffee and apple cider during the day, and have a running signup list for anyone to perform." Thanks to his connections, even bigger names were allowed to drop in and run a deck. At least that was the plan. "The next two months we have evenings and weekends booked," said Jonathan. "Except one night. Sunday August 26th." The two reached the downstairs, where the bar was, clean, remodeled. "We can't let the end of one thing be the end of everything. This," he said, "this is Dos, like 'two' in Spanish."

A familiar voice broke from under the bar. "I thought it was Dos like Dostoevsky!" Julia appeared. "Or Dos Passos." Her hair was up. Her eyes innocent. She stepped next to Jonathan and grabbed hold of his bare muscular arms. She looked at Ilya, then kissed Jonathan on the neck. "But *Two* makes sense too."

"Well?" asked Jonathan, shoving Ilya who had been staring at Julia, as always, as anyone who meets her does. "Well?"

"Well what?"

"I need you that night."

Ilya put out his hand. "It's a deal." He turned around, thinking he heard someone coming from the staircase. "August 26th?"

"End of summer."

"I'll have my EP by then."

It was a deal.

"Did you say bye to Robespierre?" asked Ilya, to Jonathan, who wanted to start opening boxes of new glassware.

"I didn't get the chance," said Jonathan, absentmindedly. "He went out west."

"To Chicago."

"On tour, I think," said Jonathan, cracking a glass as he cut open the box. He didn't get upset. "Didn't he invite you?"

"I thanked him, but declined," said Ilya, getting down and helping Jonathan remove the shards of glass. "I wanted to finish my EP first. He understood."

"I hear he's going to master it?"

"He will, as soon as I'm done adding one or two more live instruments."

"When will you be done?"

"I don't know."

Just then, both men heard a voice from the stairway: "Hello?" Everything was dark, except for the spots under the lights lighting grim. Not a sound but footsteps. Not a breath, but a greeting.

"Hello?" asked the men, turning towards it. Jonathan asked if Ilya had left the door open. Before the DJ could reply, in walked the voice.

"Hi," said Ilya. "How are you, Stacy."

Jon didn't say anything.

She took off her glasses, and tightened the jean jacket around her shorts. Then she apologized for the show the other day. "Things got out of hand, didn't they?" she said.

"In the end, no one got too hurt, right?" said Jonathan, stepping in, getting up, measuring two heads higher than her.

Stacy shook her head.

"Rock and Roll."

"I wanted to apologize to you, too, Ilya." She stepped forward, as if to hug him. Ilya stepped back.

"Nah, don't worry about it."

Stacy stepped forward again. "I'm going on tour tomorrow."

"Isn't everybody?"

"I don't know when I'll be back," she said, unfazed. "But I wanted to give you this before I left New York." She handed Ilya a t-shirt. It was his, and had forgotten it at her dorm a long time ago, from when they first met. She had kept it as a souvenir, and for the longest time Ilya would tell her to keep it, because it always gave him an excuse to see her in the dorms, to get it back, until he forgot about it. On the front read the words "KING, QUEEN, PRINCE" and had, respectively, the image of Michael Jackson, Freddie Mercury, and Prince silkscreened. Ilya had made it himself. He got teary eyed. It was easy for him to get this way.

He thanked her, then, flipped it around. "What's this?"

Stacy smiled. She had silkscreened another image on it, over a red, handwritten word:

ACE

"Man," said Jonathan, "ugly photo." It was a photo of Ilya looking up at the sky as if staring at a giant beanstalk, full of awe, and looking sexy, holy—Stacy's favorite of him.

He shed a cold one. Then they hugged for the last time.

"I gotta go," she said, turning around and out. "Thank you for letting me play with you."

"Wait," said Ilya. "How did you know I would be here?"

Stacy looked confused. "Jonathan told me."

"Oh."

"Later."

"Wait!" Ilya came up to her. "No chance of us getting back, is there?"

"We met in college, Ilya," she said. "Let the past be the past."

Suddenly, loudly, from the trapdoor appeared Julia.

"Excuse me," she announced. "A pleasure to finally meet." She reached out her hand. Stacy looked stunned. As soon as the ladies held hands, Julia led Stacy out the stairs, telling the boys the ladies had to catch up, why don't they finish unpacking then make her a drink. Then she darted her eyes at Ilya.

"If you leave before I come back, let's meet at Brighton Beach this weekend, what do you say?"

August 17th. All DJs must at one point, and with the same solemnity that medieval pilgrims had to hike the road to Santiago de Compostela, sample the Amen Brother's break. These things are part of growing up.

We are part and parcel of traditions, us DJs, albeit a very young tradition, but one that branches off of other music and arts, remember, with roots in cavemen's camp fire ghost stories accompanied by a deer hide drum bum-bum-bum. We are here to enhance the dancehall. We are here to fill a space with acoustic energy. Blah, blah, blah, blah. All this is rhetoric, Папа would say, and would be right. I do feel alone. I must be alone. I see an empty track waiting to be filled with green and blue blocks of MIDI information, and I have to do something.

And I am hearing Tiffany in bed with Jem Jem, again, probably telling him that she has a flight the next day and all week but that the sucker still has to call her and talk every day. Tiffany is a trip. She used to treat men like gladiators, sex slaves sent into a pit of leopards and tigers and other gladiators, as she watched them fight to the death, deciding, yea or nay, with a thumb in their butt, if they should live or in her case if they should see each other again, or not. But now? She's settled down. No more deluge of DMs, no downpour of Tinder super likes, no more indulgence or self-importance, just one happy Empress Voltescu with her one local white boy—call their story "The Downtowner and the Artist," romantic insofar as it is novel; O Tiff, you Romanian by pedigree, Roman by heart. Thank you for making me but a senator in your colosseum, this home.

---I just reread these entries. What a rollercoaster, what a summer. I will keep them, to prove something, or create something later. Some collage art, from hopes and dreams.

☼

Central Park was invented by a poet, said Speed once.[*]

And its sidewalk along 59th St cooked hot. And the clatter of horse hoofs brought you to the 19th century. Metropolis to one side, green biosphere to the other, a transcendent experience going in or coming out of the Park, where the rocks were those from a underground, massive, bottomless structure. Past Sixth Avenue, close to Seventh, Ilya looked up at some red letters. All the skyscrapers were still that morning, still shaking themselves. Except those static red letters. He was on his way to see *Black Orpheus* at the Lincoln center, when he looked up again, at those red letters, as if for the first time.

Essex House. It must be a hundred years old by now.

And Ilya kept staring.

A young woman with a pen behind her ear stood next to him. It was so crowded this time of day, in the summer, full of tourists, that you could tell when someone had stopped moving with the hustle and flow of the minnow people.

"They put the red sign up in 1933," she said. Ilya didn't look at her, only repeated in his head the number thirty-three, thirty-three. She continued in a striking radio announcer voice, saying, "Guests of *Saturday Night Live* stay at the Marriott's Essex House."

Ilya still didn't look at her, but could hear the pen scribbling thoughts in a note pad.

"Is it true Stravinsky lived here?" asked Ilya, checking his phone, looking up at the letters again.

---

[*] Your favorite tour guide of all time, Speed Levich.

She flipped a few pages back. "Moved to Essex House in 1969," she said. "Died April 6th 1971. Buried in Venice."

Once she left, Ilya called his father. Nikolai was surprised by yet another connection Ilya could make between Russia and America, how could he have forgotten about Essex? Nikolai, who was working on his garden, snipped a flower bud off the tip of his sage plant. Then said he was going to hang up.

But before he did, Ilya stopped him.

"What did you think about the song for mom?"

Nikolai replied that at first he had no words for "Seraph," only tears—then, he added that it reminded him of "Symphony C," or "Firebird." "Who would have thought Stravinsky's pounding rhythm would make great electronic music? My son." Nikolai rambled on, "Life can be beautiful if we make it. Stravinsky was an artist, a paragon. He made life beautiful," on and on, "and did you know Tchaikovsky wrote 'Hymn of the Cherubim?"

Yes, yes, and Ilya felt he was something in his father's eyes. When out of nowhere the following thought bubble burst from within: "What ever happened to mom," he asked. "You never told me."

Nikolai paused, snipped another bud. "You never asked."

"What happened to Maxine . . . ?"

"She was an addict," said Ilya's father. "That night she went out with you and your brother she saw the house she frequented."

"That's why she left," said Ilya, "but why didn't she come back?"

"Mystery and misery," answered the father, "are a terrible combination."

⁖⁖

December 18th 1999. Misery indeed, but mystery not so much. Anyone could piece together the story, with the police report, eye witness account, a dope dealer's note spattered in blood, and the victim's backstory.

Maybe the real mystery is why Nicolai waited until asked to say anything about it. Maybe one day, he kept saying, every year, around Christmas time, Three Kings time, he would tell the story of Maxine, a ballerina turned choreographer turned mother, after she dropped the kids at the used book store.

Yes, the skyscrapers were shimmying, shaking, shamming and showing, slowly burning, samesies sowing, soundly sewing, surely shortening.

At a minute past midnight, Maxine Gagarina, née Alexandrova, knocked on the door to Apartment #2 in a gray dilapidated building in Murray Hill, Manhattan, the same neighborhood where oddly enough Ilya ended up living in not much later in the grand scheme of things, opposite to a used book store, far from Grand Central Station, where the three family members had been headed for, now only the boys headed for, while the woman who had been a mother of two bright young boys, knocked a second time. Her old time dealer was opening the door.

"Tonight?" asked the gentleman in frayed boxer shorts, not recognizing Maxine, past his haze.

She was there to settle the score, she felt so sore, life a checkerboard of bore and mushroom spore.

"It's me," she said, pushing him inside.

Three minutes past midnight, he took off his shirt.

Five minutes past midnight, she told him the real reason she came there. She had found help and now he needed it too.

Thirteen minutes past midnight, he told her just one more hit, one more why not, after that they can quit for real, for good.

Twenty one minutes past midnight, she gathered each little rubber noodle, each burned spoon, and each baggie and started throwing things into a big black trash bag.

Twenty five minutes past midnight, he stared at his old client, stared at his old lover, stared at a stained drawing of a rainbow on the fridge that his daughter had made before passing away, daydreaming a dream she might have dreamed.

Twenty six minutes past midnight, Maxine tore open the knotted baggies and flushed the supplies down the spinning toilet bowl.

Twenty seven minutes past midnight, the gentleman in the frayed boxer shorts took a syringe from under the couch and ran the sharp point into Maxine's back. Then pressed the end down.

She moaned.

He pulled out.

She fell.

"More," he said, hurt but without feeling it. "Just one more." And he jammed the thing in again, and pushed against the end again, out and in again, and—

August 19th.

Burst into flames my darling firebird /

pain pronouncing fear /

a cry, a cry / O firebird, my firebird /

who wants you near? / to hear you scream /

who could take you in /

when all you share are embers /

and all you touch turns to ash /

and ages.[*]

---

[*] Which recalls the Russian fairy tale "Ivan and the Firebird." Which in turn reminds me, I never finished the Ilya story:

Thirty years went by, and the poor, desolate Ilya Muromets family had nothing to live on, no livestock, no crops, nothing but their silent, wide-eyed boy-child of thirty years disabled and bedridden.

The parents passed away, without so much as a word from their son, without ever asking even the smallest thing from him, for him to ever prove himself, for, given his state, what could he ever offer?

He could not even bury them, when they passed. He had learned nothing, done nothing, he couldn't even end his life if he had wanted to.

Then, in the wake of a terrible raid, after a roaming tribe had rolled through the woods stealing women and gold, three old beggars visited the hut. They were looking for safety from the violence, from the absurdity.

"Lookee!" said one of the beggars. "A good for nothing bum."

"I bet he lies around all day," said another beggar. "Doing nothing."

"It makes me sick!" said the third beggar. "To see such a youth gone to waste. Boy, if I were young again!"

Ilya lay there, driven to madness listening to these three fools spit everywhere with their vicious words and their idle chatter.

Suddenly, the young man roared. "You old men, you good for nothings, get out of my house!"

"Y-y-o-o-u-u-r house?" the first beggar spoke, laughing. "Aren't you the worthless son of the man they call Muromets? Now that was a man worthy of owning a place like this."

"Who are you?" asked the second beggar, soon to answer his own question. "You who sits around doing nothing and sucking at everything life has given you without so much as giving anyone anything, not even a kiss on the cheek!"

"Get out of my house!" roared Ilya.

The third beggar started dancing around the immobile youth. "Get . . . out? Hah! We will get out only on one condition."

The three old, warty, hairy, scheming men chuckled in unison. "We will get out if you fetch us a pail of water from your famous watering hole!"

Filled with a thing he had never felt before—pure hopelessness turned pure rage—he heaved out of bed, shaking the very foundations of the old home with the sound of his roar. The three beggars fell onto their behinds, and with their eyes followed the young man's thunderous footsteps stomp one after the other to the famous watering hole. Because the well had run so dry, and the rope wasn't long enough to reach the very bottom of the well, Ilya nabbed the three closest buckets lying around, jumped in and jumped right back out with three filled-to-the-brim pails of water.

"Here you go!" he shouted, making the old men shiver in their ragged clothes.

They drank carefully, not dropping a single drop.

Together they sighed in unison. And when they were done, there was a bright flash of light.

The three old men turned into God, St Peter, and the prophet Isaiah. They had been touring the earth, healing helpless youth and freeing them from bondage or orphanage.

Ilya Muromets dropped down to the ground, and shook the forest around with his immense body bowing.

"My son," spoke the Lord. "Have I put you here to waste away?"

"No!"

"Have I put you here to test your spirit?"

"Yes!"

"Rise, Ilya Muromets," said St Peter. "You are ready to receive your mission."

"Anything," spoke Ilya, receiving Isaiah's sword and platinum armor from the prophet himself, and nodding his head.

"You must save this country from all things evil," spoke the Lord. "And you must go now."

As Ilya rode a black horse away from where he had grown up, he kept playing those words in his mind, "Go now," and the words spoken after: "You are more powerful than any foe, larger than any army, brighter than any flame, and sharper than any blade. Fear not your enemy. Walk straight in the way of the light, back up right, your way is the truth. For God is not with strength, but with truth."

Ilya vanquished villains, and saved damsels, convinced kings to end wars and to join hands. No matter what lay ahead of him, he trusted himself: he had received his mission. Now nothing would hold him down.

Amen!

Music connects and divides, language connects and divides, but love?

And from where he stood, the young Gagarin could almost hear a ship cut across the horizon, along the line that both divides and connects both ocean and sky. He walked to the restaurant where it all started. He saw her there.

"If it isn't the poet of Brooklyn," said Julia, with a voice a little in falsetto.

"I'm not that important," he replied. "Not yet." He took a seat.

"Never be modest, young knight. Was Walt Whitman?"

"Is that the poet of Brooklyn you were thinking of? I thought you meant Biggie."

Then, quietly, Ilya, who looked so healthy these days, as if he had found some sort of peace, smiled easier too, drew something between the back of his jeans and his belt. And handed it to Julia.

"What's this?" she asked, thinking all those thoughts about his health, surprised, blushing a little.

"A mix CD I made for you."

"I know what it is, I mean how am I supposed to play it?"

"Consider it a gesture, I guess," he said, scratching the back of his buzz cut head, before admitting, "I never really thanked you for getting me a phone. So I made this. Turn it over." There was a download code on the back. While on the front, there was a Tarot card of The World, taped over the cover with the title and dedication.

TELEPHONICS, for Любовь:

1. Chromeo – "Call Me Up"
2. Lady Gaga – "Telephone" (Ft. Beyoncé)
3. Florrie – "Call 911" (Florrie Remix)
4. Soulja Boy – "Kiss Me Thru the Phone" (Enschway Remix)
5. Robyn vs Cher – "Call Your Girlfriend / Believe" (I.N.G. Love After Love Mashup)
6. Gabrielle – "Ring Meg"
7. Carly Rae Jespen – "Call Me Maybe" (I.N.G. Summer Love Remix)
8. Stevie Wonder – "I Just Called to Say I Love You" (I.N.G. Acoustic Cover)
9. Blondie – "Call me" (Original Long Version)
10. Stevie Ray Vaughan – "Telephone Song"
11. James Blake – "Why Don't You Call Me?"
12. Beck – "Cellphones dead"
13. Alla Pugacheva – "Телефонная книжка" (I.N.G. Yellowing Pages Remix)
14. Bad Bunny x Farruko – "Blockia" (No Me Llames Más)
15. Drake – "Hotline Bling" (Benji Reyes Remix)
16. E-40 – "Chip in da Phone"
17. Lady Gaga – "Telephone" (Passion Pit Remix)

Julia was visibly moved by the thank-you gift. She almost spoke up to say so, but was interrupted.

"That's my seat!"

Out from the restroom came Julia's little cowboy of a son. He ran over to Ilya and kept poking his shoulder, and repeating himself. "That's my seat! Mine!"

Ilya looked at the other two empty chairs at the table, then at Julia. She was blushing. "Alright," said Ilya. "Alright, I'll get up, Alexander." He did.

"That is not my name!" shouted the young boy, as he took the seat in front of his mother.

"My apologies, Александр, I mean," returned Ilya, taking the seat next to Julia, their knees as close as ever.

"No," said the boy. "My name is Sergio!"

Julia looked towards someone at the entrance of the restaurant, and called that someone over. Then Julia turned back to her son. "He's been watching the *Sergio and Sergei* movie," she said. "He thinks his name is Sergio."

"Hi-ho, Sergio," said Ilya.

The boy waved him hello.

The waitress arrived. Julia couldn't help herself.

"Look Alex," she pulled out the mix CD. "Our favorite DJ gave me a mix CD."

The waitress turned to Julia. "Yeah, but mine is signed." She turned to the DJ.

Ilya took a closer look at the waitress. She was as blushed as ever, but this time, Ilya interpreted it differently.

"Your name is Alex, too?"

Julia laughed. You two don't really know one another. Allow me. Ilya Nikolayevich, this is Alexandra Sergeyeva."

Alex the waitress smiled. "Everyone calls me Sashenka."

Ilya got up. Completely honored. "You're—you're the biggest—what are you doing in New York still? Didn't your tour end?"

"I had a few months on my visa left," she said. "So I figured to get a job here, at my uncle's restaurant for the summer." Suddenly, she covered her mouth. "Don't tell anyone!"[*]

Julia was already up, holding on to her boy, and about to leave. "I'll let you two . . . yes . . . Ilya, I'll see you at the show tonight."

"Wait!" shouted Ilya, like he had not too long ago.

"Yes?"

"Thank you, Julia . . ." he meant to call her by her nickname, but didn't, letting the silence say it for him.

Julia smiled, then turned down. "C'mon now, Sergio. Let's go."

"Да, мама."

They left.

---

[*] Stupid P-3 visa! No, it's great. How proud was I to become the youngest artist ever to receive the O-1, though, five years later? Very.
Now those are letters that matter!

This was the first time these two spent any time together, technically, and yet it felt like the opposite was true. The daylight hours turned, while they discussed music, the state of music, and all that. It was cute. Almost as cute as how she let her brunette waves loose from a ponytail, this Sashenka, confessing that just like the DJ she had never felt comfortable saying where she was from, having been born in Moldova, but living in Moscow all through college and the year after.* "Coming to New York was my way of not caring anymore," she added. And Ilya understood this, along with why she had acted so silly around him before. She had a crush, was blushing, yet not ashamed about it. Ilya admitted he didn't like Sashenka's music that much, the later stuff, he clarified, compared to her earlier stuff. She nodded, and said she had been making music for other people for so long now, she was looking for a break, just another reason to go to New York. Plus, the beach was nice. "Now it's time go back on the road."

"You too?"

"I'm going on tour, yes." Sashenka elbow-nudged Ilya a little, making him ticklish, making her smile. "Want to come? I could use the extra hand."

"Only if Nina Kravis pays."

"She's my manager," said Sashenka, "not the bank. But if you worked merch . . ."

---

* I wish I had more stage time in the book, but it is your story. Ilya and Sashenka. Ilona and Alexander. Sly how you played with our names. Oh husband, you are a devil, and I? Just your old DJ wife.

Why and why not, Ilya wondered. So many reasons to stay in New York, all exhausted. Could he leave? Did he have it in him to leave? Maybe not. And yet:

"Sure," he said. "Sure, I'll go. It might help me find that missing sound on the track."

Alexandra was pleased. And it was time to head back home, hit the shower, his show was in a few hours, plus he was feeling inspired. But before all that, she asked Ilya a question: "What's that on your lip? Did you cut yourself?"

Ilya told the truth: "It's a cold sore, lol."

"Ew, I get the same thing. But who cares. La di da."

"La di da?"

"La di da!"*

Ilya smiled. They walked to the station.

Not far from the train station, a jazz cool melody caused a stir. The sounds of automobiles and claps were not enough to douse the notes floating around. In the center of the big group was a tall muscular man strumming the guitar.

The couple stopped to enjoy, then one stayed a little longer to ask a question: "What's your name?" Ilya asked. Sashenka looking curiously on.

The dude didn't open his eyes nor stop plucking pleasurable notes as he replied: "Charazard James. Check out the Instagram, friend."

Sashenka told Ilya, "Let's go, we'll be late to the show."

---

* *Annie Hall.*

"Hey," Ilya said, almost turning around and leaving, but before that, saying, "I've always liked Blastoise."

Charazard James winked, inwardly falling into the same trance his riffs and rambles explored that midday, midweek of music busking. This was the music Ilya needed on his title track. A local musician. A cool sound. So right. Blown away by the second chance encounter of the day.

Down by a stool, in the open guitar case with different cash bills from around the world, Ilya tossed a sheet ripped from his notebook like a business card: with his full name, ten digits, and two words: "Wanna race?"

Show day—the remix.

The lights cut off. A rumble begins. Sparklers shoot. Go-go dancers with bunny ears and neon bracelets put their palms together. Behind the DJ booth, a video cues up, on a large screen: it's an interview with Jim Morrison, wearing his sunglasses indoors. The reporter asks him what the future of American music will be. Morrison leans forward and explains how the roots of contemporary rock are black blues and European folk music. He says that right now, as they speak, 1960s rock is dying, and artists are falling back into either of those two categories, some back to blues music, others back to folk. Morrison is then struck by an inspiration. The fog machines kick off, the strobe lights punch in, the subwoofers along the walls move the walls, and a young Jim Morrison gives his last living testament to the state of American music: saying, *"The new generation of music will synthesize rock and blues, the two American roots music, and some third thing. It might rely heavily on electronics or tapes. I can kind of envision maybe one person with a lot of machines, tapes, electronic set-ups, singing or speaking, and using machines. One person with a lot of machines, one person with a lot of machines, one person with a lot of machines, tapes, tapes, tapes, electronic set-ups, I can kind of envision, maybe one person with a lot of machines, maybe one person with a lot of machines, I can kind of envision, tapes, tapes, tapes, electronic set-ups, I can kind of envision, maybe, The new generation of music will synthesize a lot of machines, one person, The new generation, some third thing, singing or speaking, singing or speaking, singing or speaking, singing or speaking* (and here the crowd goes wild, they start chanting the words) *singing or speaking, singing or speaking, singing or speaking, singing or speaking, one person with a lot of machines* (and Ilya sets up his DDJ and laptop, a little shy, but very sharp and with one hand up, all eyes on him, under limelight), *The new generation of music with synthesize*—language—*two roots, and some third thing, electronic set-ups*, or CDs and MIDIs; *I*—We the People of the United States—*can envision*—"Science!"—*one person with a lot of machines, tapes, electronic set-ups, singing or speaking and using machines* (here Ilya picks up the microphone and turns off the video recording of Morrison to say...)

MY NAME IS I-N-G, THANK YOU ALL FOR COMING OUT TONIGHT, ENJOY!*

---

* **Final consideration.** My feeling, having been by your side as this book was in the making, is that while you were writing the first part of the book there was balance between despair and hope. The second part of the book, however, seems more about loss, and sometimes I got lost myself. My advice is we should discuss these aspects that I mentioned above, and then, the next step is to complete the work with the missing details. I'm sure the time we have left "on this planet" is enough to reflect on the right way to perfect TLTW. That way, once you start writing on it again, it will flow as quick as quicksilver. With the publishers having it in time to celebrate the 30th anniversary of your real debut album, after the ill-fated *Seraph*.

Remember these notes are not about "changing" anything in the book, but rather about ADDING on the existing version. (For example I liked this idea of an "outro" chapter so much that I went ahead and inserted similar "breaks" between your movements.)

This is in a nutshell all I could come up with. I hope I can bring a tiny contribution to bringing this book to LIFE.

Te iubesc <3,

Ya baby

Coda:

Little did you know, you are the old man. Guess who is the old woman? *It was all a dream,* sang the poet of Brooklyn.

She closes the book, we reach narrative zero. She is done editing the thing, done adding herself to the work, having very much enjoyed reading it. Just a typo here and there, of course. Plenty of distraction added with the footnotes and lovenotes. And this zigzagging cannon finale:

И я там был,

                        And I was there,

мёд-пиво пил,

                        I drank the honey beer,

по улыбке текло,

                        it flowed over my smile,

а в рот не попало.

                        but got not in my mouth.

End.

New York – Bucharest – Pyce

2018 – 2020

Acknowledgments:

I would like to share why this book is dedicated to my parents. For one thing, together they showed me that a good love will last. Individually, it was my father who taught me the beauty of playing the same song over and over. I will never forget those late night car rides blasting "We'll Be Burning," "Tomara," and "Ya Rayah (Sonar Remix)." While my mother showed me it's ok to sing off key and dance, to "Oremi," to "Central Reservation (Ben Watts Remix)," or to "Coolo" by Illya Kuryaki. The plethora of other musicians, whose music I bobbed my head to while typing this novel, is too high to list again (they are found within the pages of this book).

A shout out to the New School wolf pack, dashing through the sandy snow of Cape May.

A special thanks to my graduate advisor, who saw a version of this story as a rough graduate thesis. You are a star in the night, Sigrid, pointing in the right direction.

Raising a glass, I say cheers, to the health of the Russians in my life or out of it, especially those who struck a pitch fork inside of me when they gifted me a copy of Shklovsky's *Theory of Prose*, Ilf and Petrov's *Twelve Chairs*, Montefiore's *Sashenka*, or Bulgakov's *Master and Margarita*.

Last but most of all, I thank my editor, my marketer, my muse, and my wife: the one and only Ela. Without you my days would be quiet, cold, and gray. You are the song in my heart. Thank you. Te amo.

About the Author

With half a decade of education experience, Iván Brave lives and works in the capital of Romania, managing a professional team of assessors for a corporate language solutions company. His writing has been recognized by Public Poetry in Houston (Artlines Award 2015, in partnership with the Museum of Modern Art), and by the Vera List Center for Arts and Politics (Writing Awards 2017). To learn more, read other works, or pass the time, please visit:

ivanbrave.com.